I0749217

# A Love Match, Indeed!

A Novel of Regency Romance

Teresa Sweeney

Courting Romance Publishing
California

A Love Match, Indeed! is a work of fiction. Names, characters, places, and incidents are the products of the author's imagination or are used fictitiously. Any resemblance to actual events, locales, or persons, living or dead, is entirely coincidental.



Published in the United States by Courting Romance Publishing

**ISBN 978-1-940319-00-1**

**First Edition**

**Cover Photography by Christina & Jason Brusaca**

**By Teresa Sweeney**

*Always Rebecca*

*A Love Match, Indeed!*

*To my husband Larry, a man of impeccable character, intelligence, and charm.*

# A Love Match, Indeed!

# Chapter One

Since her introduction into Society, the Countess of Westfield was touted as being an *Original* with her honest and forthright personality. Only someone with her esteemed connections could get away with breaking the social customs that often had her as a topic of conversation. The *gossipmongers* thought her extremely lucky to have produced an heir on her first birthing, so they could not understand why she was not boasting at every afternoon tea and fete of her accomplishment. After all, Elinor had secured the title for her husband. The Earl of Westfield had no brothers, so he needed a son to keep the earldom secured in his family. Any other lady would be exclaiming how happy she was to have her duty over and done. She would expect to be pampered and rewarded for her most magnanimous act. Then, when she felt recovered, she would make her way to Town, leaving her husband to his own devices and the care of her newborn to nurses and nannies.

However, most ladies of Society could not boast that their marriage was a love match, or that their child was a blessing of their union. Almost ten months after their wedding, the countess delivered a healthy son. From that moment, the earl and his wife watched over him, never wanting to relinquish his company to his nurse. Even after two months, Elinor was reluctant to leave her baby to a caretaker, so she isolated herself from Society, receiving only family and those friends that she considered dear. Lord Felton was one of those friends.

He had come to her son's christening to stand as godfather for him. He was keeping Elinor company in her private parlour awaiting her husband, Jonathan, the Earl of Westfield to join them. Lord Felton watched Lady Elinor cradle her son as he sat languidly on a floral needlework Queen Anne chaise. He looked rather large, sprawled on the delicate sofa, supported with slender walnut-carved cabriole legs that ended in clubfeet. He was a handsome man, owning a strong square jaw, straight nose, and cobalt blue eyes. He looked formidable, aside from a wavy lock of black hair, that liked to fall forward to mar his perfect appearance.

Elinor sat in a matching winged armchair, and Lord Felton thought she made quite a charming picture: mother and child. He realized if he did not have scruples, then Lady Westfield might very well be Lady Felton. He, rather than Lord Westfield would be her husband, and proud parent. However, a year ago his conscious, and his growing affection for the newly *come-out* debutante, had driven him to be honorable by exonerating Westfield of his alleged indiscretion.

Lord Felton, had not yet received his title when he was commanded by the Prince Regent to court Lady Elinor. He was simply Mr. Edward Brentwood. During his pursuit of Elinor, he found her unwavering devotion for Lord Westfield to be affecting. He realized that he too craved a union, where love and mutual respect were the foundation. Even though he knew his alliance with Elinor would merge two vast fortunes, and provide him the title he craved, in the end he could not break the lady's trust in him to secure her. When she asked her pointed questions regarding the Earl of Westfield's alleged indiscretion with his cousin, the beautiful Lady Catherine, he had told the truth. Edward sacrificed his own hopes of winning Elinor's hand in marriage when he absolved Lord Westfield from any wrongdoing. Edward lost a bride, but he happily settled on what has turned out to be his dearest friendship, between himself and the Earl and Countess of Westfield.

"Elinor, you do have a nurse to tend to your infant, do you not?" asked Edward.

Lady Westfield smiled and responded, "You know very well, that they hover nearby, and are ready to come if summoned, but really, Edward, my son Stephen is so good. Look how he sleeps, nestled in my arms."

He asked, "I suppose Westfield is just as ridiculous as you are, in doting on the tiny heir?"

Elinor replied with glee, "You do not fool me, Edward. I know your heart all too well. You are an honorable man, of great affection and sensibilities. I can hardly wait to tease you, when you start your own nursery. I am glad you have come for the christening."

"It does you credit, to name your son after Mr. Stevens, since he raised you as a child, but are there any hard feelings with your other father, Lord Ingall?" he inquired.

"Neither Jonathan, or I, have forgotten our birth fathers. My son's name reads like a list, I fear. You are looking at Stephen Miles Roger Shelby. You see, we pay homage to all our fathers."

Edward smiled, as he remembered Elinor's story. She was separated from her noble parents at birth, and raised among commoners by a vicar and his wife: Mr. and Mrs. Stevens. They named her Rebecca. Elinor did not learn her true identity, until she turned eighteen, when she discovered that her birth parents, thought she perished in a raging river.

It seemed that Providence saved Elinor to be raised by Mr. and Mrs. Stevens. Then, fifteen years later, fate brought her and her widowed father, as the new vicar, to the Westfield and Ingall properties. Lady Ingall was immediately drawn to her. Lord Ingall, seeing how much his wife's spirit rose around Rebecca, hired the young girl to be a companion for her. Rebecca spent three years living with the Ingalls, more as a family member than as

Lady Ingall's companion, before they all learned that she was their lost daughter, Elinor.

Rebecca's life changed dramatically at the revelation. In Society, she went from being the invisible companion of Lady Ingall to the much sought-after heiress, the daughter of the Earl and Countess of Ingall, and granddaughter of the Duke of Hartford. Rebecca, now known as Lady Elinor Ingall, found herself initiated into Society, by being presented to Her Royal Highness, Queen Charlotte and her son, His Royal Highness, the Prince Regent. A lady *comes-out* of the nursery in order to make herself eligible for marriage, and Lady Elinor marked her *come-out* with her presentation to royalty at Saint James Palace.

His Royal Highness, known as Prinny to his intimates, held much sympathy for Rebecca. It bothered him monstrously that a young girl of nobility, especially, the granddaughter of his most intimate advisor, was forced to live the life of a commoner. He wanted to secure a future for her in Society. On a whim, he decided to help her acquire a suitable husband. He knew an exceptional marriage would guarantee her place in Society. In what could only be described as folly, he created a list of eligible suitors and commanded them to court Lady Elinor. However, unknown to Prinny, Lady Elinor had already fallen in love with the Ingall's neighbor, the Earl of Westfield.

Lord Felton, Mr. Edward Brentwood at the time, was one of the ten gentlemen listed as suitable bachelors on Prinny's list, and therefore, was commanded to court Lady Elinor. Edward was a gentleman of fortune and noble lineage. He was an experienced man nearing thirty. His dalliances over the years earned him the reputation as a rake. His tastes fell to the more mature woman, who knew how to satisfy his needs. Early in his majority, he learned that his wealth was not enough to earn him favor with the debutante mothers, who found his association with trade to be vulgar. Eventually, Edward grew weary of the hauteur. He began to choose his alliances with women interested in pleasing him, and in being rewarded for their efforts. There were many.

However, Edward heeded the advice of his mentor, his grace, the Duke of Hartford. Like his grandmother the Dowager Duchess of Aubry, his grace helped Edward with his entry into the *bon ton*. For years, he relied on being the guest of either his grace, or his grandmother in order to attend the affairs of the *ton*.

It was the Duke of Hartford's suggestion that placed Edward on Prinny's list. His grace reminded the Prince Regent that though Edward might be tainted with trade, he had noble blood running through his veins, and had superior connections. Prinny agreed with his grace, surmising he could settle Edward's peerage by awarding him a title if he was successful in winning the hand of Lady Elinor. Prinny, was well aware of how the *bon ton* hated the new wealth that tried to infiltrate their peerage. The aristocrats, like all gentlemen of the peerage, believed they were born to their station. They protected their exclusive circle, vehemently shunning those persons that tried to elevate their station with newly acquired wealth. Money earned through trade was not considered respectable. Edward wanted a title to gain the respectability that was denied him when his father, the son of a duke, married beneath his class.

Even though Edward had uncles, aunts, and cousins who held titles, he was still held at the fringes of Society. The *bon ton* justified if they made an exception for one, they would have to make one for another. Before long, there would be no distinctions made between the peerage and the commoners.

Edward's desire for a title, and his astuteness not to offend the Prince Regent, influenced him to pursue Lady Elinor earnestly. He soon discarded his notion that debutantes recently launched into Society were silly and naive. He found Elinor to be intelligent, compassionate, and forthright. Over time, he relinquished his pursuit, as soon as he realized that Elinor's heart was resolutely engaged to Lord Westfield. While he failed to win Elinor's hand in marriage, he did reap two priceless friendships.

Elinor broke Edward's reflection by asking, "Are you enjoying your title, Edward?"

Edward smiled. He liked the warmth he heard in Elinor's voice, when she used his Christian name. He replied, "It is only an honorary title, to distinguish that I am heir to my great uncle's estate, the Marquis of Beaumont."

Elinor responded, "I am very glad that your great uncle decided to name you as his heir. I would hate to be the cause behind you not receiving the title that you craved when you relentlessly courted me. Prinny should have rewarded you for your efforts. Clearly, you were the most diligent of my suitors."

"Elinor, you put me to shame, reminding me how self-serving I was," he replied. "Though, I must admit, it is your forthrightness and honesty that attracted me to you in the first place. I dare say, and Westfield would agree, that your directness is a magnet to those of us, who deplore the obsequious nature within our Society."

"You are too hard on yourself, Edward," she responded. "It is the way of the *ton,* you know, making advantageous connections. You did nothing that any member of the peerage, would not do. I am only thankful that you are a romantic. For who else would care that my heart was otherwise engaged when you courted me."

"Me!" gasped Edward. "A romantic! I think not."

Elinor rose with her sleeping infant son in her arms, and went to pull the bell cord that summoned the nurse, lingering nearby. She smiled, as she handed Stephen over to her, carefully cradling her son in the nurse's arms. Elinor whispered her instructions to the nurse with a softness that made the nurse smile in return. She watched them exit her parlour, returned to her seat, and then, turned to scold her guest.

"Really, Edward," said Elinor. "Must you raise your voice? You almost woke, Stephen."

Edward flushed, apologizing, "I do beg your pardon..."

Before he could finish, Elinor laughed, saying, "I will tease you no more. Relax, Edward, and explain to me why the marquis did not name you earlier as his heir, and save you the grief of being abjured by the *ton* all these years."

Edward frowned, stood up from resting on the chaise, and began to pace, before he answered. "You know, I never thought about it until you made your inquiry. My guess would be, that my uncle expected to beget an heir himself, and when he failed in that endeavor, he looked to me. He is old now, and probably realizes if he does not bequeath his title and properties before he dies, then, his assets will return to the Crown. I am sure, his sister, my grandmother, the Dowager Duchess of Aubry, had a hand in his bestowal."

Rebecca asked, "Why do you say that? Were you not close to the marquis?"

Edward replied, "He could have easily named my uncle, the Duke of Aubry, as his heir. After all, he is the senior male of my father's line, but my guess is that my grandmother, out of love for me, convinced him that I would be the better choice. You see, I would be the Marquis of Beaumont, assuming his county seat as my residence, while my uncle, the Duke of Aubry, has no need for an inferior title, or properties. A bequeath to his grace simply increases his coffers."

"But, Edward," rebounded Elinor. "You did not answer, if you are close, to your great uncle."

"Our only interaction when I was a boy, was when I was visiting my grandmother and he visited at the same occasion. He did not spend any time in the nursery, so I have no memories of anything significant," he answered. "However, since he announced me as his heir, I have made every opportunity to visit him and get to know him better. His countenance is much like his sister's, my grandmother, whose hauteur when utilized can be intimidating to those that do not know them. As common with age, he has become wiser and amiable. Jejune at times, finding joy in the simplest of things, and wanting to appease rather than argue. I think he is at a time in his life that he would like to retire from the management of his estate. I find myself liking the old coot quite well, and would like to unburden him, if I may."

"Will you miss the Season then, in order to tend to him?" asked Elinor.

"No. Unfortunately, he is pressing me to find a wife. He would like to see an heir produced before he leaves this world. While I will not wed simply to beget an heir, I will be open to marriage. It is time I set up my own nursery. I am in agreement with my uncle on that point. I would not want my family line to expire."

"Have you met anyone that interests you, Edward?" she asked.

Edward answered, "No. I am afraid since the announcement of my peerage, I have been attacked, and I do mean literally thrust upon, by *marriage mart* mothers, with their simpering debutantes, who flutter about me like annoying mosquitoes. Frankly, I find it distasteful that these same matrons, who shunned me since my majority, now find me quite exceptional in my eligibility. In my excitement of becoming the heir to the Marquis of Beaumont, I accepted what I thought to be desirable invitations. However, after attending one tedious sojourn after another this past year, I have strengthened my resolve to find a wife who is interested in me and not just my title. Someone whom I find interesting. I admit to meeting a number of beauties, but discovered them quite empty-headed. Not one of them, had a remarkable thought or opinion. These young debs have no life experiences for them to base any opinions. I found them all extremely dull, with little wit to amuse me. I think I might have even settled on one of them if I had not met you, but now I want more in a wife than just a good connection. I shall not settle on anyone unless my heart is engaged!"

Elinor exclaimed, "Jolly good for you, Edward! I would want nothing less."

"And what is that?" asked Lord Westfield who just entered the parlour and came to stand next to his wife's chair.

Edward exclaimed, "Westfield, it is about time you arrived. Where have you been?"

"Sorry, Felton. But my meeting with my steward took longer than what I thought. Where is my son? And what is it that my dear wife wants for you?" Jonathan's eyes gazed down unto Elinor, before fleeting over to Edward, with one eyebrow arched.

Elinor cut into the conversation, before Edward could respond to her husband, "He is looking for a love match, Jonathan. I told him, that I wanted nothing less for him. I shall qualify that statement, and say, I expect nothing less from him. What do you say?"

He responded, "I only hope for your sake, Prinny does not get wind of your intentions, and decide to play matchmaker for you, as he did for Elinor. You will have a devil of a time securing your woman, if he does."

Edward laughed, saying, "Do not even suggest such a folly, Westfield. I have had enough of such schemes. Does Prinny attend the christening?"

Jonathan replied, "No, he is too busy, trying to get parliament to increase his allowance. As usual, he has spent a fortune he does not have."

Elinor interjected, "You know, Edward, Prinny's list of eligible bachelors for me was absurd because I had already given my heart to Jonathan. However, in theory, the Prince Regent's approach for helping me select an eligible husband was remarkably clever. If you are vexed with the jejune debutantes that are presented to you, perhaps you should consider a lady who has already met her majority. Find a lady with a little life experience, someone to challenge you, rather than abide by you. Why don't you make a list of candidates and pursue them, instead of waiting for the perfect debutante to present herself?"

Edward frowned, saying, "Really, Elinor. I am not sure, this is a proper conversation for a lady to be having with a gentleman. Imagine, suggesting I marry an experienced woman, whom I might add, I am acquainted with many. I am speechless." Edward looked at Jonathan, for some kind of agreement, but only found humor in his face.

Jonathan, smiling broadly, exclaimed, "Do not look at me, Felton. My wife is quite independent with her opinions. However, I don't mind saying, her words have wisdom. Why do you not take a more calculated approach?"

Elinor laughed, "Thank you, husband."

"Because," retorted Edward in a haughty breath, "most women who reach their majority have done so because other gentlemen found them lacking. I am not interested in the leftovers, that my peers found unworthy."

Elinor stood with outrage, and railed, "For shame, Edward! There are many pearls that you slander as leftovers. Many ladies, who through no fault of their own are overlooked. Lady Anne is such a candidate. If her father had provided her with an adequate dowry, instead of gambling away all his wealth, I can assure you, she would have been solicited for her hand years ago."

Edward's eyes lit up with amusement. He smiled and then said to Elinor, "Ah! Lady Anne. Is that what this is all about, Elinor? You wish me to court Lady Anne?"

Elinor went to stand next to her husband, and threaded her arm through his. Jonathan looked at her, and smiled. Stifling a chortle of mirth, she responded, "I truly did not consider it, until now. She is a *diamond of the first water*, a real gem, Edward. You could do no better."

Edward pressed his lips in a grim line, replying, "I dare say, I could. I am sorry, Elinor, but she has been on the shelf too long, and it is my intent to start my nursery, not retire it. Besides, I fear, we do not get along very well."

Jonathan, who liked Lady Anne said, "I do not know your relationship with Lady Anne, Edward, but you are too hard on her. She is only five and twenty. I agree with Elinor, and fear it is her penury state, that keeps her single. Her bloodline and character are flawless. Aside from my wife, you could not meet a more engaging female."

Elinor added, "She comes to attend the christening, Edward. She is most dear to me. I shall expect you to be nothing but gracious toward her."

Edward responded, "I am yours to command, Elinor. Do not worry. I would do nothing to offend you or your dearest of friend."

Elinor smiled her gratitude to Edward, whose smile turned into a laugh, when Jonathan said, "Come Felton. Let us retreat to the nursery, and spend some time with my most outstanding son!"

The Earl and Countess of Westfield held an intimate supper for family and a few guests the evening before the christening. A large crowd was expected to witness the sacred event at the village church, and then, return to the Westfield Mansion for a day of festivities. Lady Westfield and her husband wanted a private celebration, with those dearest to them, in honor of their son's baptismal, so the quiet supper was planned.

Lord and Lady Westfield sat at each end of the expansive dining table. Elinor sat between her mother, the Countess of Ingall and her mother-in-law, the Dowager, Duchess of Westfield. Elinor's fathers, Vicar Stevens, and Lord Ingall, flanked her husband at the opposite end of the table. Lord Felton found himself sitting directly opposite Lady Anne. He smirked at Elinor's suggestion, that he should consider Lady Anne a suitable candidate for marriage. He did not know, if his seating assignment across from Lady Anne was intentional, but he found himself in a perfect position to draw her character, if he so chose. Lady Anne sat between Lord Ingall and his father, the Duke of Hartford.

Edward conceded that Lady Anne was a pretty girl. She sat with a proud posture, shoulders back, and her head held high. Her hands rested on her lap. A maroon ribbon was threaded through the braids of her straw-blond hair, fashioned in a becoming coif. A few tendril curls framed her face and brought attention to her blue eyes. Her eyes were not brilliant, but they sparkled, as if she held a secret, that only she knew. She had a straight nose, a regal one, that denoted her aristocratic bloodline. Her burgundy high-waist dress, accented her décolletage, and was more fashionable, than Edward ever remembered her wearing. He deduced, that business as a chaperone, was becoming more profitable now that the Season was ready to begin.

Elinor revealed that Lady Anne's profligate father, had gambled away both her dowry and his wealth, leaving his daughter destitute with nothing but her class to recommend her. Edward thought Lady Anne was quite clever to maintain favor with the *bon ton.* Most women in her position would have looked for a protectorate, or lowered themselves to the rank of governesses, thereby removing themselves from Society, and eliminating their chances for an advantageous connection. Lady Anne somehow managed to keep her respectability, and remain independent. She was too self-sufficient, he thought, for him to believe she was without a benefactor. He caught himself debating whether she was truly on her own, or whether an unknown gentleman saw to her needs. Edward knew without some type of family or male guardian to watch over her, she would be quite vulnerable to the rakes and deviants of the *ton.* A smug grin crossed Edward's face as he remembered Elinor's words telling him he should "find himself an experienced woman." He wondered, *"Just how experienced was Lady Anne?"*

Edward remembered the carriage ride he took with Lord and Lady Westfield, and Lady Anne to Hyde Park. The memory disturbed him. That day, Lady Anne seemed to be able to read his thoughts. Since he had always been well able to mask his emotions, her penetration into his soul was alarming. When he snubbed her, rather than take offense, she found amusement. His attempts to discomfit her always seemed to backfire, and he became the uncomfortable one. He had never noticed her before in Society, but since that outing, he found her almost everywhere among the *bon ton*. It seemed, she hired herself out as a chaperone to those mothers too tired to attend every ball or fete. Lady Anne moved quietly, never speaking, simply remaining behind her charge. She was always present to satisfy decorum, seeming invisible to the bevy of suitors around the young lady she chaperoned. It appeared she did not mind that they never noticed her.

She was a lady with significant lineage. However, her penury placed her eligibility for marriage just higher than a commoner. Edward never received a direct invitation from the crème of Society, but his wealth and austere connections made it difficult for Society not to admit him, though they greeted him with a haughty countenance.

Lady Anne on the other hand, had no wealth. She had only bloodline and respectability, yet somehow, she managed to be known as a favorite of the Prince Regent, and an intimate friend of the Earl and Countess of Westfield. As Edward watched her, he deduced that the Duke of Hartford would soon be added to her list of friends. He watched them converse, and saw the pleasure that crossed their faces. Lady Anne had an amiable disposition. She laughed as she responded to his grace. When the Duke of Hartford laughed, a good belly laugh, Edward wondered what Lady Anne said to provoke such a reaction.

Edward found himself captivated by Lady Anne's animated face. It was genuine. She had laugh lines around her eyes when she smiled that marked her inclination for mirth. Perhaps, they revealed that she did not subscribe to all the creams and concoctions that were so fashionable among the *bon ton*. He thought, she was genuinely engaged in her conversation with the Duke of Hartford. Her eyes sparkled with delight, as though everything his grace spoke was of significant importance. Edward had plenty of experience with women who played at being interested in what he had to say, and he knew a real conversation when he saw it. The moment reminded him of the conversations he had enjoyed with Elinor, discussing literature, music, and even some theological debates. He smiled, remembering their sometimes heated discussions. He was still smiling when he saw Lady Anne arch one of her eyebrows, and direct him an amused look that shocked him out of his reverie.

*"Damn!"* thought Edward. *"Does the minx think, I am flirting with her?"* Edward gave a nod to Lady Anne, and then turned to speak to the neglected Vicar Stevens, who flanked his left side.

Lady Anne wondered why Lord Felton was scrutinizing her. She was well aware that he had been observing her, but enough was enough. His lengthy perusal would soon bring speculation upon her character, and she thought it best that she check his behavior. She turned her head to look directly at him, and raised her brow. She smiled, realizing that Lord Felton was *woolgathering*, daydreaming, and probably unaware that his focus had been placed on her. She saw him flush when his wits returned to the present, and she was quite pleased to see him nod in discomfiture. She returned his nod and like Lord Felton, turned her head to converse with her neighbor.

# Chapter Two

Edward watched Lady Anne hop with her adolescent partner across the finish line in a three-legged race. Lady Westfield had organized games and races for her guests on the bowling green situated on the south side of the Westfield Mansion. Edward scanned the verdant field, taking in the festive scene. He was surprised to see Anne participating in the games. She was paired with a tenant's scraggly child, laughing wholeheartedly at their ineptitude of moving down the lane. Her clear joy was infectious, and he wanted to bellow along with her, but checked the unseemly behavior. He did not wish for anyone to note him looking at Anne, though her glowing and amused face would draw anyone's attention. He watched her hug her tiny charge, congratulating the child on her effort.

The Countess and Earl of Westfield had opened their home to every tenant and gentry family in the area who wanted to celebrate the christening of their son, Lord

Stephen, Viscount Shelby. Earlier that day, Edward was honored to stand up as Stephen's godfather, but found himself vexed when he saw that Lady Anne was honored as godmother. He thought he was a more particular friend to the earl and countess than Lady Anne. To his chagrin, he noted a spark of jealousy, knowing Anne enjoyed an equal intimacy with them.

Early that morning the clouds had broken and drifted away, revealing a clear cerulean sky that promised them a warm day. Elinor was happy the unpredictable English weather did not produce showers thereby forcing alternative plans for her son's celebration. The good weather ensured the roads would be firm and dry to travel, so anyone wishing to attend the festivities could.

According to Lady Westfield, everyone from the surrounding properties had attended. Since she knew every gentry and tenant family in the area personally, not just the Westfield tenants, but also her parent's, whose property bordered the Westfield's, the remark was received as fact. Lord Westfield and his countess were well liked among their community. Elinor was a great asset to her husband, and Edward thought he would be exceptionally lucky if he could find a woman as multi-faceted as her.

Edward continued to take in the panoramic view, where laughter and good cheer prevailed. Various children's games and contests were entertaining both the cacophonous participants, and the applauding crowd. A bevy of men clanged their tankards of ale to toast Viscount Stephen. Commoners and gentry alike, hovered around the multiple booths, that offered tasty treats and delicacies. Throughout the property, men and women, boys and girls, filled their stomachs with good food and their souls with merriment. Edward looked forward to when he could experience the warm felicitations that were being generously given to Lord Westfield and Elinor.

He was so enthralled with the scene that he did not see the Duke of Hartford, approach him in greeting, "Felton! I have not seen much of you. How do you fare, since your great uncle named you as his heir?"

Edward smiled at his grace, a long time friend of his grandmother, the Dowager Duchess of Aubry, and Elinor's own grandfather. Over the years, the Duke of Hartford, on the dowager's insistence, had championed Edward into Society whenever possible. Edward attended many balls and fetes as a guest of his grace. Over time, he developed a close relationship with him. The Duke of Hartford was like a father, mentoring him and providing him advice. Edward appreciated having someone to guide him. Ever since, he lost his parents over a decade ago in a traveling accident, he found his grace's guidance to be comforting and priceless. It was through his insistence that the Prince Regent had placed Edward on his list of candidates for Lady Elinor's hand in marriage. The Prince promised him a title, if he succeeded in winning her hand. Although Edward did not prevail, Providence intervened, and the Prince bestowed him with a title, nonetheless.

Edward responded, "I am well, your grace. Thank you. Congratulations on your grandson. I found him a remarkably strong infant with sound lungs. I have heard him, and therefore, can attest that he bellows prodigiously."

The Duke of Hartford laughed, replying, "Yes, he will not be ignored. A good trait for a future earl."

Edward smiled, asking, "Will you return to London, or home to your county seat?"

His grace answered, "I must return to Town, to do some bidding for Prinny. I fear he may be in a foul mood if Parliament did not increase his coffers, as he hoped. What are your plans? Do you return for the Season?"

Edward replied, "Yes, I must start looking for a suitable wife. My uncle is pushing me to wed and start my nursery."

Smiling, he responded, "You will make the *marriage mart* mothers happy." His thoughts were interrupted when he saw Lady Anne cross the bowling green making her way back to the Westfield Mansion. "Excuse me, Felton," he said, "I see Lady Anne, with whom I must speak. Be sure and see me when you come to Town, if I am still in residence. Give my best to your grandmother and your uncle."

Before Edward could bow and exclaim, "your servant," he watched the Duke of Hartford stride towards Lady Anne. A brisk stride at that. He wondered what his grace had to confide to Lady Anne, and decided to follow them back to the mansion.

Elinor approached and stopped him with her exclamation, "Oh, Edward! Is it not a beautiful day? Do tell me that you are enjoying yourself? Have you had enough to eat?"

He laughed at Elinor's buoyant nature. She was the consummate hostess, always worried about her guests and whether their needs were being met. He replied, "Elinor, if I eat any more, I shall not be able to keep my seat on my return to Town."

Elinor pouted, asking, "Do you return today, Edward? I so hoped you would stay a fortnight?"

Edward grinned and replied, "Do not pout, Elinor. It will stretch your beautiful face, and then Westfield will harangue me for causing such damage."

She laughed, while poking Edward's arm, and scolding him, "Fustian, you are *bamming* me, sir. Why can you not stay?"

"I must return to Town and start my search for a suitable wife. Why don't you and Westfield follow, and help me find someone worthy?" he replied.

"Stephen is too young. I will not chance bringing him to Town where the air is foul," answered Elinor.

Edward asked, "Can you not leave him?" Elinor gasped in outrage. Her eyes turned to steel, staring at Edward with profound ire. Edward quickly rebutted, "Never mind, I immediately realized my error."

Elinor laughed, "We will not come to Town, but should you organize a sojourn to visit your uncle's home, then send us an invitation and we will attend. Mind you, we will bring an entourage of nurses and maids, but if you choose, we will come."

Edward took Elinor's hand, brought it to his lips and kissed the back of her hand. He said, "You are too good."

Again, she laughed, replying, "Come, let us find Jonathan, so that you may say your appropriate goodbyes."

Lord Westfield was happy to visit the Marquis of Beaumont's Manor. Jonathan was a forward thinker. He was always interested in visiting other estates, to see how they managed their home and properties. He heartily believed in crop rotation, forced irrigation, and adding nutrients to the soil. He was anxious to see if the marquis initiated any scientific techniques, and if so, how well they produced results.

Edward understood Westfield well enough to know that he did not need to persuade him. Westfield's curiosity over how the marquis managed his properties would ensure his visit.

When Lord Felton returned to Town, he was happy that his tailor had left his card, indicating his new wardrobe was ready for a final fitting. Edward was an astute businessman. He ran his personal life with the same diligent planning he applied to his business affairs. Unlike many of the peerage, he did not wait until the Season started to take stock of his wardrobe. He had a standing appointment with his tailor before the Season began. He was measured, viewed fashion plates, and made his selection of styles and materials to produce the finest and most fashionable clothes available. He was no dandy, but he did subscribe to being an arbiter of fashion. Edward was a born leader, and it was his nature to start a trend, not to follow one.

Edward summoned his valet, Jenkins. He instructed him to be ready to accompany him to Bond Street the following morning. Jenkins had been in Edward's employ since his eighteenth birthday and was most loyal to him. He took his role seriously. He was diligent in keeping abreast of the latest fashions, and socialized with other valets of distinguished peers who were considered leaders in fashion. He took all steps to ensure that his master was never lacking in his dress. He practiced the art of folding cravats, mastering the difficult Oriental and Mathematical styles, and even took credit on occasion for producing an original fold for his lordship.

Jenkins was the nephew of Edward's father's valet. While he owned only five more years to Edward's thirty, more often than not, Edward yielded to his recommendations regarding fashion. Though Jenkins served Lord Felton, Edward considered him more family than not, since he had known him from his nursery days.

Edward was six years old when he first met his valet. His father was entertaining a lawn party for his brothers and their family. This was another one of his gestures to try and bridge the severed relationship that occurred when he married Edward's mother, and entered the business of trade.

It seemed that Providence intervened to bring Jenkins into Edward's service, for it was rare for Jenkins to visit his uncle. On that particular day, Edward's future valet found himself waiting for his uncle on the veranda, when he saw two boys, greater in size and age, began to bully Master Edward. As he was to find out later, the boys were Edward's cousins, but at the time, he only knew that the ruffians had taken the boy's cap. They were teasing him relentlessly, tossing his cap over his head in the manner of "keep away," a child's game. However, in this instance, it was a vicious version. His older cousins were taunting Edward, pushing him as he reached for his cap, and inevitably tripping him, damaging his suit with grass stains and dirt, and his knees with scratches. Jenkins did not consider the odds fair, but found Master Edward's grit, in refusing to be bullied, remarkable. In lieu of running for help, Edward changed his tactic, from jumping to try to reach his cap that was held at arm's length away, to wrapping his arms around his cousin's knees, to tackle him to the ground. Taken by surprise, the cousin released the cap, flinging his arms back as he fell in an effort to brace himself. Edward grabbed his cap and began to run away. Unfortunately, he was not fast enough, for the second boy grabbed his arm, and hurled him back, getting a better hold of him.

Jenkins intervened when he saw Edward being held by one boy while the other hooligan searched for a hefty twig, no doubt for which to strike him. Jenkins was closer in age to Edward's attackers, and while he did not outsize them, he guessed he was more versed in fighting than any noble son. He quickly entered the melee, delivering a bloody nose and a black eye, to each culprit. The ruckus brought the household of guests upon them, and Jenkins, after delivering a facer to the eldest of the boys, found himself being lifted by the boy's father, the Duke of Aubry. There were accusations, anathemas, and eventually scolds. Jenkins would have feared for his life, except that Mr. Brentwood, with an authoritative and calming air, resolved the situation by scolding each boy equally. There was a sterner warning to Jenkins, to appease Mr. Brentwood's brothers, but Jenkins did not take it to heart, since Mr. Brentwood finished the rant with a wink that only he could see. Later that evening, his uncle had given him a guinea and told him that it was from Mr. Brentwood, who said that there would be another one, should Edward ever be outnumbered, and he was able to provide assistance. Jenkins knew at that moment that his future was to be linked with Master Edward.

Edward never understood why Jenkins followed his uncle into service, since Edward knew that his own father had offered to purchase either an apprenticeship or commission for him. Jenkins said, that Edward needed him, and that he preferred his command than that of a fool. At the age of fifteen, Jenkins began shadowing his uncle, learning the service in which he took pride.

Edward spent the morning on 39 Old Bond Street. His tailor, John Weston, was one of the best-known tailors of the day, and was also the Prince Regent's tailor. While having the fashionable prince as a patron fostered Weston's elite clientele, it was the physique of patrons like Lord Felton, rather than the pudgy form of the Prince of

Wales, that showcased Weston's wares to best advantage. Weston was a skilled craftsman. He preferred to see his creations on someone like Lord Felton, whose tall and muscular body complimented the tight fitting style of the day.

After paying his accolades to Weston, Edward left the final details of his wardrobe to Jenkins, and decided to stretch his legs along Bond Street before heading over to his club. It was a weary morning, being measured for linen shirts, waistcoats, coats, and breeches. Edward was happy to leave the final selection and instructions to Jenkins, who knew his taste well.

He had just begun to stroll down the street, when Lord Mansfield and Lord Trenton, highly engaged in conversation, almost collided into him.

"I do beg your pardon, Felton," replied Lord Mansfield. "I fear Trenton and myself were quite distracted in our conversation. I was just remarking how beautiful she was, when Trenton criticized that the remark was a paltry description of her. Well, you can imagine ..."

Before Mansfield could continue, Lord Felton raised his hand in a manner to halt his conversation, saying, "Mansfield, I have no idea what you are mumbling about, but I suggest you focus on where you are going, before someone takes offense to your clumsiness and calls you out for it."

Mansfield replied, "I am sorry Felton, but if you saw her, you would understand our distraction. She is..."

Trenton interjected, "an angel," before Lord Mansfield could finish.

"Who do you speak of?" asked Edward.

Mansfield answered, "We do not know. Lady Anne was her companion, but she did not allow an introduction. While she did not give us the *cut direct*, neither did she engage our company. We were all proper, tipping our hat to her, waiting for her to greet us, but she simply nodded and continued walking. As gentlemen, you know it would be *bad ton* to speak to her, without her speaking to us first, so we could not approach her. Now we are at odds to learn the name of the young lady she chaperones.

"Are you acquainted with Lady Anne?" asked Trenton.

Edward replied, " I am slightly acquainted."

"Then hurry man!" rallied Trenton. "She stands just down the street. You cannot miss her. You must find out who she is!"

Before Lord Felton could make up his mind, Lords Mansfield and Trenton pushed him forward. Amused, Edward consented to their juvenile request, and went to find out the name of the young woman. With all the distinction he possessed, he strolled down Bond Street scanning the shops, keeping his eyes peeled for an *angel*.

He did not have to walk far, before he noticed a young woman with a radiant face, chatting animatedly with Lady Anne. The young woman was full of excitement, bobbing up, and down. Her head was full of blond ringlets, that jostled around her petite face. She had round eyes, with a small nose, and pursed mouth. Her long dark eyelashes contrasted against her light blue eyes. Her height was insignificant. Her full bosom was a stark contrast, to her otherwise petite figure. Edward found no ethereal presence in her, surmising that her endowment and animation is what Mansfield and Trenton found most engaging. Edward deduced that this was her first shopping excursion to Town, and that she was overwhelmed with the novelty of it all.

Edward had to admit, the girl was pretty in a sprig muslin dress, that accentuated her full bosom. He wondered if she had a mind to compliment her body. This past year, Edward met a number of remarkably beautiful young debutantes, but any illusions he had in considering them for a wife, were shattered once they began to speak. He wondered if this *angel* was different.

Edward smiled, as his eyes passed from the *angel* to her companion Lady Anne. He raised his beaver hat in acknowledgement to Lady Anne, pausing to receive her greeting. To his surprise, Lady Anne did not greet him. Instead, she offered a smile and a nod, while she pressed her charge forward. When Edward realized that his mouth was open, and that his hat was still hovering in the air, he quickly shut his mouth. He replaced his hat back on his head, scanned about to see if anyone noticed the affront he had just received. He forgot about Mansfield and Trenton, grumbling his malefactions as he made his way to Whites, his club on St. James Street.

# Chapter Three

Edward knew the best way to announce that he was back in residence was to attend one of the Almack's Balls. Only the *haute ton* were given vouchers to attend the weekly assemblies, held every Wednesday night during the Season. The Lady Patronesses, who judged the formal requests for vouchers, held incredible influence. A rejection of an application could be Social ruin. Applicants from the *nouveau riche* and *cits*, (wealthy merchants, who tried to join the echelons of Society), were routinely denied. In this age, where the Prince Regent increased his coffers by knighting members of trade, the Almack's Patronesses heeded their mantra. They professed that a title recommended an applicant, but ultimately, it was good manners and breeding that persuaded them to release a voucher.

He grimaced at the memory of reaching his majority and attending his first Almack's Ball. He learned quickly that his association with trade, marked him an inferior bachelor. The *marriage mart* mothers, were not interested in the addresses of a man not of the *bon ton*. Edward's bloodline was not the issue, his father was the third son of a duke. The problem was that Edward earned his money through industry. Gentlemen did not work, those that did were considered common, and the *marriage mart* mothers were not interested in marrying their daughter to someone that would diminish their consequence, or remove them from their elevated sphere. Edward soon tired of the rejections, and relinquished any hope he may have had of courting a lady of quality.

However, the Patronesses were smart enough not to offend Edward's grandmother, the Dowager Duchess of Aubry, who in her own right yielded substantial influence. Whenever Edward requested a voucher, he received it, though it bothered him that each year he had to ask for it. Lady Jersey, one of the Patronesses, welcomed Edward, if for no other reason than he increased male attendance. She was always looking for dancing partners with good breeding for the flock of new debutantes that graced the assembly rooms.

Edward realized tonight would be different. He was heir apparent to the Marquis of Beaumont, and Prinny had proclaimed him Earl of Felton. He knew that he was finally considered *good ton* when he returned from Stephen's christening and found the Almack's vouchers, resting on the silver salver that captured the cards and invitations delivered to his town home. He smiled, realizing that he no longer needed to seek out the vouchers to seek out the *ton,* for the tide had changed. The *bon ton* sought him.

"Really, milord," complained Jenkins, as he removed the ruined cravat from Lord Felton's neck, and deposited it on top of the other crumpled neck cloths that piled nearby. "That is the fourth cravat you have ruined. You must remain still, and keep your chin up, if I am to construct a proper Oriental, one with no creases."

"I will allow you one more try, Jenkins," scowled Edward. "Though I lack the patience for you to perfect the style. I get angry every time I think of the nerve of that woman!"

"I have never known you to allow a woman to so rile you. Why is this lady different?" asked Jenkins.

Edward dropped his chin and saw an exasperated Jenkins. Before he could speak, his valet exclaimed, "Please, milord, you must remain still. I cannot complete my task if you are constantly moving about. Perhaps you should consider why this woman disturbs you. I am happy to listen. Then, perhaps you will allow me to finish dressing you properly."

"Don't be ridiculous," he replied. "She does not disturb me." He then raised his chin and stood still, so that Jenkins could finish tying his cravat. His manner inclined him to contemplation. He began to analyze whether Lady Anne did indeed disturb him, and if so, why?

Edward entered the assembly rooms and was quickly greeted by the Patronesses of Almack's, who congratulated him on his peerage. Within seconds, Lady Jersey took command of him by weaving her arm through his, and tugging him towards the ballroom. She informed him there were a number of young ladies anxious for an introduction. Each of them hoping that he would favor them with a dance. Edward usually found the obsequious nature of fawning debutantes distasteful. Since he was shopping for a wife, he determined that he should keep an open mind. Especially since empty flattery and flirtations were part of the *marriage mart* game.

He had just completed the opening set of dances with the daughter of an earl, and was trying his best to maintain his good humor as he escorted the darling back to her mother. On the outside, the young lady looked promising, but the silly chit could do nothing more, than flutter her eyelashes and produce a head splitting giggle throughout the set. Edward knew the quadrille did little to foster a tête-à-tête, as the couples were apart more so than not, but he would have preferred an alluring smile, or a hint of mystery, to the girl's miserable attempt at flirtation.

He headed to the card room for a much needed reprieve. It seemed as though he just arrived, and already he ached to depart. He wondered if there was anyone here worth engaging in a conversation, when the noise from a bevy of suitors caught his attention. He was surprised to see they hovered around Lady Anne. He was used to watching her play the role of the invisible chaperone, so his curiosity regarding her popularity, piqued his interest. He moved toward the group, hoping to overhear their conversation, when he was inadvertently pushed to the front of Lady Anne's suitors. As one man departed, another one tried to move in and in his haste, the gentleman propelled Edward forward into the coveted spot, dead center in front of Lady Anne.

Edward, for the first time in his life, was speechless. He was aghast that Lady Anne might consider he favored her. He was still reeling from yesterday's slight on Bond Street, and his disposition leaned more towards punishing her than revering her. He wanted to give her the *cut direct*, ignore her, but his better judgment told him that was ludicrous, since he was the one who approached her. Besides, he was practically penned in by a ridiculous number of young men, too young, he thought, for Lady Anne. Why, most of them just made their majority. He wondered what all the energy was that surrounded her. Edward thought she looked weary of her suitors' interest, but found himself impressed with the amiable front she projected. He discerned that Lady Anne might not like the attention she was garnering, but though he hated to admit it, she was too polite to admonish it.

Edward's focus on Lady Anne's demeanor was interrupted as his brain began to grasp the questions being launched at her. "Ah!" realized Edward. "They are asking about the *angel*."

Anne thought, *"Enough is enough."* She was tired of being hounded, and felt she more than served her duty to her charge, even if the young woman wasn't in attendance. Anne's new client was the daughter of the recently widowed Mrs. Tate, whose town address was in Cheapside. She had spent the last ten years living in the country with her daughter, when the unexpected death of her husband six months ago, brought them both to Town.

Mr. Tate was a draper, who made a great deal of money selling cloth. He owned a number of stores. Thanks to the money his wife's father settled on him when they married, he was able to profit from a number of investments. Particularly those interests that brought silk back from the Orient. He did not love his wife, but treated her well. Mrs. Tate knew that her father paid a heavy price to have her, an aging spinster, married. Mr. Tate was an ambitious man and thought the arrangement satisfactory. He gained a fortune, while his wife gained a home to call her own. No one was more surprised than the couple when the consummation of their marriage produced a daughter. At first Mr. Tate was not pleased of owning a daughter. However, he soon realized that the infant kept his wife distracted, allowing him to do as he pleased without censure. His wife only had eyes for the daughter she named Annabelle, Bell for short.

Mrs. Tate loved her precious Bell. Each year, she could see that her daughter was blossoming into a beauty that would soon attract attention, not just from the local boys, but from her husband. She feared he would try to take advantage of the sweet girl by selling her off for profit. When Bell turned eight, Mrs. Tate convinced her husband to establish them up in a small cottage near Cornwall. She knew that Mr. Tate was interested in elevating himself in Society. She argued that if they could isolate Bell from the boys in the neighborhood, who were sure to want to court her, then when she made her majority they could try to secure an advantageous alliance. Surely, a beautiful daughter with a large dowry could entice any nobleman into matrimony. Her reasoning seemed sound, and before long Mr. Tate supported the move. Within days, Mrs. Tate and Bell left London, secured with a Cornwall cottage, and a dowry for Bell.

Mr. Tate never bothered to visit his wife and daughter. He did his duty to support them, but had no interest in them, until the day that Bell could be introduced into Society. He was so determined to make a great connection for his daughter, that he had instructions for his agent to sell the cottage on Bell's eighteenth birthday, and stop their living funds, thereby forcing his wife and daughter, to return to Town.

The selling of the cottage on Bell's eighteenth birthday, their lack of funds, and the untimely death of Mr. Tate, did indeed force Mrs. Tate and her daughter back to Town. Upon meeting with her husband's solicitor, she was shocked to learn that somehow her husband had taken on a partner, and lost his fortune on some bad investments. His new partner, a Mr. Archibald Brown, now owned the prosperous draper store. Except for the trust that Mr. Tate had set up for Bell, there were no funds available for Mrs. Tate and her daughter. Mr. Tate's partner even held the lien to the house in Cheapside.

Overcome, Mrs. Tate sighed to her solicitor, "What shall I do? Where will we go?"

Taking pity on the woman, the solicitor replied, "I suggest that you find a husband for your daughter, one that will provide for you, as well. Your husband did not set up any restrictions on your daughter's trust, only that it was to be used to secure a titled connection. I advise you to borrow from it, enough to present your daughter adequately to Society, without depleting the allure of its size. Then, join the rest of the *marriage mart* mothers in securing a worthy connection for your daughter."

"I would not know what to do. I have no one to sponsor my daughter. I have no connections," cried Mrs. Tate.

The solicitor replied, "I can recommend a compassionate woman who might be able to provide you with some guidance."

Mrs. Tate rose from her chair, and grabbed both of the solicitor's hands, shaking them exuberantly, saying, "Oh, thank you. Thank you."

Later that day, Mrs. Tate found herself overcome once again, as she completed her interview with Lady Anne.

"I do sympathize with your plight," replied Lady Anne. "But I do not know why my solicitor would have recommended me to assist you. I myself am in constant fear of not having enough living expenses. You see, my role as a paid chaperone is primarily seasonal work. I am forced to earn my way, so I live at the fringes of Society. I am not a member of the *bon ton*. It is only my bloodline that keeps the *crème of society* from adjuring me. I fear you have been sadly misinformed as to my influence."

Bell, who had been sitting quietly with her hands clasped on her lap, finally spoke. "Excuse me, Lady Anne, but do you suppose you could assist me in becoming a chaperone, like yourself? I am quite industrious, and have been told that I am of a cheerful disposition. Perhaps, I might excel in such a role."

Until that moment, Anne had not taken in the girl's countenance. She did so now, and began to laugh. Anne saw a girl, too pretty to act as an invisible chaperone, and too young, for any mother to place their daughter's welfare.

Neither Bell, nor Mrs. Tate could understand the humor that cultivated Lady Anne's laughter, but they found it contagious. They both began to giggle, along with Lady Anne. Once the snorts and chuckles subsided, and they all wiped away the tears of frustration, Mrs. Tate finally asked, "What is so funny?"

In reflection, Anne surmised it was an act of desperation and camaraderie. For who else but herself could understand what it felt like to be alone in the world, with little to recommend them. At least Bell had a dowry, a pretty face, and character. Who was she to say that Bell could not make a respectable alliance?

Anne agreed to help, as long as they understood that she was in no position to sponsor her. She rarely received invitations. Her entrance to balls and events was usually through her role as a chaperone, or on a rare occasion through a friendship. However, she could introduce Bell to the sights of London. Perhaps cultivate some interest among the young bucks that flocked to Town during the Season. Anne knew that the *ton* would assume that she had taken on a new client, a new arrival, since she would be unknown to anyone, and that alone would drum up some curiosity. She hoped it would foster enough interest to garner some invitations for the girl. Especially, she connived, if she refused to introduce the girl when they were out on their excursions.

Anne with the brightest of smiles, excused herself from the crowd of Corinthians that were bombarding her with questions about her new charge. Edward thought her finesse, in removing herself from her bevy of suitors, remarkable, considering she was hemmed in on all sides.

He watched as she sashayed away, swinging her hips gracefully from side to side. He was surprised to find her figure appealing. He smirked to think this woman, who discomfited him beyond comprehension, could manage to bring a grin to his lips.

Edward resolved he had enough of Society, and decided that he would head over to White's before calling it a night. He retrieved his beaver hat, greatcoat, and gloves, and exited the building, to await his carriage on the front steps. He paused before descending, spying Lady Anne waiting for her conveyance.

Anne turned her head towards Lord Felton when a footman greeted him. The servant announced that he had sent for his lordship's carriage. Edward saw Lady Anne's amused expression when she greeted, “Good evening, my lord.” He knew this was the perfect opportunity to turn his back to her, and give her a *cut direct*. Unfortunately, he was too captivated with the mirth he saw in her eyes, to do anything but stare.

He realized, seeing the gleam in her eyes, that she not only expected the affront, but found humor in it. Before he could decide his next move, the footman abounded down the steps to announce to Lady Anne that her hackney arrived. The footman opened the door to the cab, placed the carriage step down, and was about to assist her ladyship into the cab, when Edward, to his surprise, found himself offering his services to her.

He said, “My lady, Please allow me to convey you home. I think you will find my carriage a more comfortable ride, than a hired cab.”

Anne smiled with mischief in her eyes, when she replied, “Lord Felton, I concur your carriage is a superior ride to this hackney, but I argue whether I would be comfortable riding with you. I am, after all, a single woman, whose chaperone duties do not grant me the privilege to act on my own behalf. However, I do thank you, my lord, for your consideration, and bid you good evening." Anne alighted into her hired cab, amused that the indomitable Lord Felton was left speechless.

Edward strode into his town home reeling. He made his way to his study, where in haste, he removed his greatcoat and gloves. He threw them unto the small sofa that resided near the hearth. His butler would not be pleased that he did not wait to be assisted upon his entry. He placed his beaver hat on the table, next to the crystal decanters that his staff ensured were kept full of the finest liquors. Edward poured himself a brandy and took a healthy gulp. Then, he walked over to tug the bell cord, to summon his butler. Edward was in a foul mood.

After his encounter with Lady Anne, he skipped going to his club. He was too perturbed for small talk. He still could visualize her self-satisfied smile. Edward grimaced, thinking that she might liken him to a puppy that was smitten with her. He asked himself, "What in the devil's name, provoked me into offering my carriage to her? I should have ignored her. I should have evoked a proper set down." Edward swallowed another gulp of brandy, as he considered what he should have done, when Simmons entered, and asked, "May I be of service, milord?"

Edward placed his glass down, and replied, "Yes, Simmons. Please light a fire for me, and tell Cook I am desirous of a small repast. I will eat here at my desk."

Simmons replied, before moving to the hearth to light the already prepared wood stock, "At once, milord."

Edward sat at his desk. He looked through his mail. He spied a letter from his great uncle among the many invitations, to what were the routs and balls the *ton* hosted through the Season. He reflected that the large quantity of invitations should please him, but he was too distracted with the bane of Lady Anne to enjoy the moment. He opened his uncle's letter, to discover that the Marquis of Beaumont was anxiously awaiting him. His letter ended, beseeching Edward to bring a party to sojourn at his manor, as soon as possible.

He grimaced. He knew he had to find an appropriate wife, but his heart was not in it. He was more interested in visiting the marquis and learning all the man had to offer, rather than playing suitor. Edward was anxious to see Westfield and Elinor, and to enjoy some companionship. He missed the comfort of being among peers that wanted nothing from him, other than his friendship. As much as he wanted to take his leave from Town, and meet up with the Westfields, he knew he could not arrive at his uncle's manor without a party that included a possible wife.

Edward recalled Westfield's words, "Why not take a more calculated approach to selecting a bride?"

*"Yes,"* thought Edward. *"I will make a list of the attributes I am looking for in a wife. Instead of acting like an animal on the prowl for a mate, I shall create a job description that lists the attributes of an agreeable wife. Surely, the woman that meets my requirements will appeal to my heart."* Edward pulled a sheet of paper from his

desk, and placed it in front of him. He dipped the quill in his ink jar, and titled his paper, "Attributes for a Proper Wife."

He crossed out the word "proper," visualizing a very prim woman, who weaved her hair in a very tight bun at the back of her head. In its place, he wrote, "desirable," and replaced his prim vision of a woman, with that of a goddess, whose hair flowed around her shoulders. Edward laughed, as he wrote the number "One" to mark the first trait he would look for in a woman.

One. Must have a sense of humor. Edward mulled that attribute over. He was concerned that "humor" was the first trait he listed. Clearly, he thought, humor could not be the most important attribute, but he did not want to stop his thought process, and decided he could rank the characteristics later.

Two. Must be of flawless lineage. *"Yes!"* Edward exclaimed, *"My children will not suffer my fate, of living at the fringes of Society. My heirs will not be looked at as a half-caste, a nobleman tainted with trade. No, I will ensure my children are born into thc bon ton."*

Edward paused to redip his quill, as he pondered his next trait. He felt he had done his duty to his heirs, and that he must not overlook his own interest. After all, if he had to marry, he might as well marry someone that appealed to his senses. Placing quill to paper, Edward entered his next item.

Three. Must have a beautiful face and figure, a "*diamond of the first water.*"

Edward wasn't sure if his next requirement was part of number three, but decided that it was important enough to give the item its own number.

Four. Must be passionate. Edward cringed at the idea of being married to a cold fish. He deduced that he could be flexible on number three, if the lady was desirable to his touch, and he was to hers.

Edward placed his quill down, as he reluctantly recalled Lady Anne's smile. *"That woman is the most undesirable woman I have ever met. She makes me want to shake the living daylights out of her, every time I see her. I do think she laughs at me. Me!"*

He stretched his long legs out in front of him, crossing them at the ankles, as he pushed back in his chair. A vision of Lady Anne's backside came to mind. He smiled, remembering that on occasion, she was able to foster a different response from him. Wasn't he amused at her poise? Did he not compliment her finesse, in managing the crowd at Almack's? Did not the Westfields, call her friend? Is not the Duke of Hartford, an admirer? Edward frowned, as he wondered the exact relationship, between his grace and Lady Anne. He pushed aside his list, and thumbed through his other mail. He remembered seeing an invitation from his grace, the Duke of Hartford. *"He must still be in Town,"* thought Edward.

The Duke of Hartford, was indeed still attending the Prince of Wales. He was inviting Edward to join his small party at the opera house. His grace owned a box, and when he was in Town, he liked to use it. His son, the

Earl of Ingall, and his family rarely visited, so unless his grace attended the opera, or another theatrical performance, the box remained empty. Like many aristocratic families, his grace paid the yearly fee for the box, even if he did not use it. The private suites were as highly coveted as an Almack's voucher, simply for the status of owning them. It was rare for any noble family to relinquish their subscription, or for a vacancy to occur. However, unlike most of the *bon ton* that purchased their boxes to flaunt their wealth and status, the Duke of Hartford held his box because he enjoyed listening to the enchanting arias and sonatas that graced the stage.

Edward wondered if Lady Anne would make up one of the members of his grace's party. He knew he would find out soon enough, because he would accept the invitation. He knew that if it were in his command, he would never refuse a request from the Duke of Hartford, who was like a father to him.

As his master bid, Simmons brought in a tray of a cold collation for him to eat, setting the meal on his desk. He refilled his glass with brandy, and after assuring himself that he could provide no other service for his lordship, he left. Edward took another sip of the fortifying ambrosia. He finally felt his body start to relax. He had begun to eat his meal, when he glanced at his list of wifely attributes. He felt very satisfied with his effort, until he realized he had no clue how to use it, to locate his perfect partner.

# Chapter Four

Edward tugged on his white waistcoat laced with silver thread, before entering the door to the Duke of Hartford's opera box. The scarlet velveteen curtain was pulled to the side with a thickly braided gold cord. Later, the curtain would be released to shield the light from flowing into the box whenever the door to the private suite opened. Edward made quite a dashing picture with his superfine black breeches and coat. His black hair was cut fashionably short in one of the new styles, encouraging his natural wavy hair to fall forward attractively. He ran a hand through his hair to put it in its proper place, before he took in the Duke of Hartford, and Lady Anne.

Edward thought Lady Anne was far from invisible. She stood next to his grace, who wore similar attire to his. Lady Anne's coif was styled, with a string of pearls, and a blue ribbon threaded through her locks. She wore a pearl necklace around her neck, and long white gloves. Her high-waist dress, was made of a light blue crepe, that lay against a white satin slip. A matching wide blue satin ribbon, separated her bodice from her skirt, and Edward guessed that it tied into a bow on her back. Her dress was designed with a square neckline and short, puffy sleeves that were embroidered with blue silks and silver thread. The edges were trimmed with white lace, and her hemline duplicated the effect. When Lady Anne turned her attention from the Duke of Hartford to see who entered the door, Edward saw her eyes alight with recognition. He found her enchanting, though her beauty flummoxed him.

He immediately recalled her earlier effrontery, and he resorted to a churlish nature. In his most dignified air, he pulled his quizzing glass from his fob, and he inspected Lady Anne, from head to toe. Smugly, he remarked, "I hope you found your escort with his grace, comfortable, Lady Anne?"

Anne replied with laughter, "Yes, quite comfortable, my lord."

"Really, Edward," admonished his grace. "Do you not think you should greet us, before you make impertinent inquiries? What puts you in a foul mood? Surely, it is not Rossini?"

Anne intervened, saying, "Oh! Do not admonish him, your grace. I am to blame for his distemper. You see, I declined his offer to convey me home from Almack's this past Wednesday. Although it was my single state that forced my refusal, I fear his lordship took my regrets as an affront."

The Duke of Hartford responded, "Nonsense! Felton is no schoolboy, and understands what propriety dictates. Besides, he has better sense than to think someone as gracious as you, could ever be less than a lady of decorum. He should also know, that I would not place you in such a predicament that would cause the *ton* to gossip about you. Did I not have you properly chaperoned in my carriage?"

Anne's eyes held mirth, as she maintained Lord Felton's steady gaze. Edward saw her lips twitch. He could tell she was doing her best to maintain her composure. Lady Anne tried not to laugh, but when she saw Lord Felton's face relax, and his eyes open wide in amusement, her composure broke. Her chortle escaped like a bird, released from its cage to freedom.

The Duke of Hartford smiled, remarking, "That is better. Now let us take our seat, as I believe the curtain is about to rise."

Edward pulled the velveteen curtain closed behind them, and took his seat next to Anne, before asking the Duke of Hartford, "Your grace, I thought you were hosting a party? Are we the lot of it?"

His grace replied, "Basically, yes. Lady Jersey and George will arrive fashionably late. I invited them to share my box, because Sarah insisted in joining me when she heard that Lady Anne was to be my guest. It seems she is quite interested in her newest charge. No doubt the Jerseys will prove to be a nuisance chatting throughout the performance. I tried to persuade her to use her own box, and visit during the break, but she would not relent, since she does not plan to arrive until the second set."

Edward commented, "I myself have been asked about her. I hear she is being touted as an *angel*. To Anne, he asked, "May I ask the name of your charge, my lady?"

Anne hesitated. Although she knew the *ton* would abjure Bell for her class as a merchant's daughter, she could not lie, the *ton* knew the peerage, like a man of cloth knew his Bible. There was no way around revealing her background. She had spent the last few days escorting Bell around Town. They spent the days shopping on Bond Street, and taking a refreshment of ice at Gunter's. Each morning, they strolled along the Serpentine in Hyde Park, and each morning, a larger crowd of young men drew to seek an introduction.

Today, they went to visit the controversial Elgin Marble exhibit at the British Museum. The Parliament debates over the legality of Lord Elgin's acquisition, was daily drawing a large crowd to the museum. Anne thought the exhibit was another opportunity to gain more suitors for Bell. Besides, Anne loved to view the marble sculptures, inscriptions, and other building pieces acquired by Thomas Bruce, the 7th Earl of Elgin, when he was the British Ambassador to the Ottoman Empire. She always found the classical Greek pieces mesmerizing, even though she had seen them before. Anne was pleased when Bell remarked her appreciation for being brought to see such fascinating artifacts. Together, they marveled over the panels that depicted the battles between the Lapiths and the Centaurs. As they studied the pieces, they became distracted with the *on dits* circulating around the exhibition. Some gentlemen discussed the personal cost of £74,240 that the earl spent acquiring the pieces. Others, were amazed how Lord Elgin sold the collection to the British Museum for less than it took him to ship it to Britain. There was speculation that he refused higher bidders for the exhibit, and that he even refused Napoleon's offer to purchase it.

Anne overheard a lady addressing her companion, that Lord Elgin deserved praise for saving the classical art. She had read in the paper how the local Turks were burning the fallen sculptures, to produce lime for their local buildings. If not for Lord Elgin, she professed, there would not be anything left of the Parthenon to admire.

Anne grinned, saying to Bell, "I do not know the right or wrong of acquiring the pieces, for surely each side has a strong argument, but I confess my persuasion leans towards having them here for our enjoyment."

Bell grinned back, and agreed.

It was at that moment, that Anne caught the eye of Lady Jersey across the room. Before Anne could be hailed, she rushed Bell to another exhibition room, and then they both made their way to exit. Lady Anne expected it was her behavior in not making a proper introduction of her charge, was what drove Lady Jersey's desire to join the Duke of Hartford's party.

Sarah Villiers, the Countess of Jersey, was married to George Child Villiers, the 5th Earl of Jersey. Her mother was the daughter and sole heiress of the banker Robert Child, of Osterley Park, Middlesex. Lady Jersey's countenance, was cultivated from a vast fortune, in addition to a regal bloodline. She was often churlish, flouting airs, to place herself above others. She did her best to distance her reputation from being confused with her mother-in-law, Francis Villiers, a onetime mistress of the Prince Regent, by adhering to her standard of moral righteousness. She was a stickler for good breeding and manners. Anne feared the countess would squelch the interest she had created for Bell, by simply spreading the word the girl was nothing more than a *chit,* a forward and saucy girl.

Edward was surprised that Lady Anne hesitated. He noticed, she lost all color in her face at his inquiry, and then her cheeks slowly began to crimson in embarrassment. He thought, *"The minx is scheming for an answer,"* and wondered, "*why*?"

Anne finally took a breath, and exhaled, "Oh, Fustian! There is no other reply than the truth."

Both Lord Felton and the Duke of Hartford raised an eyebrow, placing their astonished looks on Anne. She continued, "I had hoped that some of Society's young bucks would form an opinion of Bell, before their mamas learned she is the daughter of a draper. Her name is Annabelle Tate, recently arrived from Cornwall, where she spent the last ten years living with her mother. She barely knew her father, as he was not interested in her, other than as a commodity. He hoped to broker her when she became eighteen. Well, the joke is on him for he has been dead this past year. Bell is now eighteen and holds a considerable dowry. She is being hailed as, his lordship mentioned, an *angel*. I must concur that her face is cherubic and her temper enchanting. She is all innocence and accommodating. Unlike many of our debutantes, she is able to put together enough words to engage in a satisfying discourse. I think she is a *diamond of the first water,* who will probably be abjured because of her connection to trade. Even though her pretty hands have never worked a day in her life!"

Lord Felton marveled at Anne's passion for her young charge. Then he remembered how, until recently, he had lived at the fringes of Society because of his connection to trade. He felt empathy for the young girl. He, of all people, understood the stigma the *ton* placed on persons associated with trade. Even now that his title gave him entree into the *ton's* elevated sphere, his commercial ventures, regardless of the wealth it produced for him, were looked upon as nothing more than a vulgar hobby.

Before he or his grace could make a comment regarding her new client, the stage curtain raised. The hush of the audience, focusing on the first act, ended Anne's heated outburst, and the three of them relaxed into their seats to watch the performance. After a few minutes, Edward noticed that Anne's shoulders began to soften, remarkably. He could see the tension leave her body, as she let the opera amuse her. Her lively face pleased him.

He could not help but smile, as he watched Anne fervently applaud. She radiated with exuberance, revealing her enjoyment of *La Cenerentola*, the opera by Gioachino Rossini. Once the thunderous applause within the theatre diminished, he asked, "How did you like Rossini's interpretation of the Cinderella fable?"

Anne replied, "A wonderful love match, was it not? I am glad that Rossini refrained from having a magical fairy godmother. I rather enjoyed that Prince Ramiro's former tutor Alidoro, came to Angelina's aid, rather than the mystical powers of a fairy godmother. Alidoro's helpful character, offers hope for those women who often feel alone when they are holding out for love."

Edward was surprised at her romantic notion, and asked, "Do you hope for love, my lady?"

"I fear my ship has sailed on that front, my lord," replied Anne. "Tell me, what did you think of Rossini, switching the evil stepmother for an evil stepfather? Were your senses offended?"

Edward tried to read Lady Anne's eyes, to determine whether her comment on love reflected bitterness or folly. What precisely did she mean, when she said her ship had sailed? He decided he would like to know more about the intriguing Lady Anne. Edward kept her gaze, grinned, and then answered, "Not at all. How about you, would you have forgiven an evil stepfather, and stepsisters, as easily as Angelina did?"

"No!" exclaimed Lady Anne. "I may not wish them harm, but I could not embrace them as she did. I am of the experience, my lord, that a leopard does not change its spots."

Anne realized she was neglecting his grace, who was listening intently to their conversation. She turned her head to him, and queried, "Did your grace, enjoy Madame Righetti's ballad in the first act?"

"Very much. Although I admit I do not have a sentimental constitution, so I can only tell you that I thought the cast performed prodigiously," replied the Duke of Hartford.

Edward laughed.

His grace raised an eyebrow, asking, "Would you like to elaborate, Felton?"

Edward answered, "I am only in amusement, that you do not find yourself sentimental. Was it not you, who cultivated my suit with your granddaughter?"

His grace, raised his hand to silence Felton, before he burst out laughing. He said, "I expect Sarah Jersey will arrive soon, and we best keep our humor checked. You know she is *high in the instep*, and would frown on our less than haughty demeanor. I must admit I am happy that she did not interrupt the performance. Nor do I mind if her company keeps me from hearing the theatrical comedy that follows. These second performances are so trite, probably because our noisy *crème of society* arrives at this fashionable hour. I am surprised how full the house is. It appears that Rossini drew an early crowd." His grace, noticed the curtain blocking the door, being pulled back by Lord Jersey. He exclaimed, "Ah! Our illustrious guests arrive."

His grace, advanced to make his greetings to Lady Jersey, before bringing Lady Anne forward for an introduction. He said, "You are acquainted with Lady Anne, are you not, my lady?"

Edward felt Anne try to shrink back, but with the palm of his hand on her back, he kept her from retreating. Anne was in good standing with the Patronesses of Almack's, but she was far from the upper echelons of Society, where Lady Jersey reigned. She would never think of approaching her ladyship, unless the countess commanded her society, so she was quite unnerved when Lord Felton thrust her forward.

Before Lady Jersey could reply, his grace interjected that Lady Anne was a dear friend of his, and his family, and that perhaps, Sarah had met her at one of the many balls she frequented.

Lady Jersey smirked and replied, "Indeed." The countess thought, *"Yes, I have seen her at many functions in the role of chaperone."* Sarah felt her husband George, the Earl of Jersey, elbow her. She understood that he did not want the Duke of Hartford offended. If his grace called her friend, then she had no other choice, than to acknowledge her. It did no good to offend a man, who had the Prince Regent's ear.

Sarah replied, "Yes, I believe Lady Westfield introduced us."

Lord Jersey made a distinguished bow, and offered, "Your servant, madam."

Anne made her own notable curtsey to them both, and noticed that Lady Jersey gave a smug approval. The countess waved her hands for everyone to take their seats. She said that their standing was drawing attention from the boxes, and she would not be the one, who would be discussed at tomorrow's tea.

His grace proffered the front row to Lady Jersey and Lady Anne, while the men sat behind them, with Lord Jersey in the center. George began to converse immediately, discussing his latest foxhunt. This led into recollections of past hunts, where his grace and Edward's father, once participated. Edward enjoyed hearing stories about his father and the Duke of Hartford, but found his ears perked to Lady Jersey's conversation with Lady Anne.

Sarah did not waste any time, and asked, "Your new charge is creating quite a stir. The Corinthians and dandies are badgering me. They want to know the name of the girl. Why is she not attending Almack's? Tell me dear, have her parents not applied for vouchers?"

Anne was expecting the question, so to Edward's surprise she answered, "No, my lady, she would not think of it. She is too well mannered to apply. I believe she once told me, that she does not ask for invitations to someone else's party. She feels, that if someone is desirous of her company, then they would display the proper hospitality, and proffer an invitation."

Edward was amazed to hear Lady Jersey laugh, and then reply, "I don't know whether to give you or the *chit* the credit. I have never heard of such a thing. You have managed to pique my curiosity, Lady Anne. Confess now, while I am in good spirits. Who is she?"

Anne continued, "She is Annabelle Tate, my lady. Her mother raised her proper in Cornwall, these past ten years. Her father, now deceased, had not laid eyes on her from the time he removed her to Cornwall. He was a wealthy man and made his money on sound investments. He left her a considerable dowry upon her eighteenth birthday, and her mother came to Town to settle with her solicitor, who made their introduction to me. Mrs. Tate wanted Bell to see some of the sights, before retiring back to Cornwall. Bell has led an isolated life, and has never been to Town. Her mother asked me to escort her on some daily excursions. I have been acting as her chaperone."

Lady Jersey exclaimed, "Do you tell me she has not attended one evening affair! Is she not out? Or has she been abjured?"

Anne replied, "She is an innocent and above reproach. No one making her acquaintance could find any fault in her. She and her mother have led a secluded life. She is of age, so she is out, though lack of a sponsor and position keeps her from being presented at court. To my knowledge, I am their only acquaintance."

Lady Jersey replied, "I have never heard of such a thing. Why have you not introduced her? I have been harangued with inquiries."

"I can vouch for her character. She is a lady, but her father made his money in trade. I have not introduced her, because I know how the *bon ton* feels about those who are connected with trade."

Sarah replied, "Yes, I see your point. I myself find it quite distasteful, seeing these commoners trying to invade our sphere. However, I think my dear you have found an aberration. She sounds delightful. I am most curious to meet her, and determine for myself, whether this girl is the *angel*, our young bucks are confessing her to be. Bring her to tea tomorrow. I will invite Lady Sefton. Together, we will determine if she is as well mannered as you say. I want no pretensions, so do not reveal who we are. If she is the innocent and isolated waif you say she is, then she should not know we are the Patronesses of Almack's. If she is to our liking, then we will provide you with a guest pass, so that she may attend Almack's with you next week. It would be precipitate of us to grant her a voucher for the Season, until we judge her behavior among our Society. However, I warn you, if she is indeed doing nothing more than foisting herself upon us to make a titled connection, then I will ensure she is revealed for the *chit* she is."

A chill went through Anne's body. She smiled and thanked Lady Jersey for her generosity.

# Chapter Five

Anne woke early and made herself over to the Tate apartments that were located in a modest, but respectable living quarter. She broke her morning fast with them, drinking a cup of hot chocolate and eating a warm currant bun. She was too anxious to enjoy it, so rather than do the polite thing and wait until everyone had finished their breakfast, she blurted out, "Lady Jersey and Lady Sefton have invited Bell to tea today!"

Mrs. Tate was in the motion of raising her teacup from the saucer she held in her hand, when Anne's outburst threw her into a excited state. She haphazardly returned the cup to its plate, moved it to the nearby mahogany table, before her shaking hands spilled the hot brew. She clasped her hands to her bosom, exclaiming, "What does this mean?"

Bell asked, "What does what mean, mama? And who are Lady Jersey and Lady Sefton?"

Before Mrs. Tate could answer Bell's question, she balked when she saw Lady Anne shake her head. Anne then remarked, "I met Lady Jersey at the Opera House last night, and she is desirous of making your acquaintance. She has invited you and I to attend her this afternoon. She has invited her friend Lady Sefton to join us."

Bell asked, "But, what about mama? Is it not rude to not have included her?"

Anne was charmed by Bell's concern for her mother. She feared that Bell might decline the invitation if she felt her mother was slighted, so she answered with what she hoped was the truth, saying, "Lady Jersey is aware that your mother is in mourning and did not want to offend her by offering an invitation. You know Bell, you are the only one seen in Society, so it was not churlish for her to invite only you."

Bell thought Anne's reasoning perfectly sound, but she still worried over her mother's feelings. She asked, "Would you mind if I accept, mama?"

Mrs. Tate grinned at having such a considerate daughter and replied, "Not at all daughter. It would please me to see you enlarge your society. My company alone must be quite dull."

Bell responded, "Nonsense! You are perfectly sufficient company, but thank you mama, I would like to attend. My lady, when should I be ready?"

Anne replied, "I will call on you at two-thirty this afternoon, so that we may arrive at three o'clock. Will that suit?"

Bell answered, "Yes, very well. Thank you."

Mrs. Tate was quite anxious to talk to Lady Anne alone, so she asked Bell to run upstairs to get the embroidery frame she was working to show it to her ladyship. She knew it would take Bell some time to find it because the frame lay on a mahogany console hidden from Bell's current sight.

As soon as Bell left the room, Mrs. Tate asked, "What is amiss, my lady? Are our hopes fueled or undone with Lady Jersey's invitation? Why do you not want Bell to know she is a leader in Society and an Almack's Patroness?"

Anne explained all. She was determined to keep Bell in the dark regarding the purpose of their visit. "After all," she said. "It can only make her anxious. Why worry her? I believe her charms will prevail and win the Patronesses over."

Mrs. Tate asked, "But what if they ask if she is seeking a titled offer. All will be undone. She will be abjured!"

Anne placed her hand over the trembling hand of Mrs. Tate. Looking into her eyes, she said, "I certainly hope not, but the reality is this. If she states she does not seek an eligible offer and one is made, these powerful women will intercede to dissolve the connection. They will accuse Bell of being nothing more than a conniving and devious commoner, trying to raise her station in life through marriage. Sarah Villiers has enough clout to ruin Bell if she chose. Let us hope that she and Lady Sefton will be as enchanted as I am with her character. Besides, every woman, noble or not, is looking for an advantageous connection. I expect they would not believe Bell even if she said she had no intention in seeking an offer. We shall have faith in her character and talents, to prove that Bell can rival any debutante. Have faith Mrs. Tate, all is not lost."

Anne and Bell arrived promptly at three o'clock at the Jersey town home located in the Mayfair District. Bell was awed by the magnificence of the house and all its accoutrements. Her stomach, hosting a flurry of butterflies, made havoc on her countenance as she anticipated meeting, what she surmised would be, very regal people.

The Jersey's majordomo escorted them into a small receiving room. Anne realized, especially with the hauteur the butler was emanating, that this room was reserved for the insignificant: solicitors, merchants, impoverished relatives, and guests of uncertain nature. The fact that they were not announced, but placed in a small room without honor irked Anne who, in addition to feeling slighted, noticed the lack of a tea tray.

It was at that moment that Lady Jersey was complaining to Lady Sefton about how reckless she acted in inviting a silly *chit* to tea. She remarked that she did not know what overcame her to act in such a careless way. She said that it was all George's fault because he ordered her to recognize Lady Anne with equanimity, thereby opening herself up to the folly of today's tea.

Lady Maria Sefton was the eldest of the Patronesses and was socially prominent among the *ton*. She held unwavering clout that allowed her to sponsor such notorious acquaintances like Mrs. Fitzherbert, the on and off again mistress of the Prince Regent. No one questioned her alliances. She was not *high in the instep* and leant a compassionate ear to Lady Jersey's tirade. Before she could counter her peer's ranting, suggesting she was of a different opinion, the butler entered. He announced that Lady Anne and Miss Tate had arrived and he placed them in the small receiving room per his mistress's instructions.

Lady Jersey waved him off and said to Lady Sefton, "Come, let us get this insidious meeting over with, so that we may enjoy our tea."

Lady Sefton smiled and followed Lady Jersey into the small parlour.

Anne did not like the look of things when Lady Jersey entered. A more grim expression on her ladyship she could not have expected. She could not understand why she and Bell were received in the first place. Surely, it would have been less churlish for the butler to announce that some unfortunate business had taken her ladyship away and that the tea would be postponed to a later date, sometime never to occur. Anne found her temper rising. She used all her will to keep her composure calm, as she prepared for her and Bell to be dismissed out of hand.

To everyone's surprise, Bell was the first to speak. You would have thought she was the hostess, greeting her guests, putting them at ease. She made a proper curtsey and then went up and took Lady Jersey's hand in greeting.

Bell exclaimed, "It is so kind of you to invite me to come. Lady Anne informed me that you wished to make my acquaintance. I think it most generous for you to extend yourself to someone like me who is most undeserving."

Anne marveled at Lady Jersey's stunned look, a stark contrast to the smiling demeanor of Lady Sefton, who said, "Come Sarah, introduce me to this charming girl."

Sarah looked at Maria and replied, "Excuse me. Lady Sefton, may I introduce Miss Annabelle Tate, recently of Cornwall. Miss Tate, I present the Countess of Sefton."

Bell made her curtsy to Lady Sefton, replying, "Your servant, my lady."

Lady Sefton then looked over and offered her felicitations to Lady Anne, saying, "You are looking well Anne."

Anne replied, "Thank you, my lady."

Maria looked to her hostess and proclaimed, "Sarah, my dear. Let us remove to your beautiful parlour and enjoy our tea before it gets cold."

Sarah replied, "If you insist, Maria."

"I do," responded Maria who then proffered one arm to Bell and the other to Anne. "Come," she said. "I do detest cold tea, do you not?"

Anne replied, "I would never be so bold to agree, your ladyship, in the event that my answer would offend Lady Jersey."

Maria smiled at Anne, saying, "Very good Anne. You are all kindness."

Sarah, to her distemper, found herself following in the rear. Anne took notice and disengaged herself from Lady Sefton. She placed herself next to Lady Jersey who acknowledged her with a smirk.

Anne overheard Lady Sefton ask Bell, "What did you bring to show us my dear?"

Bell replied, "Lady Anne told me that Lady Jersey was an admirer of our coastal lands and would appreciate my watercolors. I do not think them worthy, but I am happy to share them if by chance they should provide even the smallest amusement."

Maria smiled and glanced over to Lady Jersey who was listening attentively.

Each lady took a seat around an oval Queen Anne mahogany tea table. Unknown to Lady Anne and Bell, the Almack's Patronesses were impressed with both girls' correct posture and manner. They noted how they sat, shoulders back, legs crossed at the ankles tucked in, hands clasped on their lap. They held their posture, not touching the support of the chair where they sat. Maria received a nod from Sarah that told her she approved of their manner.

Bell offered to pour for Lady Jersey and Lady Sefton almost laughed when she saw Sarah blush. Before any offense could be taken, Bell asserted that her dear mother always found the teapot too heavy for her comfort. Bell was happy to relieve Lady Jersey of the task if she should desire it of her. Lady Jersey declined her help. Then, Bell remarked on the magnificence of her surroundings and Anne saw that Lady Jersey was not impervious to compliments. Lady Sefton asked to see Bell's watercolors and both Patronesses marveled at her skill in depicting the coastal shores of Cornwall. The time flew by. Anne knew they had stayed later than propriety allowed when she noted the hour. She told Bell that it was time to leave.

Bell apologized when she realized their visit passed the half hour and exclaimed, "I do apologize for wearing out my welcome Lady Jersey. You and Lady Sefton have been too generous with your time. Please accept my heartfelt gratitude for a most enjoyable afternoon. I look forward to sharing our visit with my mama, who I know you were unaware is out of mourning. Lady Anne informed me that was the probable reason your invitation did not extend to her. Otherwise, I would have missed the honor of making your acquaintance. I bid you both good day."

Anne bid her farewell and they left.

Sarah looked at Maria who laughed at her astonishment. Sarah exclaimed, "Am I to understand that Miss Tate would have declined our tea, if she thought her mother was neglected in the invitation?"

Maria replied, "It would appear and she had the right of it. Was it intentional on your part Sarah?"

Sarah answered, "No, just remarkably careless."

"The girl has a regal flare to her. I do not think she was impressed with our stature at all, yet I found nothing insulting in her manner. She is unique in that she seems to be comfortable in her own skin and is thoughtful for the comfort of others. Whether that was bred into her or nurtured, I do not know, but I found the girl quite up to snuff," remarked Maria.

Sarah retorted, "She is tainted with trade."

Maria countered, "Her father is dead. Her mother appears to have raised her properly. Only her dowry is vulgar and I do believe the *bon ton* does not take exception to the actual wealth that comes from trade. Why look at Lord Felton. He is not to be despised, is he?"

"No," answered Sarah. "But he is well connected and from a noble family."

"Well, I leave it to you Sarah. This would not be the first time that you have permitted someone of stellar character to attend Almack's. What was the name of that poet you so adored? The rest of the Patronesses will follow your suit, but you know the girl already has a bevy of suitors demanding an introduction. What harm can it do to give her a guest voucher? There is nothing vulgar in her and her dowry might just be the thing for a third son with no expectations. Besides, the crowd was a bit thin on beaus this past Wednesday. I expect news of her appearance would fill the house."

Sarah replied, "She was rather charming in her accommodating way. I really think she feared the teapot was too heavy for me to handle."

"Adorably sweet," remarked Maria. "Though her loyalty to her mama won me over. Do you not have a soft spot as well for your own mama?"

"Very well," resolved Sarah. "I have already admitted her into my home, why not to Almack's? I will send a guest voucher to Lady Anne to use for Miss Tate."

"You best include two and invite her mama as well, otherwise, she may not attend," countered Maria.

"Maria, It is beyond comprehension. However, I am persuaded that you may be quite right. I will send two guest passes," replied Sarah.

Anne was at her desk when she heard the front door knocker. Her means were too strict to allow for a butler, but she did maintain an abigail for propriety's sake. Mary entered her small parlour. She announced that a footman had just delivered a note from Lady Jersey and did not wait for a reply.

Anne took the note, thanked and dismissed her servant before she broke the seal. Enclosed were two guest vouchers for the Almack's Balls with a note:

*Lady Anne,*

*Both Lady Sefton and myself were quite pleased to make the acquaintance of Miss Tate. We are sending two guest vouchers for Miss Tate and her mother. We hope you, a member in good standing, are available to escort them this Wednesday.*

*Yours Etc.,*
*Sarah Villiers*
*Countess of Jersey*

Anne was dumbfounded. Certainly after yesterday's visit, she did not expect any vouchers to be forthcoming. Before Mary had interrupted her, she was in the middle of penning a note to Lady Jersey to thank her for the invitation to tea. Anne hoped to appease any *faux pas* made the day before. The quick dispatch of the vouchers could only mean that Lady Jersey and Lady Sefton did not take any offense during their meeting, and found Bell if nothing else, worthy of attending Almack's.

As soon as Anne completed reading Lady Jersey's note, she was up, fetching her pelisse, straw bonnet, reticule, and exited the front door, before Mary even realized her mistress had left.

Mrs. Tate was overjoyed with the news of receiving the much sought after vouchers. She exclaimed her delight. She had no reservations regarding Bell's success. She knew her daughter could compete with any debutante in terms of beauty and charm. Her concerns dealt with her own class of station. She worried her appearance at Almack's could only harm Bell. She argued that while Bell would draw the admiration of male suitors, she felt she could only draw the ire from the *marriage mart* mothers who would be jealous of Bell's success. Mrs. Tate argued that it would only take one of the mothers to snub her for being the widow of a tradesman for Bell to be abjured. Mrs. Tate was determined that only Lady Anne should accompany Bell.

Anne spent the next hour reviewing some of the rules of conduct that Bell would be required to follow.

1. She must never be in the company of a man without a chaperone.
2. She must wait to be introduced to a gentleman.
3. She must never dance more than three dances with the same man. Make that two dances, for three would surely draw speculation of an offer upon her.
4. She must not refuse a request to dance with one suitor and then accept the offer of another.

Bell listened attentively and only after hearing number four, did she state, "I am not sure I am prepared to dance."

Anne balked, asking, "How do you mean?"

Bell replied, "I have only been to two assemblies in Cornwall and I performed the country dances quite awkwardly. My partner needed to call out my steps to me.

I am not even sure I remember the steps. It was all so new and exhilarating at the time."

Mrs. Tate exclaimed, "Oh, my dear! How I have failed you!"

"Nonsense Mama!" responded Bell. She then looked to Lady Anne, saying, "I think I am a quick learner, if you teach me I am sure I will be ready in time."

Anne hesitated with her thoughts for a moment and then said, "You do not have permission to waltz, so we shall hire a tutor and teach you later. The quadrille is usually the opening set, so if we arrive late that is one last dance you need to learn. We will practice the basic steps and hope your partner will assist you. I am sure they will delight in coming to your assistance. We shall only stay for a couple of sets to make an appearance. You will comment that you are concerned for your mama and hope to receive another guest voucher to attend the next assembly. Hopefully, your admirers will pressure Lady Jersey for another voucher."

"Do you think it wise to leave early Lady Anne?" asked Mrs. Tate.

Anne answered, "Most definitely."

Later that day, Anne scribed a note to Lady Jersey thanking her for her kindness. She informed her that while Bell would be attending the Almack's Ball on Wednesday, Mrs. Tate unfortunately must send her regrets, but with full appreciation to the Patronesses for their generosity of including her in the invitation.

Anne was just seeing her abigail off with her note to Lady Jersey, when to her surprise she saw Lord Felton draw up on his curricle drawn by two magnificent bay horses. He looked distinguished wearing a bottle green double-breasted jacket and buff colored pantaloons that hugged his legs. The shine on his Hessian boots complimented his black hair and as he pulled on the reins to stop his cattle at her doorstep, she found herself holding her breath in anticipation.

It was near the fashionable hour when members of the *bon ton* promenaded along Rotten Row in Hyde Park to see and be seen. Anne expected that Lord Felton was making his way there and happened by chance, to be passing through her modest neighborhood on some errand of business. She watched his *tiger*, the groom wearing a yellow and black waistcoat employed to ride on the back of his curricle, jump off from his perch and run to take hold of the mares' bridles. Edward commanded him to walk them up and down the street, while he conversed with Lady Anne. He then directed his attention to her and said, "I am glad to have found you at home. I had planned on leaving my calling card, but am delighted to be fortunate to address you in person. How are you?"

Anne was surprised by Lord Felton's amiable countenance and simply replied, "I am well, thank you. May I offer you some refreshment, my lord?"

"No, thank you," replied Edward. "I would not feel comfortable having my horses idle for too long. I had hoped you might take a ride through Hyde Park with me?"

Still flummoxed by Lord Felton's friendly demeanor towards her, she replied, "But, why?"

Edward laughed. "Surely, I am not the first gentleman to request the honor of your company?"

Embarrassed by her lack of finesse, Anne responded, "No of course not, it is just I did not expect you, so I was not prepared."

Edward found Anne's discomfiture charming. Her crimson cheeks and pouty mouth made her look younger than her five and twenty years. It was, he thought, the first time he felt he had the upper hand in their conversations. He replied, "Please come with me. I would like to hear how your tea with Lady Jersey went and Oh! I forgot. I brought you the *libretto* from Rossini's performance. I could not remember if you had taken your program or left it in the opera box, so I brought you mine. I remember how much you enjoyed the opera and thought you might like to have it as a keepsake."

Anne was delighted. She remembered she had indeed set her program down during her discussion with Lady Jersey and upon leaving, had failed to reclaim it. She was sorely disappointed at the time to forget it. *"How nice,"* she thought, for Lord Felton to give his *libretto* to her. She said, "Thank you, my lord. I very much would like the *libretto*. I was sorry when I returned home and realized that I had left it behind. Give me a minute to get my pelisse and bonnet and I will be happy to join you on your ride through Hyde Park."

Anne found herself quite anxious sitting next to Lord Felton. She could not remember the last time that she was the object of a gentleman's attention. She felt giddy and did her best to check her jejune behavior. *"Heavens!"* she thought. *"What a fool he will think me if I should start giggling, blushing like a green girl just entering Society. I should say something, anything."*

While Anne contemplated an amusing retort, Edward asked, "How did your visit with Lady Jersey and Lady Sefton go?"

Anne was relieved for the question, for she still had not thought of anything clever to say. Her clammy hands were beginning to stain the palms of her white gloves, so she started to fan her fingers on her lap to try to dry them out. Edward noticed her actions and thought perhaps the pace of the curricle was more than her nerves could handle. He placed his hand on one of hers and said with sincerity, "I am quite capable of handling my cattle, my lady. Please do not worry."

Anne felt a surge of energy bolt through her and thought she might jump right out of her seat. Edward felt her tremor and pulled on the reins to bring his bays to a halt. "My dear," he asked. "Are you all right?"

"Yes, thank you," replied Anne while thinking, *"I am acting quite the ninnyhammer."* She continued, "I am sorry, my lord. I have been *woolgathering* and have not given you the attention you deserve. I believe you asked me a question."

"Not at all," said Edward. "But perhaps I should return you home. You do seem out of sorts and I do not wish to overset you. I hope you will allow me to stop by tomorrow and see how you fare. I could enjoy that refreshment you offered me earlier."

"That would be most agreeable," replied Lady Anne. "I confess to have been under a bit of strain, trying to do my duty to Mrs. Tate and her daughter. I am happy to say that I have procured guest vouchers for them to Almack's next assembly. Will you attend, my lord?"

Edward smiled. "I am happy for your success, my lady. One of the reasons I wanted to talk to you was to find out if the Almack's Patronesses approved of Miss Tate. I look forward to hearing the whole story tomorrow."

Anne felt as though she just woke from a dream. Reason sank into her mien. Lord Felton wanted news of Bell. He was not attending her. No, he was learning of Bell's fate with the Almack's Patronesses and she felt quite the fool. *"Well,"* she thought. *"It was still nice of him to bring me a libretto."*

# Chapter Six

Anne and Bell were rolling up the Aubusson carpet that lay on her parlour floor when Lord Felton surprised them. Anne had thoroughly forgotten about Lord Felton's visit. She and Bell were in the process of moving her parlour carpet and furnishing to the sidewall to make room for a dance practice.

Mrs. Tate had been passing by the front door when she heard the knocker and opened the door. She was flustered by the appearance of a distinguished gentleman. She had not the pleasure of his lordship's acquaintance, but his stature and impeccable dress clearly announced that he was an aristocrat.

Edward was about to ask to be announced when he heard the commotion from the parlour. His curiosity got the better of him and he entered without ceremony, bowing to Mrs. Tate, greeting her with a "madam," before brushing past her to enter the parlour.

He found Anne bent over in exertion with her backside to him. Edward smiled at his timing. He knew Anne would not appreciate that he found her at such a disadvantage. He gave a slight cough, saw Anne turn her head, spy him, blush, and stand to a quick attention. My lord, forgive me," she said with enlightenment. "I forgot that you were to visit."

"What am I interrupting?" asked Edward. "And how may I be of assistance?"

Anne raised her hand to her face and hair to feel if her appearance was decent. She felt her face was warm from her exertion and hoped her hair was not too out of sorts. Before she could answer, she saw Bell moving stealthily towards the door to exit. She exclaimed, "Oh! Do forgive me. Lord Felton, may I introduce Miss Annabelle Tate. Miss Tate, I present Lord Edward Brentwood, The Earl of Felton."

Edward stepped forward, gently took Bell's hand and placed a light kiss on its backside. The moment he took her hand, his eyes never wavered from hers. Releasing her hand, he made a formal bow and gallantly greeted, "Your servant, madam."

Anne was awed by the grace of his lordship's salutation and movements. She noted that he walked royally and had an elegance that made her think she had met Lord Felton in one of her romance novels. She found herself attracted to him and wondered why she had never been before. Edward's voice interrupted her reverie. She saw that he was addressing Bell with whom he was in conversation.

"I hope you will allow me to instruct you. I am sure I would be a better partner than Lady Anne, since I am of the proper persuasion. It is your goal to dance with men, is it not?"

Bell giggled while Anne with aplomb said, "We could not intrude upon you, my lord."

"Nonsense," responded Edward. "It would be my pleasure, besides my time is already yours and I would enjoy being of assistance. Does someone play or do we manage without music?"

Mrs. Tate who was watching the scene unfold from the doorway interjected, "I can play, my lord."

Edward turned to see the woman who allowed him entry. He replied, "Very good."

Anne approached Mrs. Tate and brought her to face Lord Felton. She introduced them. "My lord, may I present Mrs. Tate, the mother of my charge. Mrs. Tate, Lord Felton."

Mrs. Tate curtseyed and Edward bowed. He said, "Shall we begin?" Then, he commanded Anne, "Come be my partner, my lady. I suggest a demonstration is in order before Miss Tate begins."

As in a trance, Anne complied. She looked into Lord Felton's bewitching eyes. She did not balk when he placed one of his hands in hers and the other around her waist. He began to glide with Anne before her dreamlike state was interrupted by Bell's exclamation, "Oh! The waltz." Anne stopped in her tracks. Bewildered, Edward asked, "What is it?"

"I am sorry," replied Anne. "Miss Tate does not have permission to waltz, so today our plan was to revisit the basic reel steps. Bell is only planning to engage in two sets until she learns the quadrille and has permission to waltz."

"Ah!" exclaimed Edward. "I forget the intimacy of the waltz is still considered scandalous! Only those young debutantes who seek the Patroness's permission may dance it, otherwise they place their reputation at risk. Do you plan to sit out the quadrille or arrive late?"

"Late," answered Anne.

Anne could not remember the last time she laughed so hard, not that Bell was an ill student, for she was not, but Lord Felton was quite the droll instructor. Using exaggerated moves and poses, he instructed Bell on the common steps of the assembly dances. Bell found they were no different than the basics of a country dance and she picked up the steps easily.

Edward struck a hauteur pose and playfully chided Bell when she forgot to simper like most debutantes making their *come-out*. He remarked, "Where is your demure smile, Miss Tate?" Next, he would admonish her, "No, not like the *angel* you are, but more like this," demonstrating a ridiculous smile. Everyone realized he was joking, for only an imbecile would take him seriously.

At one point, Edward picked up a fan that he spied on a console table near the wall and started demonstrating the various uses of a lady's fan. He struck one pose with the fan in front of his face and said, "See how my eyes are displayed to their best advantage?"

To Anne's surprise, he winked. Everyone laughed. Anne thought Lord Felton's boyish behavior most charming and wondered what to make of it all. Was he a possible suitor of Bell's or was he amusing himself for pure folly? Whatever the reason, Anne was happy that Lord Felton had revealed his playful side to her.

After almost an hour, Anne summoned her abigail Mary to bring some refreshments. While they waited, Lord Felton took what seemed mere minutes to put the parlour to rights. As Mary entered, they each took a glass of lemonade from her tray and sat down. The pleasant mood prevailed and Lord Felton was the first to speak.

"We will continue the lessons tomorrow at my home. I will hire a proper dance instructor who will tutor Miss Tate in the quadrille and waltz. Your mother, Miss Tate, shall act as chaperone."

"But Lady Anne is my chaperone, Lord Felton," corrected Bell.

"Indeed," replied Edward. "But in my home she will be my guest."

Edward looked at Anne and asked, "You will come, won't you?"

Anne had to remember to close her mouth. For her jaw had dropped when Lord Felton acknowledged her as a peer. Invitations for herself were so few, that his gesture was received with extreme appreciation. *"He is of the old school,"* thought Anne. *"A man of true gallantry."*

"Yes," answered Anne. "I will come. But you must let us bear the cost."

"Nonsense," replied Edward. "The tutor is for my primary use, for today's exercise proved I am in great need. I am inviting you to help me practice."

Anne smiled and retorted, "But of course, we are of the proper persuasion, are we not?"

Edward laughed and answered, "Precisely. Should we make tomorrow's practice an early hour and then perhaps after a rest you will allow me to take you all for a ride during the fashionable hour in Hyde Park? I would like to try again, if you please, my lady?"

Anne looked at Bell whose eyes begged her to accept. She had yet to experience the fashionable hour and so wanted to go. Anne answered, "Yes. That would be nice as long as Mrs. Tate has no objections."

Mrs. Tate, who was still concerned she was a liability for her daughter, remarked, "I have no objections for Bell, though I must decline. I do hope you understand, my lord."

Edward looked steadily into Mrs. Tate's eyes and said, "completely." Reading his eyes, Mrs. Tate thoroughly believed he did understand.

Edward grimaced as Jenkins diligently tied his cravat. He was in the process of admonishing himself for his childish behavior yesterday at Lady Anne's and could not understand why he would reveal himself to her so freely. He could not remember the last time he felt so relaxed, letting his guard down, behaving as though he was among family. True, the Tates and Lady Anne had no pretensions. However, to allow them to witness him behaving in such a ridiculous fashion, where they could later mock him, was completely against his character.

He spent his whole life acting in the most proper way when engaged in Society. He honed his manner, so if anyone dared to laugh at him, they would find his wit more than capable of a full set down. His tongue could be lethal. Most gentlemen feared his influence in the business arena. Edward's business acumen was well respected among the *bon ton,* so a word from him to a banker or financier could squelch a hopeful prospect.

Jenkins asked, "What is it milord? Why are you fidgeting so?"

Edward responded, "I do not fidget. Are you almost done tying your wretched knot?"

"I beg to differ milord, but will not trespass on whatever is befuddling you," retorted Jenkins. "I expect it is Lady Anne for whenever the two of you meet, you seem to walk away very much affected."

He exclaimed, "Enough of your insubordination! I am not affected, simply preoccupied with some business affairs. It is coincidence that my discomfiture corresponds with Lady Anne and the Tates visit. Has Monsieur Devereaux and his accompanist arrived yet?"

"Yes, milord. They are awaiting you in the ballroom. Your majordomo has instructions to bring the Tates and Lady Anne there as soon as they arrive."

"Very good," he replied.

Edward was surprised to see that Lady Anne and the Tates were already awaiting him in his expansive ballroom. There was a staging area flanked by some potted palms at the end of the room where a piano resided. Monsieur Devereaux's accompanist sat on the bench and Lady Anne and Monsieur Devereaux were in a deep discussion nearby. Miss Tate stood next to her mother who both seemed to be taking in the grandeur of the room. Mrs. Tate was the first to notice Lord Felton enter the room. She advanced quickly to greet and praise him for his generosity in hosting a dance class.

"My dear Mrs. Tate," replied Edward. "I would hardly call the three of us a dance class." He then escorted Mrs. Tate back to the rest of the group, joining Lady Anne and Monsieur Devereaux whom he hired to perform the day's instruction.

"Monsieur Devereaux," greeted Edward. "So good of you to join us and on such short notice. May I present my guests or have you already made their acquaintance."

"Oui, My Lord Felton," replied Monsieur Devereaux. "I am well acquainted with Lady Anne, who most properly introduced me to my pupil Miss Tate."

Edward wondered how Anne was acquainted with Monsieur Devereaux. He found it interesting, how someone he never paid any attention, seemed to be well ensconced in his Society. Technically, it was her Society as well. Her penury state lowered her eligibility, but she was a respectable and titled lady. It was her profligate father, a marquis, who lost his wealth in gaming. Even though his luck was known to come about to replenish his coffers, his early death prevented him from reclaiming any of his fortune for his daughter to inherit.

Monsieur Devereaux continued, "It is Providence, is it not? I am happy you encouraged me out of retirement to bring two of my old pupils together again, my lord."

Monsieur Devereaux's comments surprised Edward. It had been twenty years since he engaged in a class of his. Although he had found his instructor most obliging and amiable towards him, his reflections produced a more disheartening memory.

Edward's father was determined for him to receive the education and privilege of a gentleman, so that he would never feel inferior among the titled. Edward almost always found himself among the *ton's* precious heirs when he yielded to his father's direction, and dance class proved no different. Edward was the only student in Monsieur Devereaux's class whose family resided at the fringes of Society because his parents engaged in trade. At the age of ten, Edward had enough experience and knowledge to understand that he was not considered an equal among the children of the titled. If he forgot, it took only one lesson with them to be reminded of that fact.

Edward remembered that Monsieur Devereaux had difficulty finding him a partner for practice. Third sons were challenging enough for a dancing maestro to partner, but a young man tainted with trade was impossible. Even at five years old, the daughters of the *bon ton* were tutored to know that only first-born sons were desirable partners and anyone affiliated with trade was beneath them. Edward frowned when he realized he had invited into his home a woman who must have shunned him. To further his gall, he was helping her.

Anne observed Lord Felton's demeanor. She was surprised when his eyes steeled and his face became hard. She wondered if he remembered her when she was a young girl and found the memory distasteful. Those days were not pleasant reflections for her either. She was a tall and gangly girl that towered over the boys and girls of her age. She felt gargantuan among the commonly petite debutantes, even though her mother was constantly assuring her that her body would catch up to her long legs. She remembered how diffident she became when they laughed at her height. The boys blatantly refused to dance with her, claiming she was too tall for them. If not for Master Brentwood, to her embarrassment, Monsieur Devereaux would have claimed her as a partner. Then, she would never have experienced that one-day of joy in dance class.

Anne recalled that Edward was five years her senior, so her height was not that spectacular to him, but she knew the other students made fun of him for having to partner with her. She knew he could have joined in their mockery and earned some respect from those that looked down on him, but he did not.

That day, Anne remembered that Edward was not happy when Monsieur Devereaux escorted him over to partner them. He said nothing, but bowed properly. Taking her by the hand, he led her onto the dance floor where the other couples were forming. He never took his stern eyes off of her and she reflected how they eventually softened as he started to exaggerate his steps in jest. She shortly joined him, mirroring his moves, until they both started laughing. She had so much fun and looked forward to being paired up with him again, but after that day, Edward never returned to class and she never knew why.

Anne greeted Edward cautiously, "My lord, do you not remember the extremely awkward child you once saved from the observation seats?"

The tightness in Edward's face slackened and merriment danced in his eyes. He laughed and responded, "Are you the girl that was forced to come to my aid because no other would associate with me?"

Anne laughed and replied, "You are under a misapprehension, my lord. It was you that was forced to dance with one whose height repelled all of Monsieur Devereaux's pupils."

She continued, “I always appreciated your nobleness though I felt bad that you were forced to partner with one that could only have embarrassed you. The other pupils used to gossip that the experience forced you to stop your lessons.”

Edward was astonished and saddened that his actions had caused Anne embarrassment. He remembered telling his father that he would not return to class where he was not welcomed and where Monsieur Devereaux was placed in a position to force a nice girl to dance with him. From that day forward, Edward took private lessons at home with the master, benefitting himself and his valet’s younger sister, who became his accommodating partner.

Monsieur Devereaux interrupted their varied recollections and said, “You were both attentive pupils who learned well. Please, my accompanist will play and you both will demonstrate the waltz for Miss Tate, who is most anxious to learn.”

Edward saw Anne blush and lower her eyelashes. He thought it charming that a woman, considered on the shelf at five and twenty, could still become flustered by a gentleman’s touch. His eagerness to envelope her into the waltz position surprised him. He wondered, *“What is it about this woman that makes me feel excited about doing the most ordinary things?”*

Anne found herself in familiar territory, sitting across from Lord Felton in an open carriage as they promenaded along the avenue known as Rotten Row in Hyde Park. She remembered a similar ride during last year's Season, before Lord Felton received his title and was known to her as Mr. Edward Brentwood, one of Lady Elinor's suitors. Edward had secured an afternoon ride to Hyde Park with Elinor, and Lord Westfield had engaged Anne as a willing consort to scuttle Edward's courtship by imposing on the couple's outing. Anne recollected how Edward wanted desperately to win Elinor's favor. She could tell that he was smitten with the beautiful, straightforward, and refreshingly innocent debutante. She could not help but compare his previous behavior towards Elinor with his current attention to Miss Tate.

Anne noticed Lord Felton's pleasure in watching Bell experience Hyde Park's fashionable hour for the first time. The *crème of society* came in their best finery, mounts, and equipage during the late afternoon hours to see and be seen. Edward smiled, looking at Bell as she marveled at the smartly dressed and ostentatious *bon ton*.

"I have never seen so many people in one place before," remarked Bell. "They are all so spectacularly dressed. Did you see that woman with the five ostrich plumes in her hair? Or that man in the carriage with that adorable poodle?"

Edward replied, "I did not see the woman, but I expect the man was the Honorable Frederick Byng, a friend of the Prince Regent. His friends call him "Poodle Byng," thanks to Beau Brummell, who nicknamed him because he is never without that ridiculous dog!"

"Oh, how sweet!" exclaimed Bell.

Edward laughed.

Anne smiled and directed Bell's attention to the approaching carriage. She could see that Ladies Jersey, Sefton, and Cowper, all Patronesses of Almack's, were prepared to acknowledge them. She was surprised when Lady Jersey asked her coachman to stop, so that she could greet them.

"Lord Felton, Lady Anne, Miss Tate," greeted Lady Jersey. "I am glad to see that Miss Tate is finally ensconced in Society. What do you think of our esteemed Hyde Park, Miss Tate?"

Bell brought both her hands together in a clasp and exclaimed, "I think it is most prestigious, Lady Jersey. Thank you for asking. I also want to thank you and Lady Sefton so much for the guest voucher to Almack's. I am so looking forward to attending tomorrow's assembly."

Lady Jersey and Lady Sefton smiled. Sarah responded, "The pleasure is ours dear girl. Now, let me introduce you to Lady Cowper."

"No need for formalities, Sarah," replied Lady Emily Cowper. "I heard all about Miss Tate. I am glad that you will be joining us tomorrow."

Bell responded, "It is an honor to make your acquaintance, my lady."

Lady Jersey interrupted, and addressing Bell's companions said, "I expect to see the both of you tomorrow night as well." She then directed her coachman to move on before Lord Felton or Lady Anne could answer.

"My," stated Bell. "They do take one's breath away. Will everyone at tomorrow's assembly be so overwhelming?"

Edward chuckled, "Do not fear Miss Tate, you will manage quite well."

"Felton!" called the Duke of Hartford.

"Your grace," responded Edward. "It is good to see you."

The Duke of Hartford's mount came up to rest on the side of Edward's carriage. He responded, "Thank you. You are well?" Before Edward could answer, his grace turned to look at Anne and said, "It is good to see you, my lady. I have been meaning to call on you and see how you have fared, but Prinny has kept me quite occupied." He then looked at Miss Tate and asked, "Is this your new charge?"

Anne blushed and answered, "Oh, how thoughtless of me. May I present Miss Annabelle Tate to you, your grace. Miss Tate, I present his grace, the Duke of Hartford."

Miss Tate replied, "Your grace, It is a pleasure to make your acquaintance."

His grace replied, "Nonsense, the pleasure is mine." He then went on to say, looking directly at Anne, "Will you both be attending Almack's tomorrow?"

Before Anne could reply, Bell burst forth with an answer, "Yes, your grace. We will be there."

Felton grimaced as Lords Riverdale, Mansfield, and Trenton on horseback approached the carriage on the other side. Anne heard Edward hiss under his breath, "We will never move this carriage forward if we continue to be accosted."

Anne thought his remark on the strong side, but dismissed it and continued to give his grace her full attention.

"Felton," said Lord Mansfield. "You must introduce us."

His grace smiled and bid his goodbyes before giving his mount his heels.

Edward accommodated the trio and saw Bell blush and flutter her eyelashes with each introduction. Anne noticed Lord Felton's changed mood and wondered if Bell's popularity with the young trio made him jealous.

# Chapter Seven

Edward waited impatiently for Lady Anne and Miss Tate to make their entrance into Almack's. He had arrived hideously early, a first for himself, but he did not want to miss the arrival of the ladies. He knew they were to come late in order to skip the opening set of the quadrille, but they also planned to leave after only two dance sets, which meant there was no way to time their attendance.

He had promised Miss Tate the first set of dances and did not want to let her down. He knew she would be nervous and wanted to offer her his support for the evening. He caught himself fidgeting. He almost laughed out loud as he recalled the remarks his valet Jenkins made, while he helped him to dress earlier that evening. "Perhaps, your nervous disorders are founded in alchemy. Has Lady Anne bewitched you by chance?"

Edward's thoughts were interrupted by the reduction of noise as he noticed gentleman after gentleman, stop their talking and turn to see the newly arrived. Bell created a charming picture, standing alone in a pastel jonquil gown that shimmered, as the light caught the glass beads that trimmed the neckline of her heart shaped bodice and flounced hem. Edward knew all the young debutantes wore pastel colors to denote their youth, colors that usually paled against their alabaster skins, but Bell glowed in her yellow high-waist satin dress with puffed sleeves.

Her blond hair was set in bouncing curls around her face. Her skin was a warm hue that marked the time she spent outdoors. Her beauty and radiance lit a path for her suitors like a beacon that guides its ships home.

Even from his distant vantage point, Edward could tell Miss Tate was nervously scanning the room, he surmised she was looking for him. He was about to make his way to her and put her at ease when he saw Anne. Edward thought she never looked lovelier. She wore a high-waist gown that accentuated and revealed her bosom. The dark slate blue silk underdress and matching chiffon layers made her look more like a debutante than a woman of five and twenty. White lace trimmed both her short puffy sleeves and square neckline, the finished hems were decorated with petite red rose buds. Anne dressed her hair to the side so that a ringlet of curls rested just above her décolletage and Edward was captivated.

As the bodies of suitors pressed forward, Edward reacted and forcefully pushed his way through the crowd, incurring more than one gentleman's wrath. He saw the merriment in Anne's eyes when he finally reached them in greeting. He said, "I thought you would never arrive, but I have been more than rewarded. Your beauty takes my breath away."

Anne's smile broke as she absorbed Lord Felton's compliment. Before she could respond, Bell intervened and asked, "Is this not our dance, My Lord Felton?"

Anne could see that the bevy of suitors were becoming overwhelming for Bell and she was hoping that Lord Felton would lead her away from the mob unto the dance floor for a reprieve. He did so, but not before grinning sheepishly at Anne.

Lord Felton offered his arm to Bell who made her curtsey before accepting his escort. She begged the pardon of the numerous gentlemen requesting to be introduced to her and happened to block her path to the dance floor. Edward felt bad leaving Anne to deal with Bell's many ardent admirers, having to inform them that Miss Tate was only dancing two sets, and that both sets were already promised.

Edward laughed as he saw face after face of dejected admirers begrudgingly look upon him dancing with Bell. He felt quite glib being the first gentleman to have ever secured Bell's hand in a dance and even more gallant, knowing that she looked to him to guide her through her newly learned steps. He was enjoying himself profusely and looking forward to dancing the next set with Lady Anne.

When the music ended, he escorted Bell over to Lord Riverdale. During their jaunt in Hyde Park, Riverdale had stealthily managed to secure a dance with Bell. Lords Trenton and Mansfield were quite affronted when they learned their friend had outmaneuvered them. They believed since they had saw her first, they should logically be first to dance with her. Riverdale could care less for their reasoning, and even less for drawing straws.

Upon releasing Miss Tate to Riverdale, Edward headed towards the area he had left Lady Anne. He was feeling a bit put out not finding her there and then restless when he heard the strings announcing the second set was ready to begin. He searched the crowd to no avail and then he heard her laugh. He knew that laugh because more than once, he had felt it directed at him. He turned his eyes to the dance floor and found her partnered with the Duke of Hartford. Edward wondered, *"What the deuce brought him here?"*

Anne saw Bell with Lord Riverdale and thought they made a fine couple. She could see that he reveled in helping her with the steps of the dance and saw Bell giggle as she erred in a turn. She thought it gallant of his lordship to err on purpose to distract the *marriage mart* mothers from making her *faux pas* tomorrow's *on dit*.

His grace remarked, "I must be quite dashing if I can make you smile without any effort."

"That you are, your grace, but I am smiling from seeing that my charge is being nicely attended to by Lord Riverdale," replied Anne.

"Ah yes. Miss Tate," responded his grace. "I do not think you have much to worry about there. She seems to be attracting much attention. Is Lord Felton among her conquests?"

Anne was dumbfounded. She was pretty sure the answer was "yes," but for some reason she did not want to publicly declare it to be true. She instead answered, "He has been most attentive and helpful in tutoring Bell in dance."

"Has he?" replied his grace. It was at that moment that he saw Lord Felton standing akimbo with an angry face. He bemused, "I do not think Felton appreciates that others are enjoying the rewards from his benevolence."

Anne followed his grace's gaze and saw a very disgruntled Lord Felton. She exclaimed, "Oh, dear, He does look out of sorts. Does he not?"

"Quite so," laughed his grace, very much to Edward's annoyance.

Edward knew that Anne and Miss Tate planned to leave at the end of the set. He had thought to escort them home, but after seeing his grace lavish his attention on Anne, he was so affronted that he left without saying goodbye. He soon found himself in his suite arguing with Jenkins. "I tell you," countered Edward, "I am not sulking!"

"Yes milord," responded Jenkins. "But something is amiss and unless you come to terms with what seems to bother you so, you are going to manifest your affectations into some sort of serious malady."

It was into the early afternoon hours before Edward rose from his bed. Jenkins had been kind to keep his room darkened by not pulling back his heavy damask drapes. He realized Jenkins must have entered his suite earlier, noting that his pitcher of water that he used for his morning ablutions had grown cold.

Edward's head felt heavy and his body wearied. He sat on the edge of his bed recalling his restless night and bad temperament. He questioned why he was angry with Anne. She had not promised him a dance, so why did it bother him to see her with the Duke of Hartford? He wondered what his grace was about attending Almack's. He couldn't remember the last time he joined the *marriage mart* assembly. Surely, he wasn't looking for a bride? Lady Anne was young enough to be his granddaughter. He knew many debutantes who married men old enough to be their father, but old enough for a grandfather? He thought not. No matter how extraordinary a connection, he could not see Lady Anne as the next Duchess of Aubry, even if he believed she would make a fabulous duchess.

Edward remembered how lovely she looked and was sorely disappointed that he was not able to spend any time with her. *"Well,"* he thought, *"so be it. If she doesn't want to engage in my company than I shall not impose on her anymore."*

He rose from his bed, but before he could pull his bell cord, Jenkins entered his room. "Ah, good. You are awake," exclaimed Jenkins. "Would you like me to draw you a bath, milord?"

It was near two o'clock in the afternoon before Edward headed down the stairs to his study. He had some ledgers to review before he made an appointment with his man of business, but he found it difficult to concentrate. He had already made up his mind not to call on Lady Anne, but he determined that it was appropriate to call on Miss Tate and her mother. After all, she had done nothing to affront him. He reasoned propriety dictated a call since he danced with her the night before. Besides, he wanted to assure her that he would continue the dance lessons. He surmised that Bell still needed to master the quadrille and waltz. *"It would be ungentlemanly not to continue to help her,"* thought Edward. *"And if I must put up with Anne as a chaperone then I shall be tolerant of her, but definitely not amiable towards her person."* Edward smirked as he pictured Lady Anne's remorse face, wondering why she was not in favor with him. Edward thought it quite appropriate for Lady Anne to stew over his disfavor for a while. Perhaps in time, he would forgive her.

Anne, ecstatic, hurried to the Tate's apartments to inform them of their success. Early that morning, she received a letter from Lady Jersey with the much-coveted Almack's vouchers, not guest vouchers for the Tates, but

Seasonal vouchers that marked Bell's approval by the Almack's Patronesses.

Bell opened the door to a very exuberant Lady Anne and knew she had some very exciting news to reveal. Bell called to her mother who begged them to adjourn to the parlour to sit down. Mrs. Tate then summoned for a pot of tea and biscuits to be brought in. No sooner had everyone taken their seats than Lady Anne, with trembling hands, hastily removed a letter from her reticule. She unfolded the letter and saw the anxiety in Mrs. Tate's eyes. She soothed, "No, no, Mrs. Tate. It is good news."

Anne went on to read the letter describing how the Almack's Patronesses found Bell all that was proper and expected of a Lady in Society. They remarked that Bell looked quite the debutante in her most appropriate Jonquil evening dress and that the gentlemen of the evening were quite put out by her early departure. Lady Jersey went on to say she heard that Bell's concern for her mother was what drew her home early, but the *on dit* is that she was not an experienced dancer and did not want to embarrass herself or her partner. Lady Jersey applauded her common sense on both counts, but insisted that she be allowed to resolve any concerns she might have regarding her dance. She commanded them all to attend to her the next day at her town home, for she had arranged for a dance instructor to tutor Bell. She also said that Lord Riverdale had volunteered his service, so Bell did not need to worry about a dance partner.

Anne looked up after reading this bit of news regarding Lord Riverdale and saw a gleam in Bell's eyes. Bell responded, "It is very nice of Lord Riverdale to assist me. Do you not think?"

Mrs. Tate commented, "Very gentlemanly and extremely generous of Lady Jersey."

Anne added, "This is more than we could have hoped. It seems Bell's popularity with the young beaus last night is persuading Lady Jersey to champion Bell. I cannot remember the last time Almack's was so crowded with eligible gentlemen. I expect Lady Jersey is bringing Anne into fashion to amuse herself, since the rumor mills are thin on scandal. Bell's raging success at last night's assembly will definitely be today's parlour chat. I am sure the Patronesses hope that Bell's continued attendance will keep Almack's packed with the lords that lately have been looking for amusements elsewhere."

The ladies conversation veered into discussions about what Bell should wear to the next assembly and both Lady Anne and Bell tried to convince Mrs. Tate to attend. Mrs. Tate stubbornly refused, adamantly arguing her presence was a detriment to Bell's success.

Anne was just finishing up her cup of tea, bringing her visit to an end, when the Tate's butler announced Lord Felton's arrival. She surprisingly was disappointed that he was paying a visit to Bell instead of her residence and then cheered, realizing she was not at home to receive him. *"Perhaps,"* she thought, *"he came to seek me out."*

Anne, Mrs. Tate, and Bell rose in greeting as Lord Felton was ushered in.

Edward made his mannerly bow and gave Bell a beaming smile. "Ah! I am so glad to have found you at home." He walked over to Bell and proceeded to take her hand and press a light kiss on the back of it. He then remarked, "You are to be congratulated, Miss Tate, the *ton* is marveling at your success as we speak."

Bell replied, "Do you really think so?"

"Quite so," replied Edward, who then directed a nod to Mrs. Tate in greeting, "Your servant, Madam." He continued, "What is your estimation of your daughter's success?"

Mrs. Tate answered, "I would find it difficult for anyone to find fault with my Bell. Lady Anne has informed us that she has the approval of the Almack's Patronesses, so I am truly hopeful."

Lord Felton's lack of conduct surprised Anne. She wondered why he failed to acknowledge her and questioned whether his behavior was meant to be a *cut direct*. It seemed a ridiculous notion since they had held camaraderie over helping Bell, but his neglect concerned her. She ignored the *faux pas* and interjected into the conversation.

"We are celebrating Miss Tate's success. Lady Jersey writes she has won the Patronesses favor and has sent the Almack's vouchers noting she is a member in good standing. She no longer holds the title of guest."

Edward directed his remarks to the Tates and replied, "That is excellent news!"

Anne was stunned at his rudeness. Clearly, Lord Felton had no interest in her. She was hurt by his ill manner. A piece of her wanted to call out his behavior and chastise him for it, but she decided to take her leave instead. She would allow the Tates to deduce what his manner was all about.

"I am afraid that I must leave," said Anne. "I will see you tomorrow Mrs. Tate, Miss Tate. Thank you for the delightful repast. I will inquire to see when Lady Jersey expects us and send you word. Good day to you, my lord." Anne did not stay to see if he would return her greeting, but turned and left without a further adieu.

Edward had mixed feelings about his behavior. He could tell that he offended Anne with his lack of address. At first, he felt pleased that she should feel the sullenness he experienced, when she failed to save him a dance last night. Then, he saw the sadness in her eyes when she bid him goodbye and he felt very small. As soon as she left, he regretted his behavior.

Mrs. Tate thought Lord Felton's treatment of Lady Anne odd and asked in a circuitous manner, "Have we done anything to offend you, my lord? You do not seem to be yourself."

Edward smiled at Mrs. Tate's tact and said, "You are quite right, Mrs. Tate. I am not myself and must beg your forgiveness. I believe I might have affronted Lady Anne. I shall do my best to make it up to her and you both. I have come to invite you to another dance lesson. Perhaps I can humble myself before her and she will agree to waltz with me."

Before Mrs. Tate could answer, Bell responded, "Oh, my lord. It is so nice of you, but we have accepted Lady Jersey's offer of instruction. We are to attend her tomorrow!"

Lord Felton looked at Mrs. Tate for confirmation. "It is true, my lord. Lady Anne came with the news. I fear we cannot decline Lady Jersey. I hope you know that we sincerely appreciate all that you have done for us and that you do not think ill of us for not accepting your gracious offer."

"No, not at all," replied Edward. "You may not need my tutor, but perhaps I can aid this endeavor as a partner for Bell."

Bell retorted, "Oh, but Lord Riverdale is to be my partner!"

Mrs. Tate gave Bell a warning look that she understood and quickly rephrased, "Thank you, my lord. That is most generous of you. I am sure Lady Jersey would welcome you. Should I have Lady Anne alert her to your participation?"

Edward laughed, "No need. I shall speak with Lady Jersey myself. Until tomorrow."

By the time Lord Felton arrived at Lady Jersey's town home, he found the dance lesson in full swing. He noted Lady Jersey had hired a four string quartet, two dancing masters and had arranged a table of refreshments. To his chagrin, he also noted that Lord Riverdale did not come alone. Along with him, he should have guessed, came Lords Trenton and Mansfield. He knew he should not have been surprised as the friends were also referred to as the Lords Trio.

Edward had hoped that he might partner with Lady Anne and beg her forgiveness for his churlish behavior. Indeed, his behavior was ungentlemanly. He did not understand why he acted so out of character, why he engaged in a tit for tat battle when Lady Anne did nothing malicious other than forget him. That is what Edward surmised, that Lady Anne simply forgot to consider that he would wish to dance with her, to celebrate Bell's success, to spend time with her. He reasoned that he was the only one that felt there was a lack of consideration. Miss Tate made no reference to Lady Anne not dancing with him, nor did Lady Anne admonish him for not requesting a dance. Only he seemed to think that feelings were involved in this oversight.

That reasoning brought him back to how Lady Anne always managed to get under his skin. *"Feelings!"* He thought, *"Since when did I ever let feelings dictate my behavior?"*

Lady Jersey saw Lord Felton cross her threshold. She waved him forward, saying, "My Lord Felton, You have come. Although I do not know why, unless you favor the young girl."

Edward's surprised face made Lady Jersey laugh. She then said, "Well, what is it then. Surely, a man of your consequence has better things to do than oversee a dancing lesson."

"As a man of consequence, I can afford to be a man of leisure and it is my friendship with the Tates that brings me here. You see, my lady, you usurped my role as a dancing tutor and I have come to ensure that I relegated my job to a worthy master."

"You are no *fribbler*, sir," said Lady Jersey. "But I will not question you further regarding your business. Do you come to dance or watch?"

"I am no wallflower, my lady," stated Edward. "I shall dance. Perhaps, Lady Anne will partner with me since Miss Tate seems to have eyes for only Lord Riverdale."

"Yes," said Lady Jersey. "I have noticed that Lord Riverdale's eyes are just as fixed. I do not know how his mother, the countess, will condone such an alliance. You know trade and all."

"But," retorted Edward. "Miss Tate is not in trade. Her dowry came from that line of industry, but she herself does not engage in the business as I do. The business that continues to increase my wretchedly full coffers, with more wealth than I know what to spend it on."

"Must you be so vulgar, Felton?" remarked Lady Jersey. "Your great uncle finally raised you into the sphere you always craved. Must you remind us how ridiculously tainted your wealth is?"

"Forgive me, my lady," replied Edward. "I forgot how fickle the *bon ton* is in issues of acquiring wealth. Perhaps, I should refuse his lordship's interest in one of my business opportunities citing his wife's, your disapproval, my lady, for the refusal."

"I do not find that amusing, sir," replied Lady Jersey. "I shall forgive your impertinence and suggest you hurry up to secure Lady Anne's hand for the next dance before Lord Mansfield does."

Edward smiled and replied, "Your servant, madam." He then strode across the dance floor and wrapped Lady Anne up in his arms into the waltz position. Lord Mansfield balked just before reaching his target and then turned and left the floor begrudgingly. He caught Lord Felton's gaze and knew better than to try and collect his promised dance with Lady Anne.

Anne was quick to inform Edward that she had promised the dance to Lord Mansfield, but Edward just laughed. It upset her that Lord Felton commandeered her without protocol. Even if this was only a lesson, he still should have sought her permission.

Edward found Anne's body stiffening and he noticed her mouth was ready to admonish him. He tried to appease her into compliance with his apology before she exploded with wrath. Edward looked deeply into her eyes and said, "I have come to apologize, my lady. You must forgive my jejune behavior. I know you are unaware of the affront I felt, but I hope that you will pity me for behaving so immature."

Edward's hold on Anne was too strong for her to do anything, but listen to him. She did not know what to expect, but an apology was not one. She was not even sure what he was talking about. She insulted him? When? He looked so sincere that she found her only response was a chortle. She replied, "My, you do run hot and cold, my lord. You have taken me unawares. I expect you are apologizing for abjuring me yesterday at the Tates, but I do not know when I fell from grace in your eyes. What affront did I cause?"

He smiled and said, "I am wounded. Was I the only one who suffered? Here I thought you had wickedly sought to cause me injury by not saving the second set of dances at Almack's for me."

Anne was dumbfounded, saying, "I never promised. You never asked. I did not know you wished it."

"A Cheltenham Tragedy, I think," retorted Edward. "I fear I am responsible for my own misery. I have come to realize that the fault is mine. There was no promise or offer, only an expectation that was sorely unfulfilled. However, I hope to make it right by offering for the first waltz at Wednesday's Ball. You will accept, will you not?"

Anne did not know what to think as she walked with Bell into the Almack's Assembly Room. She was not an ingénue. Her role as chaperone placed her as a mature woman at the fringes of spinsterhood. Any hope for marriage evaporated with her father's downfall, when his death left her without a living or dowry.

The only inheritance she had was the town home that for some reason her father had not mortgaged. Perhaps he had thought he had, or maybe he remembered his daughter and had intentionally set it aside for her. Regardless, thanks to her father, she was able to recommend herself to the *bon ton.* Her title and fashionable address in the Mayfair District marked her an appropriate chaperone. Even though she could not afford to reside in the town home, she was able to profit from it, by renting it out for an exorbitant fee during the Season. Between the rent and hiring herself out as a chaperone, she was able to secure a small apartment in a respectable neighborhood and live prudently.

Her only hope of marriage dissolved during her third Season, when the man she thought loved her, quickly changed his tune when he learned her fortune changed. She was not bitter, probably because she never really loved him. Her heart had never really been engaged or therefore at risk until now. At least, that is what she deduced. For why else would she be so nervous around Edward? This was not her first ball, or even her first dance with a handsome peer, yet, somehow her anticipation felt as if everything was being newly experienced. Her senses piqued whenever he neared her. She was so discomfited in his presence that she nearly took her leave of him, until her common sense prevailed. Through sheer will, she managed to control herself and while she wanted to run away and protect her heart each time he captivated her, she knew any hasty departure could only draw unwanted attention to her. As a hired chaperone, she could not afford to create speculation regarding her behavior, so she did her best to check her emotions. She admitted she was attracted to Edward, to his looks, strength, and character. She acknowledged when her guard was down, she experienced a delightful ease that fostered a camaraderie, complete satisfaction in being in each other's company. Even if her emotions moved from peace to exuberance, she could not refute how much he affected her. She wondered if Edward's apology and confession were made in jest, or if he actually had feelings for her.

Anne remembered his words. He said he suffered because he had an expectation that was sorely unfulfilled. Is that what she could anticipate if she did not check her feelings for him?

With anticipation, Anne searched the ballroom and was disappointed not to see Edward. Lord Riverdale greeted them first and was quick to secure Bell for the opening set of the quadrille and the last waltz. Lords Mansfield and Trenton vied for the second and third dance sets. Bell's dance card filled as she tried to accommodate the bevy of suitors that flocked to her.

As Anne watched the flurry around Bell, Lady Jersey approached her and commented, "Well, I hope Miss Tate's performance in the quadrille honors my patronage. It would be quite annoying to have gone to all that trouble and not be allowed any bragging rights to it." Anne raised her eyebrow to her ladyship who added, "It is no secret that the girl could not dance, so don't give me the air that I am being disingenuous."

Lady Jersey saw Lord Mansfield approaching and commented before she walked away, "I see that you are in fashion as well Lady Anne. I hope you are smart enough not to waste the opportunity that chaperoning Miss Tate has bestowed on you."

Anne reflected on Lady Jersey's comment while she danced with Lord Mansfield. It was true that she no longer felt like the invisible chaperone. Bell treated her more like a friend than a servant. Bell respected her. She included her in her conversations, asked her for advice, and kept her at her side, versus having her off at a distance. Bell's behavior, she realized, made her feel more like a participant in the Season than an observer of it. She found herself taking more care in her dress and hair. She accessorized and spent her precious coin on fripperies. For a woman who lives on a tight budget, a new fan or a new piece of ribbon are extravagances, but how marvelously she enjoyed the attention she was receiving. She understood the Lords Trio were only interested in friendship. She clearly was a link to Bell, so treating her amiably could only place them well in Bell's favor, since she knew that Bell valued thoughtfulness. Regardless of her logic, Anne knew the real reason she took care of her appearance was because she wanted to make a good impression on Lord Felton. She wanted him to think her attractive and if he was harboring expectations of her, perhaps, she had caught his eye. She only wished she could catch it now because she had yet to see him. As the waltz approached, she feared that Lord Felton's confession was nothing more than a hoax. A mean joke at her expense, *"An expectation unfulfilled, indeed,"* she thought.

If she was not Bell's chaperone, she would have left early, but she was required to put her best face on and not reveal how humiliated she felt. She was not angry. She was embarrassed. Lord Felton struck her vulnerability, her spinsterhood. *"How funny he must think it is to toy with an overage maiden,"* thought Lady Anne. She racked her brain to think if she said or did anything to suggest how thrilled she found his favor. *"No,"* she thought. *"If he comes, I shall just say that I forgot all about the ridiculous dance. After all, I am here as a chaperone. I shall tell him, I do not overly engage in dancing."* Her thought appeased her countenance somewhat and since it seemed that Lord Felton had no plans in making an appearance, she began to relax and not feel self-conscious.

It was just before the second waltz that the Duke of Hartford approached Lady Anne. She was pleased to see him and smiled in greeting. "Your grace, I did not expect to see you here, but I am glad you have come."

His grace replied, "I am on a mission though I fear I am late. On my way here, I was detoured with a command from the Prince Regent. I just barely made it through the doors before they closed them to latecomers. I have a message from Lord Felton apologizing for his absence. He was summoned to his great uncle's estate, some kind of emergency. He asked me to stand in his stead for the first waltz with you, but perhaps you will settle for the second if you are not otherwise engaged."

Anne's face alighted when she realized that Edward's intentions were honorable. He did not stand her up or make a mockery of her. "I am not engaged, your grace," answered Anne. "I would very much like to dance with you."

The Duke of Hartford proffered his arm and escorted her to the dance floor. He acted like a suitor and she was touched by his generosity. While they danced, she asked, "Do you know what the emergency was that took his lordship away?"

His grace answered, "No, but I do know that I am charged to invite you and anyone you wish to make into a party to Beaumont Manor. I am planning on going to visit my great grandson. Elinor and Jonathan will be there, so I think Felton thought you would like to visit them as well. I believe he thought you might like to invite the Tates, though anyone you desire would be more than welcome."

Anne smiled.

# Chapter Eight

Edward wasted no time packing a bag. He took his mount and rode hard to his great uncle's estate. Beaumont Manor was not far from London. A singular rider with a full moon could reach the estate within an hour. Jenkins was charged to pack his luggage and follow the next day in his carriage.

He had no idea what was wrong. The summons he received from his uncle simply read:

*Edward,*

*You must come immediately. Situation complex. Please make haste.*

*Beaumont.*

Edward was concerned, but not overly since there was no indication of an accident or illness. No emergency was mentioned, only a "complex situation." He almost waited to leave in the morning. He did not want to miss his dance with Lady Anne at Almack's, but his uncle never made urgent requests, so he did not hesitate to depart.

He was at White's, when his footman arrived with the missive. He was enjoying a brandy with the Duke of Hartford, hoping to investigate his grace's interest in Anne. Instead, he ended up encouraging their society, by requesting that his grace honor the waltz that he had secured for himself. He hastily wrote a note of apology to Anne realizing that he did not know how long his absence would be, so he decided to extend the invitation to her to Beaumont Manor. The Westfields had promised to visit his great uncle's estate when he was in residence, so he found it a perfect opportunity to create a party for Anne. Edward was sure she would invite the Tates, she might even include Lord Riverdale whom he noticed Bell especially favored. Perhaps he would round out the party and invite his cousin Lady Catherine as well.

He asked the Duke of Hartford to convey his invitation to Anne and then invited him to join the party. He was greatly attached to his grace. Regardless of the man's relationship with Anne, he was determined not to sacrifice the friendship of someone he regarded as a second father. Besides, he knew his grace would enjoy the opportunity to visit his great grandson.

By the time Edward arrived at Beaumont Manor, the sun had long since set and he had to awaken an ostler to care and feed his horse. He was exhausted and hungry when he entered his future home and was disappointed to learn that his uncle had already retired. Nothing seemed amiss. The butler did not seem overly concerned. If anything, he was surprised to see him. He alerted him to his valet's arrival the next day, requested a bath to be drawn, and a cold collation sent to his room. He proceeded to retire for the evening.

Edward deduced that whatever the *complex situation*, it could have waited until tomorrow. He was beginning to regret that he departed in haste instead of waiting for the morning. He so wanted to claim his dance with Anne. He reflected on the time he waltzed with her at the Jersey town home. He marveled at how much he liked embracing her and seeing her discomfiture at his nearness. He told her that she had affronted him and found her outrage adorable. He enjoyed tightening his hold on her, so that she would not bolt. When he looked into her eyes, he had to remind himself to breathe. He relished the way she made him feel and began to question his motives towards her.

Exactly what were his intentions towards Anne? Was he enjoying the sparring that she so ably was capable? Or did he harbor more intimate feelings? Were those feelings of a trifle nature that, like his mistresses, lost their edge over time? Or were they of a more serious nature? What did he say to Elinor when she championed her candidacy for his wife, *"Ah,"* recalled Edward. *"I am starting my nursery, not retiring it."*

He laughed. The passion he felt for Anne was far from retiring and he was fairly confident that she was more than capable of bearing children. Her lineage was impeccable. Anne was the daughter of a marquis, a penurious one, but still a member of the *ton*, so he had no fear of any children from such an alliance being shunned. He suffered from such abjurations as a child and he would want better for his own children. His wealth negated any need for a dowry, but still he was not sure if Anne would make a suitable wife. After all, marriage should be a pleasant affair and there were many instances that he could recall when her company riled him. In fact, she caused his emotions to stir to the point of rage. Well, maybe not rage, but definitely she piqued his senses to the point of discomfiture.

Edward thought, *"Will she think my invitation a prelude to paying my addresses to her? What if she doesn't invite the Tates to attend her? It will look as though I plan to offer for her."* Edward panicked and decided that in the morning, if he ever fell asleep, he would have his cousin Catherine make up a party to bring to the manor, thinking there was safety in numbers.

This was not the first time that Edward woke to a heavy head and weary body. His restless night over-analyzing his intentions towards Anne kept him from a peaceful sleep. Perhaps, as Jenkins thought, he was bewitched. He was ready to admonish his valet for not waking him sooner when he realized that Jenkins was not here. His valet was probably just now making his way from London.

Edward finished his morning ablutions and dressed himself before making his way to his uncle's study. Now that he was in residence, he wanted to send a letter to the Westfields and his cousin Catherine, inviting them to visit. He wanted to have the letters sent off before he sat down to eat.

He felt much better once he sent his messengers off with the letters. His rumbling stomach reminded him that he was hungry, so he made his way to the breakfast room, only to be disappointed not to see his uncle. He deduced that Beaumont either broke his fast earlier or, like himself, had slept later than expected. Edward made himself a plate from the buffet that offered a wide range of eggs, fish, meats, and breads before taking his seat. The lavish spread surprised him, but upon further consideration, he determined that cook must have been informed of his arrival and prepared the feast to impress him. Edward asked the attending footman if his uncle had eaten yet. The servant replied, "No, milord. Only Mr. Cowper broke his fast. I believe he retired to the library."

Edward knew better than to question the staff regarding guests, even though he knew they were kept better abreast than anyone of what went on in the manor. Instead, he finished his breakfast and made his way to the library to learn what business Mr. Cowper had with Beaumont.

As he entered the library, Edward spied a young man with brown hair reading a book and sitting rather stiffly, as though waiting to be called into a magistrate's office. He sat on an aged mahogany Sheraton settee marked by its signature design of cylindrical tapered legs finished in brass toe caps. His dress clearly denoted him a commoner, yet one who was educated and who held enough arrogance not to stand when a better entered the room. Edward raised his eyebrow and stared at the intruder before stepping closer to him. He was prepared to ask, *"Who are you? And what is your business?"* Instead, he took into consideration that the man was a guest of his uncle, and with much forbearance, asked, "I do not believe we have met?"

The young man assessed Edward and admonished him like a child accusing another of stealing his toy, "Ah! So you are the interloper. I, sir, am the rightful heir of Beaumont!"

Edward raised his eyebrows but did not make a verbal response. With aplomb, he simply turned and went to find his uncle, quietly hissing under his breath, "*Complex situation*, indeed!"

The Marquis of Beaumont was breaking his fast in his suite when Edward knocked on his door. Edward waited and when no response for entry was heard, he slowly turned the doorknob and cautiously made his entrance. He did not see his uncle, so he called out his name. He was surprised when his uncle uncharacteristically peeked out from his dressing room.

"Edward! Finally you have come," exclaimed Beaumont.

Edward asked, "Are you hiding, uncle?"

"I fear I am, though not from you," answered Beaumont.

Edward remarked seriously, "I believe I have met your *complex situation.* According to him, he is the rightful heir to Beaumont. Do you have news you wish to share with me?"

"Well, yes of course, though it is not what you expect. The lad showed up on my doorstep demanding an audience with me." Beaumont walked over to his desk and opened the top drawer. He took out a letter and handed it to Edward, continuing, "He gave this to me as proof of his parentage, although he misinterpreted the meaning."

Edward looked at the yellowed parchment that looked quite old. He carefully unfolded the fragile letter and was surprised to see his uncle's signature at the bottom of it. It read:

*Dear Alana,*

*I am grieved that you have refused my suit, but since all I ever wanted was your happiness, I will abide by your wishes. Please know that I am always at your service, should you or the child need for anything.*

*Your most obedient servant,*
*Geofferey*

Edward folded the paper, handed it back to his uncle and replied, "It seems he may be justified to think he has a claim, but clearly the boy is too young to be your son. A grandson, perhaps?"

Beaumont replied, "Nay, he is not mine. He is just grieving over the loss of his mother and cannot see what is in front of him that bespeaks the truth."

Edward inquired, "And what truth is that, uncle?"

Beaumont laughed. "The eyes, my boy. You have blue eyes, I have blue eyes, Alana had blue eyes. He has brown eyes."

"Perhaps," replied Edward. "His father had brown eyes. Have you no other proof than that?"

"Nay," said Beaumont. "Only my word that I never knew Alana in that way. I loved her. I offered her my protection, but I never bed her. She gave herself to one she would not reveal to me. The letter was my last attempt to protect her and keep her family from sending her away. I never heard from her or saw her after she left. It broke my heart that she would not marry me."

"Have you spoken of this to the lad?" asked Edward

"Nay, I have not the heart. I thought, perhaps I could help him, since I was never able to help his grandmother," answered Beaumont.

"Does that include making him your heir?" asked Edward.

"Don't be ridiculous, Edward," retorted Beaumont. "I may be getting sentimental in my old age, but I am no fool. I do not know what help I may offer, for I do not know the boy. I thought you could help settle it all once you arrived."

Edward smirked, "Well it must be settled, for within days you will have a household of guests. I would not enjoy trying to explain an interloper among them. For the record, it is Mr. Cowper and not I, to whom I refer."

"What guests?" asked Beaumont.

"I am hosting a party to help me find a wife per your wishes, uncle," answered Edward.

"Oh, very good, Edward!" smiled Beaumont who seemed relieved to unburden himself to his nephew. He then placed his hands on Edward's back, pushing him to exit his room. He said, "I shall dress and meet you in my study, so that you can see to Mr. Cowper and then we can all relax."

Edward turned his head and looked at his uncle before he exited to say, "I do not expect the interview to resolve his claim as heir. Let us hope it was his mother who had the brown eyes."

Edward saw his uncle fidget nervously in anticipation of their interview with Mr. Cowper. Both men awaited him in the study while a footman tracked Lawrence down to request his immediate presence. Edward took a seat behind his uncle's desk while the Marquis of Beaumont stood behind him with his hands clasped behind his back. They both looked at the study's threshold when the young man entered. Edward noticed his tense body, hardened face, and thought, *"He is bitter."*

Aside from his countenance, he also thought that Lawrence Cowper was a nice looking man, slimly built with shortly cropped light brown hair and brown eyes. He stood about five foot ten inches and at nine and ten years, would probably grow an inch or two more. His keen eyes showed the intellect that he possessed and shrewdness that concerned Edward.

Edward remarked, "Mr. Cowper, I am glad you have joined us. Please have a seat."

"It appears, " said Mr. Cowper, "that my seat is already taken."

Edward frowned at his impertinence; he was ready to rise and throw the young pup out the door. He began to push his chair back when he felt his uncle's hand on his shoulder.

Beaumont said, "Your churlish behavior is unwelcome Mr. Cowper. You are a guest of my bidding, not of your outlandish assumptions. You are no heir of mine, but you are the grandson of a woman I once cherished in my life. It is in her memory that I welcome you into my home and nothing else. Do not make me regret my kindness. It will benefit you none."

"You lie, sir," retorted Mr. Cowper. "The letter proves you are my grandfather."

Beaumont responded, "The letter proves I cared for your grandmother and offered her my protection, which she refused." He continued, "If you cannot accept this, I will have to ask you to leave. I have guests arriving and do not want them disturbed."

Mr. Cowper scowled, "What if I do not accept it? I have waited two days to conference with you, sir. Only now, that your heir is here, you inform me that my claim is negligent. I think not."

"It matters not what you think," Beaumont argued. "I offered you hospitality because I loved your grandmother. I was too overcome to meet with you until now. I am afraid your arrival unleashed a wealth of emotions I was not prepared to deal with at the time. I shall have you removed if you choose to hold on to this ridiculous and offensive claim of yours. I have guests to think of and will not burden them with your impertinence."

"You need not worry, sir," retorted Lawrence. "I am a gentleman. As your rightful heir I would not think of creating a scandal or disturbing our guests."

"If you were my heir," stated Beaumont, "then I would rejoice, as would my nephew, who knows that my greatest regret in life is that I produced no children. But alas, you are not. However, I am interested to learn more about your family, your grandmother in particular. If you can behave yourself, I will allow you to stay. Out of respect for your grandmother, I would like to offer you some sort of assistance, but be warned, Mr. Cowper, I owe you nothing. Do not provoke me to end my generosity."

Edward understood his uncle's need to learn about what happened to his *mon ami,* so he stood and said, "Mr. Cowper, it seems that our housekeeper relishes having a guest in the house. No sooner have we broke our fast that she has set up a tea tray with some cakes and other delights in the dining parlour. I confess I am far from hungry, but prefer not to question Mrs. Applebee's reasoning. Let us adjourn to the parlour and perhaps you will be kind to answer my uncle's questions regarding your grandmother."

Mr. Cowper's body relaxed. He realized that until that moment every muscle in his body was taut with tension. When he walked in, he recognized Beaumont's heir, the man behind the desk. He expected that his person would be evicted from the manor's premise with exceptional haste. Then, all his hopes for answers would be lost to him. Ever since his arrival and the marquis refused to see him, the idea of them having a civil discussion never occurred to him. Now that it looked like it might prevail, over tea and cakes of all things, his demeanor softened. He answered, "Yes of course, but only if you answer some of my questions as well."

Beaumont saw only a young boy with the weight of the world on his shoulders, so he took no offense to his abrupt tone. If anything, his forlorn expression made him want to do everything possible to aid him. He answered, "Of course, my boy," as he placed his arm around his shoulder, guiding him towards the dining parlour.

Edward followed in rear and as an afterthought, asked, "Mr. Cowper, tell me what color were your mother's eyes?"

Mr. Cowper answered, "Blue, of course. Just like my grandmother's."

"Of course," replied Edward.

Edward did not interject much during the noon meal. He noticed that each of them picked at the food on their plate. No one, including himself, was eating very much. They were each focused on either asking questions or listening to answers. Beaumont and Mr. Cowper volleyed their queries back and forth. Edward thought they looked like long time friends reminiscing. He took note of Mr. Cowper's manners and was surprised that they were excellent. It appeared this young man was tutored in all that was proper and expectant of a man of consequence. Someone had armed him with the ways of the *ton* so that he could hold his own among them, much like his father prepared him. Edward's contemplation was interrupted by the question he knew his uncle was waiting to ask.

Beaumont inquired, "Do you know where your grandmother lived when she gave birth to your mother and how she lived her life?" With a quivering voice, he continued, "Did she ever marry?"

The teary eyes of the marquis surprised Lawrence Cowper. *"Clearly,"* he thought, *"this man cared for my grandmother."* Mr. Cowper began, "My mother was born in the seaside resort of Worthing. I lived my life there until my dear mother died. I knew my grandmother well, for she lived with my mother and me. My father was a sea merchant, gone more than not and died at sea when I was a young boy. I thought I would join the merchant marine as a ship's boy to help support my family, but my grandmother forbade it. She said that I had regal blood and that my destiny would take me to a more esteemed future, though I know not what she meant."

"Did she ever marry?" Beaumont asked again.

"I assumed," replied Lawrence. "I never knew my grandfather. I once asked her who he was when I was younger. She only said that he died in service to his king. She was quite grieved when I questioned her so I never did again."

"And your mother?" asked Beaumont. "Did she not know anything?"

"She believed her mother was a widow for she informed me her mother told her the same tale as a young girl regarding her father. Like me, she asked no more questions, not wanting to distress her mother," answered Lawrence.

"How did you live? I understood her parents cast her off when she refused to give up her child?" asked Beaumont.

Lawrence replied, "I do not know how my grandmother supported my mother when she was alone, as best as I can remember, both my grandmother and mother gave lessons in the pianoforte and watercolors to the young women in the area. They even tutored the boys in Latin and French, though that was not common knowledge."

Lawrence asked, "Now, sir, if you please, what can you tell me of my grandmother? Do you know why she refused your offer of marriage? Why did you not insist upon it, if you knew her parents would disown her and her child?"

Beaumont sighed, "If it was in my power to do so, I would have, but while I loved your grandmother, she loved the man she gave herself. I believed that he would do right by her because she was so confident in their love. She would not name him. I was in a rage when I learned of her situation and would have called the man out. She said her love for us both kept her from revealing his name. I tried to learn who she had been keeping company with, but deduced her parents must have thought him to be ineligible because my inquiries were fruitless. When she ran off and never returned, I assumed she eloped with her lover. She knew she could count on me for assistance, but she never applied."

"I believe you," remarked Lawrence. "Your affection for my grandmother is most revealing. I believe if she was still with us you would take care of her now."

"Yes," responded Beaumont. "She was the love of my life."

Mr. Cowper announced, "I will trespass on you no longer. I know I am not your heir and will depart immediately."

"No," countered Beaumont. "There is still much I want to hear about your grandmother. I have determined now how I might help you. My means were limited as a young man, but as a marquis, I am more resourceful. Perhaps, between the three of us, we can learn your bloodline. Your grandmother said you had an esteemed future. I believe she spoke of some type of inheritance. Let me help you find it."

Beaumont turned to his nephew and asked, "You will agree to this, Edward. Will you not?"

Edward smiled at his uncle's pleading eyes. "Your wish is my command, sir."

Beaumont beamed, "There, it is settled."

Edward asked, "Do you ride, Mr. Cowper?"

"Not very well," replied Lawrence.

"It would please me if you would accompany me this afternoon," stated Edward. "My uncle would like me to assess the work that is being done to some tenant cottages."

Lawrence hesitated. He figured he had no choice since the earl's pleasure was stated as a command and not a question. It was clear that Lord Felton wanted a private interview with him and he could do nothing but accommodate him. "Very well," answered Lawrence. "Will you provide a horse, sir? I was conveyed here by hospitality of a local farmer."

"Of course," replied Edward. "Shall we say twenty minutes? I will have two mounts saddled and brought to the front driveway."

They rode at a leisurely pace, side by side; Lawrence did his best to keep his seat. He kept glancing at his lordship waiting for the private conference he expected to transpire. He could tell that the earl was watching him, clearly not impressed with his equestrian abilities.

"Sit up straight, Mr. Cowper," commanded Edward. "Do not hold so tight on the reins. I have selected a gentle bay for you. You can relax, he will not increase his pace unless you give him a good heel."

Lawrence made a nod in gratitude and after a while, he began to feel more comfortable, able to take note of the direction of their ride. They left the estate behind them, for Edward had taken them off the dirt road unto the grassy meadow that flanked the manor. He was just beginning to enjoy the landscape when Edward began his interrogation. He asked, "What are your intentions, Mr. Cowper? It seems to me, you allayed your claim quite easily. I would deduce that you knew from the beginning that my uncle was not your grandfather. Why are you here?"

Lawrence thought his lordship was a man of consequence and not one to trifle with, so he decided it best to be forthcoming. He said, "I had nowhere to go, my lord. No family that I know. I was angry that my mother died at such a young age when, had we afforded proper medical care, she most likely would still be alive. Since a young boy, the only name that I knew about that could have made a difference in my family's life was the Marquis of Beaumont. My grandmother extolled his virtues. She was very fond of him I think. Why she never applied to him, I will never understand. I guess I just wanted to meet the man that was worthy of her praise. When Beaumont refused an audience with me, I am afraid my temper inspired my claim."

"May I ask, how your mother died," queried Edward.

"I mentioned that my grandmother and mother made their living by tutoring young gentlemen. When my grandmother died, my mother took on the employment solely, only to find the task overwhelming. Some of her patrons complained they were not receiving the same level of attention, so eventually she lost students and our income decreased. When my grandmother was alive, her policy was to cancel lessons on cold and rainy days. She said it was not worth risking our health to venture out when the weather was foul. My mother changed that policy, fearing I believe, the loss of still more income. She was weary tired. I believe she went out one too many times in the wet weather. She eventually took a chill and never recovered. I live with the guilt that I could do so little for her though I tried."

"I am sorry for your loss," consoled Edward. "I lost both my parents at around the same age as you, so I do understand your sorrow. Thankfully, I had my grandmother to counsel me and lend support. I do not know how I would have survived without her." Edward pulled the reins on his steed to stop his progress and looked at Mr. Cowper who checked his mount in unison. Edward said, "I am sure your grief is constricting your body even as we speak, so much so that each breath you take is a burden."

Lawrence inhaled slowly through his nostrils and exhaled in relief, responding only with an affirmative nod.

Edward continued, "My uncle is a good and sentimental man. If you have been honest and there is no perfidy on your part, then an ally in him and me you have. But if you are scheming for something of ill consequence, let me assure you, you will not prevail. I am known to be quite ruthless in dealing with those who have done me or my family harm."

Lawrence exclaimed, "Nay! I am not of that caliber. I am only looking for answers and Beaumont is the only link I have to my grandfather. I wish your uncle no harm and would leave today if that is his wish."

"Then unless you prove your intentions are different than what you state, I will welcome you and do all in my power to assist you in your investigation. Be hopeful, I am quite proficient in uncovering information that I seek," responded Edward.

Lawrence beamed and replied, "Oh, how I hope you can discover something and that I will not regret learning of the information."

Edward gave Lawrence a sympathetic smile and exclaimed, "Do you think you can manage a canter? My mount is chewing at its bit and I would like to give him his legs. I promise you, if you keep your heels down, hands down and your back straight, you will keep your seat. What do you say?"

Lawrence, without thought, agreed with a simple nod. He watched the Earl of Felton ride off and then, convinced that his lordship's words would keep him from falling, he quickly heeled his bay's flanks and followed in pursuit. The adrenaline pumped through his body, as the brisk wind crossed his face and the powerful bay rocked beneath him. His horse instinctively followed and began to slow when the earl's steed came to a halt. With a diligent pull to his reins, he found himself alongside the earl once again and then with relief laughed. For a moment, the weight of the world was removed from his shoulders and he felt the long lost feeling of joy.

Edward was pleased to see Mr. Cowper make his way to him with a smile on his face and could not help but join in the laughter that had taken hold of the young man. He thought it was probably a while since Mr. Cowper allowed himself to feel anything other than sorrow.

As Lawrence regained his composure, he took in the verdant landscape and asked, "This is fertile land. Your uncle prospers, does he not, my lord?"

Edward answered, "Beaumont Manor, is my uncle's primary residence, but only one of his many properties. He is a good and honorable landowner who takes exceptional care of his tenants. He prospers when they prosper. He is vigilant in staying abreast of the land conditions and what it yields. He inspects his tenants' cottages each year to resolve minor problems before they become major ones. Today's errand is evidence of my uncle's attentiveness. We are to visit three tenant cottages that needed their roofs repaired. My uncle tasks me to ensure the work is completed to his satisfaction."

He continued, "Are you employed, Mr. Cowper? How do you make your living or did your mother leave you some means?"

Lawrence laughed, "I have no means, sir, aside for the few coins left over from settling my family's affairs. I was raised as a gentleman, so the only experience I have in the line of employment is tutoring young boys in Latin, French, and mathematics."

"You are good with numbers?" asked Edward.

"Yes," replied Lawrence. "I managed the household accounts for my mother."

"Perhaps," inquired Edward. "You would be interested in a position where I could utilize your talents? Or do you prefer to enjoy the sojourn that my uncle offered?"

"I would prefer the employment, sir. I do not think I could remain longer than a sev'night if I could not contribute in some way," responded Lawrence.

Edward asked, "You do not wish to be paid, Mr. Cowper?"

"Only what I am due after you have subtracted room and board, my lord," he replied.

"Nonsense," retorted Edward. "Room and board we provide for all our servants. My uncle welcomes you as a guest and I will honor his wishes by not removing you from your suite. Besides, we offer you the same hospitality we would provide any gentleman."

"But," he retorted. "A gentleman of consequence would have the means to repay in kind. I do not, therefore will not receive what is not due my station."

"Your reasons are noted, Mr. Cowper," rebutted Edward, "but in this instance, you will yield in deference to my uncle's wishes which take precedence over your pride. Agreed?"

"Agreed, my lord," replied Lawrence. "Though I feel I take great advantage of your munificence."

"Nonsense," replied Edward. "It is given willingly and benefits us as well. Do not berate yourself."

"Very well, my lord," said Lawrence. "I will follow your lead and join in those activities you think your uncle would approve. Otherwise, I will do my work and keep to myself."

"I do not think you understand me," said Edward. "My uncle extends his hospitality to you because he wishes to enjoy your company and learn more of your grandmother. Therefore, you shall consider yourself welcome to enjoy the manor. I extend an offer of employment to you because my man of business needs help and I thought you would like to establish yourself of independent means. In time, if you choose to leave us, should you do your job well, you may expect a letter of recommendation."

"Thank you, my lord for thinking ahead," said Lawrence.

Edward smiled at the youthful boy that rode by his side and said, "You are most welcome, Mr. Cowper."

# Chapter Nine

The Marquis of Beaumont sat in his library ensconced in his most comfortable and favorite Sheraton tub chair enjoying a glass of port. Edward situated himself near the hearth for warmth and Lawrence perused the wall-to-wall selection of books. Lawrence had already spent two days enjoying the room, back when he awaited an audience with Beaumont.

The library was Beaumont's favorite room. As a great reader in his youth, he spent many hours there reading and as an adult he enjoyed adding to his collection the most sought-after editions. It pleased him to know his heir enjoyed reading as well and that his new guest marveled at his collection.

Edward had already informed his uncle of what transpired between himself and Lawrence. Beaumont was relieved that his nephew had found a way to aid the young man, by giving him some occupation that would secure his future and divert him away from his present grief. He concurred with his nephew that Lawrence would be a great asset to his man of business. He hoped that over time he would prevail in discovering the identity of Lawrence's grandfather. Until then, Beaumont was interested in learning more about Alana and was glad of Mr. Cowper's company.

Beaumont began, "I remember Alana always laughing. She had a hearty laugh that would make others join in without understanding. Half the time, I would chide her, telling her 'it' was not funny, but she would just laugh more." Beaumont's grin burst into a guffaw when he said, "and before long I was chuckling though I knew there was no basis for it other than mirth."

Beaumont looked at Lawrence and asked, "Did she ever laugh again, Mr. Cowper?"

Lawrence read Beaumont's sorrowful eyes and was pleased to answer, "Yes, my lord. She loved life to the fullest. We never failed to spend the evening meal together sharing our day with one another. Mama would relate some of the funny questions and answers from her students, and grandmother, with her wit, would have us laughing."

Lawrence's face gleamed in amusement at the memory. His good humor affected Edward who had to stifle his own laughter with a cough when he saw his uncle's sadden face.

In a somber tone, Beaumont asked, "Did she suffer when her time came?"

Lawrence answered, "No, my lord. She seemed just to diminish before our eyes. I will never understand what made her lapse. One day she was full of life and the next, she was not. I remember the precise day when her countenance changed. Our tutorship was doing well and we had acquired a nice profit from our spring quarter. We went to Bath to purchase an item for each of us in celebration of our success. I wanted to order a new mystery subscription, my mother wanted a new pair of kid slippers, and grandmother wanted nothing more than to share some tea and scones at the local inn. We had just finished our repast and made our promenade down the avenue along the shops, when my grandmother stopped in her tracks. She was quite pale. I feared it was her heart, but she assured me she was fine. I thought I had heard her exclaim, 'he lives,' but when I questioned her later, she refuted me and said her outcry was because she had stubbed her toe. The next day, she did not arise from bed. She said she was tired. She would not eat. My mother and I could not make her come about. She would not talk of what ailed her nor would she allow us to send for a doctor. She had no fever and did not complain of any pain. She simply seemed to retreat into herself. My mother and I took turns sitting with her, trying to get her to eat and talk to us, but to no avail. I went to bring her some tea one evening and found her with her eyes closed. She had been sleeping most of the days away. I supposed that she preferred her dreams to reality. When I tried to wake her and found her body without warmth, I knew she was gone.

I could not speak to call for my mother. All I could do was weep." Lawrence's eyes shed tears down his face. He bowed his head, his arms hanging in defeat and made no sound. He stood like a statue, still and silent.

Edward looked at his uncle and saw him bereaved. He knew not who to counsel, but instinct told him to go to the boy. He wrapped his arms around him and felt him tremble. Moments later, his uncle had taken the boy into his arms and apologized heartily saying, "I am so sorry, my boy, that I did not offer a more forceful hand to your grandmother when I had the chance. The fault is mine. I shall never forgive myself."

Edward mastered his voice and said, "No uncle, the fault is the boy's natural grandfather, not yours. It is not ours to reason why Alana decided to give up on life. You must accept that her will was done and that she is at peace. She would not want to see those that she loved burdened by her death. You must both be strong."

Edward looked at Lawrence and said, "Perhaps, when the memory is not so raw, we can look at that day again for a clue. Maybe you heard your grandmother correctly. Maybe she saw someone that was important to her. Maybe your grandfather lives."

Lawrence was shocked to attention. Edward patted his shoulder and said, "Not now, tomorrow we will talk again."

The next day, Lawrence found Edward in the study speaking with a man close in age to the earl. He was a scholarly looking man with short blond hair. His blue eyes peeked out of his wire-rimmed glasses and as Lawrence entered the room he looked at his fob watch before glancing him over.

"Am I interrupting, my lord?" asked Lawrence.

"Not at all. You are right on time," answered Lord Felton. "Allow me to introduce you to my man of business, Mr. Alistair Chapman. Mr. Chapman, meet your new aide, Mr. Lawrence Cowper."

Lawrence bowed at his waist, replying, "Your servant, sir."

Edward continued, "Mr. Cowper, you will spend the morning with Mr. Chapman getting acquainted with your new duties. I advise you to be attentive, for you can learn much from him. I will meet up with you both at the home farm before we retire for our noon meal." Edward then looked at Mr. Chapman and said, "Alistair, we will finish the rest of our business tomorrow. You may proceed on what we have reviewed today."

"Very good, my lord," answered Alistair. "I will take Mr. Cowper and leave you to your correspondence."

"Thank you, Alistair, and good luck to you, Mr. Cowper," replied Edward. He then picked up his correspondence and was pleased that he had received multiple letters: the Duke of Hartford, the Westfields, Lady Anne, and his cousin Catherine all wrote to accept his invitation to visit. He expected them to arrive by the weekend. Lady Anne wrote that she was bringing the Tates and Lord Riverdale. Lady Catherine wrote that she hoped that Edward had organized some type of entertainment to keep them amused. She said she would not convey a party, because if Edward was not up to snuff to keep her mildly entertained then she would return to London. She explained it was easier to leave alone than to exit with a large party. Edward grinned at her impertinence and intellect.

Lady Catherine's missive got him to thinking. He forgot about entertainments, usually planned and organized by the mistress of the estate. He decided to consult with his uncle and went looking for him.

Edward found his uncle in his favorite chair in the library. He was enjoying one of his favorite books, a collection of Wordsworth poems. He looked up when he heard Edward enter and asked, "What is it, nephew? Is Mr. Cowper well?"

He replied, "Mr. Cowper is in the competent hands of Mr. Chapman. I expect that he is thoroughly ensconced in accounting at this very moment. I have come to inform you that our guests arrive in two days and that I have realized that we have not planned any activities for their amusements. Do you have any recommendations, uncle?"

Beaumont frowned and replied, "You have reminded me why all these years I have not entertained. I will have to reflect back when my mother was mistress and hostess to a large party and try to remember the types of events she planned for their entertainment. They may appear too-old fashioned for your young group."

"Very well," replied Edward. "I am off to the home farm. I expect to meet Mr. Chapman and Mr. Cowper there to make our final count on our sheep. It is time for shearing, though I expect we could wait until our guests leave, for I would like to oversee the work being done."

"That's it Edward!" exclaimed Beaumont.

He asked, "What is?"

"Why the shearing, of course," replied Beaumont. "In my parents' day, it was a grand event. We had sheep shearing contests to determine who could shear the fastest and other festivities during the day. Then we reconvened in the evening here at the manor for a grand feast and country dance to celebrate our wool harvest. We mixed with the commoners of course, but our company is not so *high in the instep* to mind. What do you think?"

He answered, "I think it is a grand idea. I will have Alistair and Mr. Cowper plan the details. I expect our guests will stay a fortnight, so they can enjoy our grounds and take in a few excursions as well. We can discuss what kinds of activities our guests might like to partake in over our noon meal with Mr. Chapman and Mr. Cowper."

Edward found it amusing to watch the animated Mr. Cowper talk, "I never saw so many sheep gathered in one spot before. Until today, I could never have imagined how much noise a herd of sheep can make with their baas. Mr. Chapman says that they were all bathed before they were brought to the home farm."

Edward laughed, "Yes. That is correct, Mr. Cowper. We get more money per pound when the wool is clean. It is to our profit to bathe them before they are sheared." Edward looked to his man of business and asked, "Alistair, what do you think of our plan to reinstate Beaumont's Spring Sheep Shearing Festival?"

"I think it a grand idea," answered Alistair. "Though reinstate might be the wrong word." Looking to the marquis, he asked, "Have you forgotten, My Lord Beaumont, that you have always provided a feast for your servants at the end of the shearing season?"

"Well, no, but I have not attended," responded the marquis. "This festival is different because it is a celebration that the lord of the manor oversees. A day event with booths for our tenants to show off their talents and wares. We can have exhibitions in spinning and frame making. Oh, I am sure our tenants will have plenty of ideas. During my childhood, my father gave out awards for the best pie, jam, and quilt. Plus, we must not forget the prize to the fastest sheep shearer. We will open the house for a big feast and a country dance in the evening, just as we did when I was young."

Alistair looked at Lawrence and said, "We will need to solicit the aid of our tenants to organize the booths. The rest of our staff should manage well in serving the food and drink, though I expect we will need to hire more kitchen help and house servants to tend to everyone that sojourns with us. We will need extra ostlers for the evening as well."

Edward was happy his man of business needed no further direction. He knew Alistair was more than competent and acknowledged it publicly, "I place it all in your capable hands, Alistair. Do not spare any expense for I want the festival to be memorable."

"Very good, my lord," he responded. "Our tenants will want to know if you will be participating in the shearing contest?"

Edward looked at Beaumont with his mouth opened. When his uncle started to laugh he realized his exasperation and closed his mouth. He asked, "Is that expected?"

Beaumont answered, "Ay. I forgot that it amuses our tenants to see us wrestle with the sheep. It takes quite strong and adept hands to hold and shear the little monsters. The choice is yours, Edward. I remember I used to partner with my father because the task was beyond his means. I would hold while he sheared."

"Very well. It is all in good fun anyway. Mr. Cowper, will you second me and hold my sheep while I attempt to shear him?"

Lawrence smiled and with alighted eyes responded, "Yes, my lord. I would enjoy that very much."

Alistair interjected, "Perhaps, you could arrange for some practices before the competition, my lord. The shears are quite sharp and there is the possibility of injury, especially if you are racing through it."

"Excellent idea, Alistair," answered Edward. "We begin our tutorship tomorrow morning. Agreed, Mr. Cowper?"

"Agreed," replied Lawrence.

Edward asked, "How many days before our fete, Alistair?"

"We have a flock that is a little over twenty-two hundred and enough shearers to complete the task in a sev'night. We could have the fete on the following Saturday," he answered.

"Excellent," replied Edward. "That should give Mr. Cowper and myself enough time to practice. Now who should be our tutor?"

Alistair offered, "If it pleases you, my lord. I have been partaking in the harvest these past years and have grown quite adept. I would be happy to instruct you, if it is your will."

"Your talents never cease to amaze me, Alistair," remarked Edward. "I do not know what I would do without you. We begin tomorrow morning. I wish to look competent even if I am not by the end of the week."

"Very good, my lord," responded Alistair.

Edward could not remember the last time he dressed so inappropriately. It seemed to him that if he was to wrestle with a sheep, he need not dress what was due a gentleman. To Jenkins' dismay, he walked out of his private quarters with only his riding pants, a crisp linen shirt, and his Hessian boots. He wore no cravat, waistcoat, or coat. There were no accoutrements befitting a gentleman, not even one ring did he wear. Edward thought he looked like a pirate with his black hair, and that all he needed was a sword to complete the picture.

He found Alistair and Mr. Cowper awaiting him at the stables, ready to mount. Edward took note of their attire and felt he had dressed accordingly. Neither man bore the look of a gentleman. If anything, the three of them looked more like highwaymen than sheep shearers. Only Alistair's spectacles ruined their rough and ready look.

The baying of the flock reached Edward's ears before the smell or sight of them. The home farm had several pen areas that were built specifically for holding the sheep during the shearing season prior to their fleecing. The pens kept the sheep's coat clean and made it easier to navigate them into the larger barn where they were being sheared.

When they arrived, one of Beaumont's shepherds was awaiting them in the small barn that Alistair had secured for his lord's tutorial. The shepherd smiled at them and Edward called out, "Gabriel, so good of you to tend to us. Do you have a sound sheep for me to shear?"

"Yes, milord," answered Gabriel. "Whenever you are ready."

Alistair remarked, "I think it best that I show you how to handle the shears and explain the process, my lord. Gabriel is the most proficient shearer you have in your service, but he is uncomfortable tutoring you. If you will allow it, I will provide the demonstration, I am most capable."

"Yes, thank you, Alistair" responded Edward.

Alistair walked over to the stool near Gabriel where the shears lay. Edward and Lawrence followed. He picked up the shears and showed it to them. He said, "Notice the sharp points on the two blades. You will want to keep the points clear of the sheep's skin so as not to cut or poke them. It is easier to shear a calm sheep versus one agitated from fear that a cut incurs. The best way to shear is to gently press the broad part of the blades upon the skin."

Alistair directed Gabriel to bring a sheep in for the demonstration. Edward was surprised to see Alistair remove his shirt. He explained, "My lord, aside from the dirt and sweat that such an activity produces, our long blousy sleeves could be a hazard. It is best to be shirtless. It is common among shearers."

Edward asked, "Are there no ladies present?"

"Women, yes, my lord," he answered. Our servants and tenants enjoy the excitement of the exhibition, but usually ladies of genteel birth would not be present, I cannot speak for your guests."

"But," Edward reiterated. "It is customary to be shirtless for safety purposes?"

Alistair confirmed, "Yes, my lord, all the shearers will be shirtless while fleecing."

"Very well, Alistair," said Edward. "I will comply. What of Mr. Cowper?"

"It is to his advantage, my lord," answered Alistair, "but not necessary."

Edward raised his brow to Mr. Cowper and asked, "Do I stand alone in this folly, Mr. Cowper, or will you join me?"

Lawrence laughed, "I defer to your judgment, my lord."

Edward smiled and remarked, "Very good." He removed his shirt and saw that Lawrence followed suit. He then told Alistair to continue.

Gabriel brought the sheep over and Alistair quickly placed the animal on his rump. He expertly clipped the wool off the sheep's stomach, down the belly to the groin. Next he opened the wool up on the throat and sheared around the left side of the neck and head. Then, he rolled the sheep over and clipped down the right side of the body. Last, he laid the sheep flat on the ground to take the fleece off the hindquarters and tail. Edward was amazed at Alistair's skill and strength in holding the sheep while he clipped its fleece. He looked at Lawrence who stood in awe and laughed. He said, "I do believe we have our work cut out for us."

Alistair spent the next half hour showing Lawrence how to hold the sheep in the various positions for shearing before Edward had his chance at clipping. After two hours of hard and perspiring work, they were glad to finish their task.

Alistair had ordered ale to be brought to the barn at the end of their shearing lesson. He also commanded that an area be set up for his lord's ablutions. Edward was pleased to see that Alistair had taken care of every detail towards his comfort and as they cooled down, each enjoying a pint of ale, he remarked, "Thank you, Alistair, for seeing to everything."

"I am only doing my job, my lord," responded Alistair.

"A job well done," remarked Edward. "We will need to continue with the same regiment each day if we do not want to embarrass ourselves. I suggest we make an early start each morning. Then we can return in time to break our morning fast with our guests. That will allow me to be a proper host during their stay. What do you say?"

"As you wish, my lord," responded Alistair. Lawrence simply nodded in agreement.

Edward concluded, "Very good. Let us return to the manor."

The three of them were surprised to see a regal carriage at Beaumont Manor when they arrived. Alistair took Lord Felton's mount as he made his way to the manor's front door. Edward hated to greet his guests in such dishevel and self-consciously ran his fingers through his hair in an attempt to better himself. As he passed the carriage he recognized the Duke of Hartford's crest, but was surprised to see Lady Anne alighting from the carriage door.

"Lady Anne," exclaimed Edward. "I am glad you have come. Are the Tates with you?"

Anne, surprised by Lord Felton's sudden appearance, was greatly affected. She had never seen him look more spectacular than he did at that moment. He reminded her with his tousled hair, opened shirt and fitted breeches of the rogue hero in one of her novels and found herself speechless until she smelled him. Her nose twitched and she caught herself placing a finger under her nostrils to block the odor.

Edward gasped and stepped back. He said, "Forgive me, my lady. I am far from presentable. I shall leave you to my majordomo and uncle until I have made myself respectable." He turned and began to walk away. Before he crossed the manor threshold, Anne called out, "Wait! Lord Felton!"

He stopped and turned to face her. She continued, "You must satisfy my curiosity. What is it that I smell?"

Edward laughed and before leaving answered, "sheep."

He did not see the smile on Lady Anne's face.

# Chapter Ten

Jenkins was appalled at his master's appearance and aghast that any of his guests should have seen him, not merely in disarray, but reeking of a foul odor. He was expecting his master's arrival and ordered a bath be made ready for him. The kitchen staff was keeping pots of water boiled. He only needed to summon for their delivery when he spied his master. He had been keeping vigil at his lord's window and pulled the bell cord as soon as he saw him approach the manor. To his dismay, his guests arrived at the same time.

Edward was pleased upon entering his room to find a warm bath waiting for him. He quickly dropped out of his filthy clothes and sank into the tub of warm water. Jenkins disgustedly picked up his soiled pantaloons and boots. He tsked, "I think your pantaloons are ruined, my lord. I shall have them burned."

"Nonsense," replied Edward. "I will need them for the rest of the week unless you prefer I ruin more than one."

"You must return tomorrow, my lord?" asked Jenkins.

"I must return all week if Mr. Cowper and I do not want to embarrass ourselves," answered Edward.

Jenkins looked at the pantaloons and said, "I shall soak them, but I do not know if they will dry by tomorrow. I fear you must ruin another pair. May I ask how you managed to save your shirt?"

Edward grinned knowing he was about to shock his valet and answered, "I took it off. It was a necessary safety precaution."

Jenkins was about to comment when his master held up his hand to say, "When in Rome we must do, as the Romans do. I will hear nothing on this subject, Jenkins. Trust me, I offended no one."

"Very good, my lord," retorted Jenkins. "I have laid out your clothes for you on your bed. I will return to help you dress as soon as I remove these foul clothes. Do you need me to help you with your ablutions?"

Edward answered, "It is not necessary, Jenkins, but do see that Mr. Cowper and Alistair know to join us for their noon meal and see whether uncle was intuitive enough to push the meal hour out to accommodate our guests and myself.

"Yes, my lord," replied Jenkins, before he left.

Edward felt in command of himself again once he donned his gentleman's attire. He looked quite dapper in his super fine midnight blue double-breasted day coat and buff pantaloons. Jenkins accessorized him with a fob watch and placed a sapphire stickpin in the centerfolds of his starched cravat. He wore a matching sapphire ring and felt quite polished as he walked into the main parlour where he expected to find his guests.

For the first time, he noticed how dreary the curtains, rugs, and upholstery looked. The room was exquisite with its mahogany and ornamental furniture, but its wear over the years was beginning to show. Edward noted it was time to refurbish and liked the idea of commanding his wife to the task.

He found Lady Anne immediately, looking out the bay window marveling of what he knew to be a superior view. That particular window provided a look at his uncle's knot gardens. He knew the geometric pattern of the verdant shrubbery and colorful flowers provided an exceptional picture.

Mrs. Tate was the first to speak. "My lord, so kind of you to include us in your invitation."

Edward smiled, walked over to Mrs. Tate who sat on the faded Queen Anne sofa. He took her hand, pressed a light kiss to the back of it, and greeted, "Mrs. Tate, the pleasure is all mine. Thank you for accepting." He then bowed to Miss Bell Tate, who returned his greeting with a smile. Edward turned to find his uncle hovering nearby, and asked, "You have met everyone, uncle?"

"Yes, Edward," he answered. "Lady Anne was kind to make the introductions."

Surprised, Edward queried, "You have a prior acquaintance with Lady Anne?"

"Nay," responded Beaumont. "But she took charge of putting us all at ease as though she was the mistress of the manor."

Edward smiled at Anne. She blushed and bowed her head from his focus. He then walked over to her to make her welcome. Anne made her curtsey. Edward took his bow and then in a quiet voice, he said, "Thank you for your consideration." He directed her attention back to the bay window and remarked, "I too enjoy the view from this window."

Anne smiled, replying, "It is beautiful. Thank you, my lord, for offering me the pleasure of seeing Beaumont Manor. Your invitation honors me."

"I would argue that the honor is all mine," responded Edward.

Once more embarrassed, Anne crimsoned. Edward noticed her blush and gallantly turned his attention to his other guests offering Anne a chance to recollect herself. He asked, "Where is his grace and Lord Riverdale?"

Having composed herself, Anne answered, "His grace went on to Westfield Mansion to escort Elinor and her family. They arrive tomorrow. Lord Riverdale, I fear was summoned home."

Edward looked to Mrs. Tate, surprised at Riverdale's absence. Mrs. Tate said, "Lord Riverdale has been most attentive to Bell this last week, my lord. Lady Anne informed us that his behavior is the latest *on dit* among the *ton* and that the news probably reached his family's ears. We are hopeful that he is not dissuaded to join us."

"Ah," replied, Edward. "Do not fear Mrs. Tate. Riverdale is not one to dally with a lady's affection. I am sure he will come, if it is within his power. We must not exclude that it was of a different nature that called him home."

Bell forced a smile and then was distracted as she saw two gentlemen enter the room. Lord Felton quickly introduced his man of business and Mr. Cowper to his guests.

Edward was pleased. His day was going exceedingly well. First, he and Mr. Cowper engaged in some rather fun sport learning how to shear a sheep. Then, he arrived home to find that Lady Anne had arrived. Next, the noon meal conversation turned out to be amusingly funny and engaging as his guests found much humor in his morning's activities. They all became excited when they learned that Beaumont was hosting a Spring Sheep Shearing Festival in their honor.

After their meal, his guests excused themselves to their rooms for a rest before supper and Edward convened with his steward to conclude a few more business matters. The last item dispatched Alistair with Mr. Cowper to Town to purchase some new clothes. Edward knew that Lawrence was ill funded and guessed that the sheep shearing activity was consuming what little wardrobe he owned. He wanted to compensate Mr. Cowper for partnering with him in his folly to amuse his tenants and guests; he also wanted to make sure that Lawrence had proper dress attire for the upcoming country dance. Edward surmised that if Mr. Cowper was indeed of noble blood, then he needed to make a good first impression into polite Society and that included dressing the mark of a gentleman. Besides, he reflected, he liked the boy and related to his struggle of trying to make his way into the *bon ton*. Regardless of who his father was, his grandmother, like his own, was of the aristocracy.

Edward entered his private rooms to change into his evening clothes when he spied Lady Anne through his bedroom window. The view from his window faced the formal knot garden, the same garden that Lady Anne had marveled at earlier. Instead of ringing for Jenkins as he planned, he exited his room and headed straight to the knot garden, where he hoped Lady Anne still stood.

Lady Anne marveled at Beaumont's intricately laced knot garden. She found it difficult to make out the geometric design of the garden because she needed a bird's eye view to see the pattern in its entirety. She expected it was a spectacular picture and wondered if one of the staterooms provided the view she needed to see it. She was walking with her hands clasped behind her back inhaling the multiple sweet smells the flowers and herbs emanated. She could identify the sweet sage and rosemary in one spot and the lavender and chamomile in another. The vibrant colors of the canary daffodils and scarlet peonies were breathtaking. The low standing boxwood hedges that framed the design in verdant hue brought the colors even more alive. She felt at peace in this garden and closed her eyes to breathe its scent one more time before she retreated to dress for dinner.

She still had her eyes closed when an intruder broke her reverie. She recognized Edward's voice as he softly chanted,

> I wandered lonely as a cloud
> That floats on high o'er vales and hills,
> When all at once I saw a crowd,

Before Edward could finish his prose, she interrupted him and completed the stanza to his surprise.

> A host of golden daffodils;
> Beside the lake, beneath the trees,
> Fluttering and dancing in the breeze.

Anne turned to face a smiling Lord Felton and burst out with a chuckle at his amusement. He complimented, "You are an admirer of Wordsworth, Lady Anne?"

She replied, "Who is not? His poem "Daffodils," is one of my favorites. And you, my lord, are an admirer?"

"My uncle is more so than I," answered Edward. "But yes, I respect his work, though I do not consume his sentimentality on a daily basis as my uncle does."

Anne responded, "I would not have thought the marquis to be sentimental. He has never married and is known to be a tyrant on occasion."

Edward answered, "Perspective is always relevant, my lady. It is true that Beaumont has never married; however, I would guess it is because he never relinquished his unrequited love for another. And while I can attest that he is a tyrant when it comes to protecting his interests, I have found him to be a very compassionate and sentimental man. These gardens were his mother's and you can see that they are immaculately kept, a tribute to his love for her. I am sure that you noticed the interior of the house is ready for some refurbishing. I expect it is hard for him to change those things that are familiar and reminiscent of his childhood. Perspective is in the eye of the beholder and I find my uncle most sentimental."

"I stand corrected, my lord," replied Anne who smiled and said, "In all honesty, your uncle has already endeared himself to me. He has been most welcoming to me and the Tates."

She asked, "You said that these gardens were your great grandmother's?"

Edward reflected as he realized that was true. He liked the idea that Beaumont's mother was his great grandmother. It made him feel more connected to the manor and deserving of inheriting it. He responded, "Yes, she was my great grandmother."

Anne continued, "This garden is lovely. I wished I could view it from a higher vantage point to discern its pattern."

"I fear the best view is from my bedroom window, but perhaps if we gather everyone together to take a look it would not be so inappropriate for you to enter my bedroom."

Anne blushed and in an effort to distract the tension her body felt, she asked, "Is the pattern based on a tapestry or rug from the house?"

Edward laughed and replied, "Yes, indeed. There is a tapestry in the Green State Room from which I am told my great grandmother took the design. Perhaps after dinner I may be allowed to show it to you."

She answered, "I would like that very much, my lord, but for now I must excuse myself and dress for supper." She curtsied, turned, and hurried off before Edward could offer to escort her back into the manor. To his amusement, he found himself grinning, happy to have enjoyed a private conference with her.

Edward was in high spirits and anxious to descend to meet his guests in the parlour. "My lord," chided

Jenkins. "I will never manage this fold in your cravat if you do not remain still. Why must you fidget? Has Lady Anne affected you again?"

Edward was about to admonish his valet when he realized the truth in his words. It was time he admitted that Lady Anne did affect him and that perhaps it was time to take their casual acquaintance to the next stage. Should he, he wondered, *"Kiss her?"* He determined that before he considered courting her, he should know what it felt like to embrace her and kiss her. What if her spinsterhood had turned her frigid? He knew that the woman was constantly in his thoughts. He found himself greatly attracted to her, both physically and intellectually. Although he took great pleasure in her company, he also knew what it felt like to be at the end of her calculating and irksome wit, and while he enjoyed their repartee, he did not want a sparring wife. *"No,"* he concluded, he must kiss her and see if any emotions would stir between them. Edward decided his invitation to visit the Green State Room to view his great grandmother's tapestry provided him the perfect opportunity for an intimate moment. He smiled envisioning their embrace, holding her soft body against his while he brushed his lips on hers to see if she would welcome him. He would not seduce her. He argued. *"She must be a willing partner. I will not spend my life the initiator of our co-mingling. My wife must want me as much as I want her."* *"Yes,"* he affirmed. *"I will initiate a kiss in the state room."*

Edward found his uncle and all their guests in the parlour ready to make their way to the formal dining room. He had instructed his servants to group everyone at one end of the long mahogany table for a more intimate and convivial setting. He gave his uncle, the head of the table that his rank demanded and placed Lady Anne between his uncle and him. Edward noticed when he entered the parlour that Bell was already the focus of Mr. Cowper's attention, so he sat Lawrence, opposite him between Bell and her mother.

Anne did her best to control her anxiety. Something was amiss and she was not sure what. Lord Felton, she noted, entered the parlour in high spirits. A grin from ear to ear graced his face and he looked as though he possessed the knowledge of a prank ready to be perpetuated. She felt vulnerable and feared for her reputation. It had been years, since before her father died, that she received a respectable offer. A lady lacking a dowry or connections had little chance of marrying well. One without a male family member protectorate was vulnerable to the rakes and deviants who preyed on them. She constantly found herself in the uncomfortable position of refusing vile offers from men who either wanted to dally or offer her a *carte blanche*. She learned early that a lethal tongue was more dissuasive to a man's advances than the weak pleas of an innocent, so she honed her wit as her weapon of choice. Her heart quickly hardened to flirtations and she never fell for the insincere accolades of her solicitors until now. There was something about Lord Felton that touched her and moved her in a way that she could not command her body to ignore. Her nerves were sensitized to his touch, her stomach fluttered at his observance, and her heart beat loudly at his nearness. She feared that he knew she was attracted to him and that he would take advantage of her. She distressed mostly that he was toying with her, especially since their meeting in the knot garden. His demeanor changed from a man of brooding to a man of cheer. She realized she was more comfortable when he disliked her. She would much rather cause him ire than glee. Sitting next to him at the dining table unnerved her and she had to focus all her energies on slowing the rapid beats of her heart. She feared that she would swoon if she did not calm herself.

Edward felt Lady Anne's tension. Her rigid body astounded him. This was not the relaxed woman he talked to in the knot garden. He hoped by engaging her in a light conversation, he could break her stressed mood.

"Did you know, my lady, that we have more than one garden here at Beaumont Manor?" he queried.

Edward's voice broke into Anne's wandering mien and like one that is scared out of hiccupping, she came to attention and found the interruption calmed her composure.

"No," she answered, happy to have regained her equilibrium.

Edward continued, "At the backside of the knot garden, there is an arbor walk that exits to a meadow that flanks the manor. Years ago, groves of cherry, crabapple, and almond trees were planted. My great grandmother designed a gravel walkway that wraps around and through some places in the grove. She had her gardener plant wildflowers in the open meadow that edges the walkway. You will see bluebells, daisies, and other species dotting the landscape. This is the most colorful season to enjoy the walk. Perhaps, you will allow me to escort you on a stroll when the weather permits."

"Thank you, my lord," responded Anne. "I would like that very much. What other gardens are there? You mentioned multiple gardens, did you not?"

"Yes," answered Edward. "There is the rose garden, the cutting garden, the kitchen's garden, the notorious maze," Edward leaned over to whisper to Anne, "and my great grandmother's secret garden."

Anne opened her eyes wide, looked to Beaumont on her right side and then looked back to Lord Felton before asking in a whisper, "Why is it a secret garden?"

Edward answered, "It is a private garden whose location is unknown except to the head gardener and the Marquis of Beaumont Manor. My great grandmother designed it as a retreat. My uncle said his parents used it to commune with nature, but I think it more likely it was a romantic getaway for a very public couple. I know that my uncle goes there to meditate, always taking his volumes of Wordsworth for company. He took me there once, but I have not visited on my own, fearful that I might intrude on him. He is known to sneak away and lose himself with his poetry in the garden."

Anne smiled, "It is easy to imagine. I found myself easily captivated in the knot garden. I can imagine how hypnotized I would be in a *Garden of Eden*."

She noticed that Beaumont had finished talking with Mrs. Tate and had turned to address her. He said, "Did I overhear you say that you liked my knot garden, Lady Anne?"

"Oh, yes," she exclaimed. I understand the design came from a tapestry located in one of your state rooms."

"Quite right, my lady," replied Beaumont. "I shall show it to you and any of my other guests that are interested after we retire from supper."

Anne smiled and looked at Lord Felton who to her surprise looked quite irked. She wondered what transpired to cause his demeanor to change. She turned back to Beaumont and engaged him in a conversation regarding poetry that kept her bound to him until the conclusion of the meal. As Beaumont rose, he suggested the ladies retire to the parlour while the men took their port in his study. He reminded them that since they were a small group, they would not be longer than half the hour. Anne grinned at her thoughtful host and took the lead to escort Bell and her mother to the parlour. Edward watched her go and realized that their kiss would have to wait until another day.

# Chapter Eleven

Edward found Lady Anne with his uncle in the parlour. He could tell they were discussing one of Wordsworth's poems. He was disappointed that he had missed breaking his fast with her, but the interview he held with Mr. Cowper that morning had taken precedence over his own personal wishes.

He had noticed that Mr. Cowper was rather quiet while they shared a pint of ale after their training session. Normally, after wrangling and shearing their sheep, they were chatty and exuberant from their hearty workout. But this morning, Edward was mindful of Lawrence's somber mood.

He asked, "What troubles you, Mr. Cowper?" And then with a grin queried, "Are we not progressing as quickly as you would like, or does Miss Tate distract your mien?"

It seemed that Lawrence did not even hear Edward's tease when he asked, "I was wondering, my lord, if whether your agents have located any information on my grandfather?"

"I am afraid you did not give us much to go on, Mr. Cowper. Your grandmother's parents, as you know are deceased. Their only son and heir died from an unchivalrous duel years ago. My uncle thought that Alana had a younger sister, so we are trying to locate her. The years have diminished the links that were once easily visible," answered Edward.

Lawrence responded, "I see. Perhaps, it is futile and I should not impose myself on your household any longer. I should think about how I am to go about managing my future, it is weighing heavy on my mind."

Edward asked, "Are you unhappy aiding my steward?"

Lawrence pulled back his shoulders and raised his chin like a rooster about to crow when he replied, "No, but I am aware you manifested the work in charity towards me and I am gentlemanly enough not to take advantage of your generosity."

Edward sympathized for the orphan that sat before him and asked in a voice that commanded attention, "Alistair, has not complained of your work. Are you telling me that you are reluctant in your duties?"

Offended, Lawrence exclaimed, "Never! I would always do my duty to my employer. I have my pride I dare say."

"I expect it is your pride that blinds you to the facts then, Mr. Cowper. I will not tell you what to do, but I can assure you that my steward needs assistance and should you relinquish the job, then I would require to fill it with another person," stated Edward. "In addition, I do not think my uncle is prepared to see you leave. Your presence has brought him much joy. Be patient. Let us see if we can locate Alana's sister. Hopefully, she still lives."

Edward felt for the boy and decided to enlist the help of the Duke of Hartford when he arrived. His grace, was a man of many resources, but more importantly, his knowledge of the aristocracy was extensive.

As Edward crossed the threshold to enter the parlour, he saw his uncle and Lady Anne look up and smile. He grinned in return and asked, "Where are the Tates? Do not tell me they are still abed?"

"No," replied Anne. "Mr. Cowper has already taken possession of Miss Tate and they have ventured to the library. Your uncle informed Mr. Cowper that he had Sir Walter's latest novel *Rob Roy* in his collection. I believe Mrs. Tate followed as chaperone. She fears Mr. Cowper's attention may be developing into something more and I think she is protecting Lord Riverdale's interest, until she hears he has withdrawn it."

Beaumont laughed, "Mr. Cowper is a pup. I do not think he sees anything more in Miss Tate than camaraderie. They are of the same age and come from an isolated background. Neither of them was sent off to school and I believe they were both raised on the seaside."

"I agree," said Edward. "But just in case, I will send a missive to Riverdale informing him of a gentleman that is enjoying Miss Tate's pleasure."

Beaumont and Lady Anne chuckled. She said, "That is most intuitive of you, my lord, and the perfect test to see if he is worthy of her affection."

Edward stared at Lady Anne intently, releasing an "Ah" in comment. He asked, "Is a test necessary in the attainment of one's suit?"

Anne stood captivated by his gaze and answered, "A man in love would be a true gallant. He would rise to any challenge to secure his betrothed."

"Do we speak of fairy tales or real life?" asked Edward.

She answered, "Only time will tell in the case of Miss Tate and Lord Riverdale."

Edward smiled and concurred, "Yes, only time will tell."

Beaumont interrupted them and asked, "How goes your sheep shearing training and how are the plans for our spring festival progressing?"

Edward answered, "My skills are progressing as are Mr. Cowper's. He is learning to hold the sheep and Mr. Chapman is organizing the festival and dance. He is very capable. You only need to worry about what you will wear."

"Very good," replied Beaumont. "That reminds me, what about Mr. Cowper's wardrobe?"

"Already taken care of," he answered.

Anne interrupted their conference and said, "I will leave you to your business, my lords." Before she could rise, Beaumont apologized, "I am so sorry, my dear. I fear I have neglected you horribly. Let us all retire to the library and see how our other guests are managing, shall we?"

Edward proffered his arm to Lady Anne. She felt a pang of excitement as he tucked her arm through his and held it firm with his hand. She should have resisted the intimacy of such an escort and lightly placed her hand on his sleeve, but she felt powerless to do so. Lord Felton was a man that took charge and where she ordinarily took offense to such arrogance, she found that with him, she enjoyed it.

When they entered the library, they found Mr. Cowper reading Sir Walter Scott's novel *Rob Roy* aloud. Lawrence informed the new arrivals that he assured Mrs. Tate that he would skip any brutish passages, so she had allowed the read. The narrative proved to be quite haphazard with its obvious gaps in the storyline. Lawrence seemed to be the only one enjoying the story for he was silently reading the missing elements. His eyes gave away his rapture to Miss Tate's frustration. The rest of the audience found Mr. Cowper's performance exceedingly amusing, so much so that they failed to notice the Duke of Hartford and the Westfields enter.

His grace announced, "Beaumont, I hope you do not mind. We did not stand on ceremony, but simply followed your man to find you."

Beaumont answered, "Not at all, your grace. You are most welcome."

The introductions were made. Lady Anne and Mrs. Tate followed Lady Westfield to visit with her baby, Viscount Shelby. Beaumont, Edward, his grace, and Jonathan retired to his study to enjoy a glass of port. Somehow in all the excitement, Mr. Cowper and Miss Tate managed to stay behind to continue their read of *Rob Roy* that slowly became uncensored to Bell's delight.

The next morning, Lord Westfield and the Marquis of Beaumont accompanied Lord Felton and Mr. Cowper to the home farm. To Edward's chagrin, Jonathan was exceedingly enthusiastic to see him at his training. Having Jonathan watch him made Edward self-conscious and the task of shearing became a fiasco.

Edward growled, "Westfield, if you dare make an insidious remark, I shall personally throttle you!"

Jonathan laughed, "You are a brave man to dare to incite my wife's wrath. I do not think Elinor will respond kindly, should you treat me other than one who is held in high esteem."

"You dare hide behind Elinor's skirts?!" retorted Edward. "Have you no pride?"

"I have an abundant amount of pride, especially in Elinor. You know, you risk her good will if you so much as touch a single hair on my head. Unfortunately, I would as well if I ever throttled you. For some reason, she has developed an annoying affection for you, so I fear our words must be our weapon of choice."

Jonathan laughed as the sheep wrangled free of Mr. Cowper's hold, its fleece hanging off its shoulders like a cape. Jonathan teased with joyful amusement, "Felton! If you were still a child in short pants, I would commend your effort."

Mr. Cowper started laughing before Edward could respond in kind. He said, "I would like to see you try your hand at shearing."

"Could I?" asked Jonathan.

"Perhaps tomorrow," responded Edward. "You are not dressed for the task and I have promised to take Lady Anne for a walk. I dare not be late. Do you and Elinor join us?"

"No," answered Jonathan. "I have already done my courting as evidenced by my little viscount. I ride instead with Beaumont to visit some of his tenants, after he fulfills his promise of showing me around the home farm."

Beaumont interrupted, saying, "Yes, indeed Westfield. I am good at my word, but first I need to speak with my head farmer. Meet me at his cottage, will you?"

Jonathan replied, "Of course." He then watched as Beaumont commandeered Mr. Cowper to escort him. He surmised that perhaps Edward wanted to speak to him privately and turned back to face him.

Edward asked, "Why do you think I am courting Lady Anne?"

"Well, I certainly hope it is not Miss Tate that has captured your eye. She is much too jejune for you, Edward. Mark my words, you will tire of her before you celebrate a month's anniversary. Besides, I thought Riverdale favored her."

He inquired, "And will not Riverdale suffer the same fate?"

"No," answered Jonathan. "His tastes lean to an obliging and green girl. Besides, they are closer in age and will evolve together. He will enjoy teaching her, while I expect you would enjoy being the student as well as the tutor."

He asked, "And you think Lady Anne is the lady I seek?"

Jonathan answered, "That is for you to discern, but I will tell you that I first fought my attraction to Elinor, fearing she was not what was expected for a man of my station. I lost valuable time trying to contemplate what she meant to me, instead of listening to what my heart was telling me. I count my blessings that someone like you did not steal her away from me."

"Could never happen," replied Edward. "I should know. I tried, but Elinor always knew her heart."

"Then perhaps," continued Jonathan, "you should listen to yours."

Edward entered the parlour to find the rest of his guests hovering over Elinor's child. The Duke of Hartford, Lady Anne, Mrs. Tate, Miss Tate, and Mr. Cowper all grinned over baby Stephen, Viscount Shelby's antics. Elinor held him so that he could face his audience. He was a well-tempered baby and had everyone amused with his wide eyes, flailing arms, and gurgling laughter. Elinor bounced him on her lap while his grace remarked that he was all that a baby should be.

Edward almost asked to hold the little tyke, but remembered Jenkins would be genuinely hurt to see his masterpiece cravat ruined. He had just left his valet and his man had taken great care to tie his neck cloth and brush his coat. He discerned he owed him his allegiance not to have his cravat ravaged or his coat drooled upon, even if the perpetrator was in swaddling cloth. He made his felicitations and asked, "I am escorting Lady Anne on a walk through the meadow and grove park. Is anyone interested in accompanying us? The weather is cool but inviting."

Lady Elinor and her father declined the invitation, wanting to continue their play with Stephen. Miss Tate wanted to go and looked to her mother for permission. She found her mother waved her off in approval, probably she thought, because Lady Anne made up part of the party. Anne smiled, knowing that to be the case and wondered whether Mrs. Tate noticed that Mr. Cowper held the novel *Rob Roy* in his hand. Anne guessed that the duo were looking for a quiet place to continue their read, and that once they started on their walk, they would find a way to escape her chaperonage.

Anne settled on wearing her spencer while Mrs. Tate insisted that Bell wear her pelisse, cautioning her not to jeopardize her health. If the sun or wind proved too extreme, she was commanded to return immediately to the manor. Both ladies gave their assurances to take care as they donned their kid gloves and bonnets.

As expected, Mr. Cowper and Miss Tate raced ahead as soon as they reached the arbor. By the time Anne and Edward cleared the tunnel of vines, they had lost sight of the conniving duo. Edward smiled and commented, "Do not worry. They will come to no harm. They only want to read."

Anne grinned. She was still captivated, transitioning from exiting the darkened arbor to entering the enchanting and brilliant meadow. She felt like she was leaving the real world to enter a fantasyland redolent with sweet smells and vibrant colors. The gusty wind made the wild flowers and grass in the meadow sway from side to side. Anne thought the motion lyrical and set her mind to find a tune that would play to its rhythm. She soon found herself humming. Edward stopped their walk to ask her what she sang.

"I do not know," she replied, turning to face him. "Do you not find the landscape calling to you? The meadow is alive and I find it beckons me."

He asked, "You are a romantic then? You wish for magical kingdoms, happy endings, and perhaps, a prince charming?"

Anne quivered as she responded to Edward's closeness. She wondered what his intentions were. She panicked, saying, "I think we should check on Miss Tate and Mr. Cowper. Her mother after all, entrusted her care to me."

Edward threaded her arm through his and resumed his escort, holding Anne's hand firm. He sensed her nervousness and feared like a young filly she was ready to bolt. However, he was not ready to relinquish her, not until he had a chance to learn more about this woman that caused his heart to flutter. He continued their walk along the gravel path until they came upon a fork in the road. One path retreated into the grove, while the other changed into a dirt road that wrapped around the hill. It was off the dirt path that they spied Bell and Mr. Cowper hovering over what they presumed was the *Rob Roy* novel. Anne laughed as she realized that there would be no way of covering up the grass stains that their repose would cause.

She was trying to visualize Mrs. Tate's outrage, when she felt herself being pulled along the gravel path into the grove park to be ensconced in a bounty of fruit trees. Edward smiled. He released her arm and then he pulled a small knife from his coat pocket. Anne marveled at his secretive manner and then she chuckled when she saw him cut off a cluster of cherries from a nearby tree.

He walked her over to a stone bench situated along the gravel path. She noted as she looked down the avenue of trees that more than one bench graced the grove. She watched Edward pull out his linen and place the cherries on the square piece of cloth. He used his knife to pit the fruit and then he offered her the prize.

Anne held out her gloved hand, but Edward simply grinned and shook his head. "No," he said. "They will stain your gloves. Open your mouth and I will place a ripe cherry on your tongue."

Anne felt sinful. Her mind told her that Lord Felton's behavior was totally inappropriate, but her body ached to participate in this dance of seduction. She realized that she was a willing participant. She knew she should stop the interlude, but she also knew she was not in any real danger. She did not fear Lord Felton, but at that moment, she discovered she desired him. She wanted to explore her feelings. She didn't even comprehend that she had opened her mouth until the sweet juices seeped across her tongue. Instinctively, she closed her mouth and chewed. She saw Lord Felton's eyes alight. He said, "It is good, is it not?"

Her body was full of anticipation, her mind taking note of every sensation fluttering through her body. She felt warm and wanting. Then, like a bucket of cold water thrown into her face, Anne's mood broke when her mind understood that Lord Felton was asking her a probing question.

He asked, "When we were at the opera, I remember you saying that your 'ship had sailed' regarding holding out for love. I have always wondered, what you meant. Did you lose your great love, my lady?"

Anne noted that Lord Felton had pitted another cherry and was ready to offer it to her. Fully cognizant and aware of what to expect, she opened her mouth for the sweet morsel and halfheartedly enjoyed it.

He asked, "Well?"

"Delicious, my lord," she answered with courtesy.

Edward clarified, "I meant, was your heart broken? Is that why you have given up on love?"

It surprised Anne that Lord Felton had no desire to relinquish his question. She wanted to tell him her personal life was none of his affair, but his inquiry displayed an air of sincerity that she did not wish to rebuke, so she answered honestly. "I do not think any woman gives up on love. I believe, my 'ship has sailed' simply because most suitors see me as *on the shelf,* past my prime, even though I am only five and twenty."

"What of a broken heart?" pestered Edward. "Was there a love lost?"

"I was actually engaged before my father died, but I released him of his obligation. He was a third son who greatly needed to make a profitable connection. I had imagined we were in love but was mistaken. I realized what we felt was nothing more than attraction, because the minute he begged me to release him, I found him to be lacking. No, my lord, my heart was never broken, only my pride was hurt."

"I am glad you did not suffer over one so unworthy of you," said Edward.

Anne asked, "And what of you, my lord, was your heart ever broken? But wait! I know the answer. You are lucky that Elinor is the kind of woman that can turn an ardor into a meaningful friendship. Not all women have that gift."

Edward responded, "Elinor had made her intentions known early so that I had not yet engaged my heart. But she had and continues to have my admiration. I could not ask for better friends than the Westfields and will confess to you that I have great affection for them."

Anne asked, "Am I also to be called your friend, my lord?"

Edward, out of sheer frustration that this woman could only see him as a friend, without thought, grabbed both of Anne's arms and pulled her towards him. He looked into her astonished eyes and pouty mouth. He closed his lips to hers and then whispered, "No, I hope to call you more than friend." Anne closed her eyes and released a small sigh before Edward's lips brushed against hers. She instinctively raised her arms around Edward's neck, he embraced her and deepened their kiss. Anne felt like she fell into a warm pool of water, her body weightless and floating until she became aware of the cool air that brushed her face. She opened her eyes to see Lord Felton grinning.

"Come," he said. "It is time we collected Miss Tate and Mr. Cowper, and return them to the manor before Mrs. Tate becomes concerned." Awestruck, Anne followed. Later, she could not remember their walk back to the manor, or how she ended up in her room.

# Chapter Twelve

Lord Felton was on his way to the Westfield's private suite of rooms. He was summoned, or rather commanded to seek an audience with Lady Elinor, the Countess of Westfield, before supper. As he walked, he reflected on his interlude with Lady Anne. He thought, he need not worry that Anne was a cold fish; he found her most engaging and was even more surprised at his own bubbling emotions that she provoked in him. He felt young and vital, his exuberant stride evidence of his joy. He was happy that Lady Anne was looking for love and decided that he would prove to her that he was her prince charming.

He remembered when the Westfields first suggested her as a possible wife for him and he rebuked them for the idea. However, since then, he found the things about her that once provoked him, made her charming and desirable. Her razor sharp wit and engaging personality amused rather than annoyed him. He acknowledged her incomparable beauty and he admired her poise. Edward laughed as he once again recollected his cutting remark to the Westfields in regards to her as a possible wife: *I want to start my nursery, not retire it. "How wrong I was,"* he admitted. *"She will make me a wonderful wife. I cannot imagine that I will ever grow weary of Anne."*

He found himself in front of the Westfield's door and knocked. He heard Elinor call "enter," and turned the door handle to make his way into her suite. He was surprised to find her alone and chided her. "Elinor, this will not do. Where is your abigail? Where is Westfield? What are you thinking, receiving me alone?"

Elinor laughed, "My abigail is on errand and Jonathan said while you have his sympathy, he will not stay to witness your chastisement. He has removed himself, saying he will hopefully see you at dinner. Besides, you know that Jonathan is quite at ease with you. You proved yourself to him by caring more for my wishes than your own. He is most comfortable if I am alone with you. He considers you family, as do I."

"That is beside the point," Edward chided. "What of your reputation?"

Elinor replied in mirth. "I am above reproach, Edward. Have you forgotten I am an *Original*? The *bon ton* tolerates my occasional slips from propriety because of my blue blood, superior connections, and wealth. The *gossipmongers* would not dare disparage me. Why, his grace alone would send them into exile if not the gallows."

Edward chuckled at the truth of her words and asked, "Well, what have I done that you wish to send me to the chopping block?"

She asked, "I want to know what you mean plying your wares at Anne."

He responded, "Plying my wares? I am afraid you must elaborate, Elinor."

"I mean, what the devil were you doing, kissing her in the grove when you told me and Jonathan that you were not interested in courting her. I warned you that she was dear to me and could not bear to see her harmed. Explain yourself, Edward!"

In a quiet and thoughtful voice, Edward asked, "She told you what transpired in the grove?"

Elinor answered, "Yes! Well no, not exactly. I came upon her in her room in quite a dazed state. I thought her ill and begged to know what I could do for her. She simply looked at me and said, 'He kissed me.' I asked who and she said you did. Then, she asked me what could it mean?"

"Well?" Elinor demanded. "What does it mean, Edward?"

He laughed and replied, "It means it is none of your business. If you want to worry about anyone, Elinor, then worry about me. I fear I am swimming in deep waters. Anne is looking for a prince charming. I expect I am too jaded and unromantic for the role. She informs me a true gallant would rise to any challenge to secure his betrothed. I can only hope that I do not fail again in securing one that is superior to me in all that is important."

"Edward," consoled Elinor. "Your heart was not yet engaged with me, so do not play on my emotions. Are you telling me that you have found love with Anne? You know, I wish nothing less for you."

"Only time will tell," replied Edward. "But I am hopeful that indeed it is love that is blossoming in my heart."

"Oh, Edward," sighed Elinor. "I did not know you were poetic. I fear you are in love."

Edward laughed and asked, "Did Anne mention if my attentions were welcomed, or do you think my suit pure folly?"

"Do not play the innocent, Edward. You are far too experienced in the petticoat line and I know it. If it is Anne that you desire, than I am confident you are more than capable in securing her. She too is looking for a love match and I dare say a little romance. She may be leery, for she has shared her confidences with me. I know that there were several men that trifled with her. She has all my respect to have protected her virtue and remained above reproach all these years, but I fear in you, she has let down her guard. Do not fail her, Edward. I do not think I could forgive you if you did."

Edward concluded, "I shall do everything in my power to court her appropriately and maintain your affection. Shall we descend for supper before Jonathan has my head?"

Edward and Elinor saw from the great hall that a flurry of excitement was taking place in the parlour. It seemed during their tête-à-tête that Edward's cousin Catherine had arrived and brought with her a singular female guest. Elinor remembered Lady Catherine from when she sojourned through Edward's invitation at the Duke of Aubry's estate. The sojourn was planned by the Dowager Duchess of Aubry, Edward's grandmother, in an effort to forward Edward's suit with Elinor. It was during her visit that she learned that Catherine had a prior connection with Jonathan. Elinor found Catherine's forward and intimate behavior towards Jonathan offensive. If she was honest, she was jealous of the beautiful woman who openly displayed her affections for the man she loved, but was not allowed to claim until the end of her *come-out* season. She feared that Jonathan may have recalled a previous obligation to Catherine, but thanks to Edward, she was able to resolve her worst fears and secure herself in the knowledge that Jonathan loved only her.

Elinor had a marked resentment for Catherine's frivolous lifestyle, the woman seemed to engage in only what amused her and Elinor wondered why Edward had invited her.

Edward entered the parlour, and relinquished Elinor's arm before he called, "Cousin! I thought you had changed your mind and chose not to attend."

"No, not at all," replied Lady Catherine. "You know that I would at least allow you to try to amuse me, Edward.

I was detained because my family had visitors. Edward, allow me to introduce you to Miss Rachel Morgan. She is a distant cousin of ours. I have discovered that mama is her godmother. She sponsored her *come-out* and I have decided to take her under my wing."

Edward thought the young girl common but pretty. She had an oval face with large brown eyes, a small nondescript nose, and brown hair to match. She was a petite girl, rather shy, characteristic of a young debutante. He bowed to her and said, "It is a pleasure to meet you Miss Morgan. I am glad you have arrived in time to enjoy our spring festival."

Rachel blushed and replied, "Thank you, my lord, for receiving me. However, I do feel that I am intruding upon your festivities."

Catherine barked, "Oh, do not start that again Rachel." She looked at Edward. "It took me a day and a half to convince her that you would welcome her. In fact, I told her that you would offer her the first set of dances at your country ball in honor of her *come-out*. Do not call me a liar, Edward."

Edward checked his temper. He had wanted to ask Anne for the opening set, but would only embarrass everyone if he refused to offer for Miss Morgan. Forcing a smile, he looked at Miss Morgan and asked, "I do hope you will do me the honor and save the first set of dances for me Miss Morgan."

Rachel blushed, bowed her head before replying, "Of course, my lord. The honor is mine."

After supper, Miss Morgan retired to her room. She claimed exhaustion from traveling, but Edward surmised that she felt awkward among the esteemed titled. Edward hoped to explain himself to Lady Anne and secure the second set of dances, but it seemed his plans would not take precedence to the whirlwind he knew as Catherine.

"You must help me, Edward, or Rachel will never make an advantageous connection," commented Lady Catherine. "She is too meek in Society. She is quite likable once she is comfortable and able to be herself. Grandmother approves of her, in fact, she told me she thought she would do well for you."

Edward flushed and curtly replied, "Catherine, mind what you say!"

Catherine replied, "Do not be so harsh Edward. We are among family, aside from the Tates and I know that their aspirations lay in another direction. Where is Riverdale anyway?"

Edward answered, "He has not arrived yet and I am afraid you have failed to notice Lady Anne."

"Oh, yes," replied Lady Catherine, "the chaperone."

Edward calmed himself before retorting, "No Catherine, not the chaperone. Lady Anne is my guest."

The room became uncomfortable and before Edward and Catherine could volley anymore remarks, Lady Elinor excused herself, asking Anne to accompany her to check on her son. The Tates followed suit, retiring for the evening, while the remaining males followed Beaumont into his study.

Edward growled at Catherine who exclaimed, "What?!"

He sent her to retire after his diatribe where he made sure she understood that he was not interested in pursuing Miss Morgan and that his interest lay elsewhere. When she asked, "Where?" He said it was none of her business and sent her off to her room. He then headed to the study where he hoped to solicit the Duke of Hartford's help in finding Mr. Cowper's grandfather.

Edward heard his uncle call his name as he crossed the study's threshold. He noticed that the men were deeply engaged in conversation. He made his way to the side console and poured himself a glass of port. He was still reeling from his discourse with Catherine and needed the drink to calm him down. He swished the dark liquid in his glass, inhaled its essence and then took a sip. The sweet liquor pacified his frayed nerves. He looked at his uncle and then to the Duke of Hartford who just patted Mr. Cowper's shoulder. He wondered what transpired during his confrontation with Catherine. He asked, "What have I missed?"

Beaumont answered first. He said, "We have just finished telling his grace of Mr. Cowper's quest to find his grandfather. He was not familiar with Alana's family whose county seat was in northern England."

His grace interrupted, "I will speak with Prinny who surprisingly is all knowing when it comes to the aristocracy. Also I will check the royal registry for Alana's lineage. If she had a sister, it would be noted there. Beaumont, have you thought to ask your sister, the dowager?"

Beaumont replied, "No, thank you. I did not think to do so. My sister married the Duke of Aubry after Alana left the protection of her family. My sister would not have known at the time, any of the families in northern England, aside from the Duke of York of course."

He continued, "I myself, met Alana in Town during her *come-out* Season. I courted her there and when she refused my offer and ran off with her beloved, I simply returned home. I never heard or saw from her again."

His grace responded, "Gossip has a way of turning into oral history, your sister may know much to aid you."

"I will write to her immediately," replied Beaumont. "Thank you."

The Duke of Hartford added, "Even if we found your grandfather Mr. Cowper, there is no way to prove who you are without a family member to vouch for your lineage, unless you possess documentation or something else like a family heirloom that validates you as an heir."

"I have nothing of significance," answered Mr. Cowper. He paused and then laughed.

Beaumont queried, "What is it?"

Mr. Cowper untied and removed his cravat. He opened his collar and moved his short brown hair behind his ear. He bowed his head to the side and said, "My grandmother frequently commented it was a mark of nobility. I always assumed she was teasing me so I never took her seriously, but perhaps, there is some truth in it. My mother had the same birthmark."

All the gentlemen looked at the crescent shaped birthmark on Mr. Cowper's neck. His grace mused, "Very interesting Mr. Cowper and perhaps it may be relevant, but unless someone connected to Alana's family, a witness who can attest to its lineage, then I fear it will not help you to stake any claim."

"In all honesty, your grace," responded Lawrence. "I am searching for my grandfather, because I am curious to know if I have any family left in this world. It is amazing how lonely one can feel, when they know they are not connected to anyone at all."

Edward looked at his uncle who he thought was ready to break his composure in sympathy. His face was overcome with emotion. He watched him as he placed his arm around Lawrence's shoulder, announcing, "You are not alone my boy. You may call me family. This most titled and esteemed group are pleased to call you friend. Is that not right gentlemen?"

The men who had been nursing their own glasses of port, raised them in toast to Lawrence, and shouted, "Hear, hear!"

Beaumont then bid good evening to his guests and asked Lawrence to escort him to his room. Jonathan reminded Edward that he would accompany him in the morning to the home farm before retiring himself.

Edward found he was alone with the Duke of Hartford and asked, "Before you retire, your grace, I would like a word with you about Lady Anne?"

"Really?" he responded. "And what entitles you to speak about her?"

Edward stiffened and practically growled at the Duke of Hartford, "Your response suggests that she is under your protection. Am I unaware of a connection between the two of you?"

His grace replied, "Any friend of mine is under my protection. You are a prominent example. Perhaps, you best relate what is on your mind, before I take you to task for your flippant inquiry?"

"I was wondering," began Edward, "why you have been attentive to her, signaling her out in Society? For heaven's sake, your grace, you attended Almack's!"

The Duke of Hartford put on his most hauteur manner and asked, "And what business is it of yours who I favor with my attention, Edward?"

Edward's ire rose as he answered, "If Lady Anne is the one you favor, if you have any designs of intimacy with her, then it is very much my business!"

"And why is that?" he asked.

"Because," retorted Edward. "I plan to make her my wife and I would hate to lose your friendship in the process!"

His grace smiled and said, "Then you have nothing to worry about. You only risked my friendship if you were to cause Lady Anne harm. Since your intentions are honorable, you may still call me friend. Is she aware of your intentions?"

Edward was dumbstruck. "I have not made my intentions known to her, for I just discovered them myself, though Elinor is in my confidence. I have only decided to court her, but was concerned that I may be encroaching on your suit, though in all honesty, it would not have stopped me in trying to claim her."

"Nor should it, if you love the woman," said his grace. "Is it a love match, Edward?"

"I do believe so," laughed Edward. "But tell me, why have you been showing her favor?"

"Aside from her amiable disposition," answered his grace, "Elinor asked me to bring her into fashion. She did not like the way the *ton* was reducing her station to one of servitude, simply because she offered herself as a chaperone. Elinor thought my attentions would aid her in Society, and remind Lady Anne of her rightful place among the *ton*."

"Your granddaughter is a good and compassionate woman," complimented Edward.

"Indeed," replied his grace. "What of Miss Morgan? How does she fit into your plans?"

Edward grimaced, "She does not. She is nothing more than an aberration of what I had hoped was a straight path to Lady Anne's heart. Aside from the opening set of dances that I felt compelled to offer her so as not to embarrass anyone, she is nothing more than a guest in my uncle's home. I informed Catherine very clearly that my intentions lay elsewhere, though I did not state where."

"You have my felicitations, Edward," responded his grace. "Lady Anne is a remarkable woman. You could do no better. I believe that you both complement one another and will find happiness together if you do not mess it up."

Edward laughed. "Thank you for your confidence, your grace. You will keep our interview private until I have secured her hand. I am not sure of her feelings for me and would be quite shattered to become pitied by my friends, should she decline my suit."

"You need not ask, Edward," answered his grace. "I keep all my interviews private, as you should know."

They made one last toast to Lady Anne before retiring to their rooms.

# Chapter Thirteen

Edward and Jonathan began laughing again as they met up at the top of the stairs. They had both just finished their ablutions and change of dress after a very sporting and comical morning. Yesterday's fiasco, reminded Edward that he would be performing in front of an audience. Today, to prepare himself for the contest, he gathered the farm servants to watch his and Mr. Cowper's performance. He wanted to practice their concentration skills, so as not to repeat the mistakes they made when Beaumont and Westfield observed them. The strategy proved effective because during the session, Lawrence and Edward were oblivious to the rants and cheers of the crowd. It was not until the end, when the task was done that their mien cleared and they heard the crowd applauding their skill.

Jonathan on the other hand, thought Edward a fiend to have a mob of witnesses at his first try at the sport. Even though Edward had a knowledgeable shearer to instruct and hold the sheep for Jonathan, without any experience, the task was daunting. Jonathan became further vexed when the shearer kept "tsking," nodding his head from side to side in disapproval, as pieces of fleece fell off in chunks versus the desired coat of one piece. Jonathan thought he would have to compensate Beaumont for the lost fleece. In the end, he bowed to Mr. Cowper and Felton for becoming proficient in the very arduous sport. Edward felt quite vindicated when he looked at the mound of fleece remnants, and could retort, "You know Westfield, if you were still a boy in short pants, I would commend your effort."

"Touché!" rebounded Jonathan. They both bellowed in laughter before Lawrence handed them each a pint of ale. They finished their drinks in good humor. Then, they went over to inspect the progress of the shearers in the large barn. All week, Edward and Lawrence had practiced in the small barn that was normally used for extra storage. Tomorrow's festival and dance would mark the end of the shearing season and Edward wondered if the shearers would finish in time. Only the sheep needed for tomorrow's contest would be left unshorn. They all marveled at the site of the shearers at work, respecting their skill and speed of work. Edward was happy that he would be able to honor them with tomorrow's fete.

Edward and Jonathan could not stop laughing over their morning sheep shearing. They volleyed witticisms at each other as they descended the staircase, mocking each other's ability. Their good humor stayed with them, while they made their way outdoors to join the rest of the party on the west lawn. They found Elinor, baby Stephen, and Mrs. Tate relaxing on an Aubusson rug that was placed on the grass for their comfort. Jonathan immediately bent down to pick up his son cradled in his wife's lap. While Jonathan raised Stephen into the air in playful gesture, Edward asked, "Where are the rest of our guests?"

Elinor replied, "They have ventured into your notorious maze. I should say, Mr. Cowper, Miss Tate, and Miss Morgan entered first. Then, when they did not exit, Mrs. Tate begged Anne to seek them out."

Edward frowned. He did not like Anne being treated as a servant and being put to task for a person, who was perfectly capable of completing the deed herself. His thoughts were interrupted when Beaumont's butler announced a guest had arrived. Following in his footsteps, to the butler's disapproval, was Lord Riverdale. He said, "I did not think you would mind if I did not wait to be announced."

Edward and Elinor laughed, while Mrs. Tate looked relieved to see the one she hoped to call family. At that unfortunate moment, Bell's infectious laugh was heard. They all turned their heads to see Miss Tate burst out of the maze with Mr. Cowper in chase. To Riverdale's displeasure, he caught her.

Edward asked, "Where is Lady Anne and Miss Morgan?"

Mr. Cowper and Bell regained their composure upon hearing Lord Felton's voice. Miss Tate responded before Mr. Cowper to say, "We know nothing of Lady Anne, my lord. Miss Morgan separated herself from us soon after we entered. We did indeed look for her, but I fear we found our exit before we found her."

Edward glared at them and then strode off to search for the missing ladies. Bell started to laugh, but checked herself when she saw that Lord Riverdale had arrived. She exclaimed, "My lord, you have come!"

Lord Riverdale bit his ungracious retort. He was glad that Felton had sent him the missive alerting him to Miss Tate's possible suitor, but was quite disturbed to learn that she was not adverse to the man's attention. He said, "I see that Felton has made up a very congenial party."

Elinor's eyes alighted at Riverdale's sarcasm and then grinned when she saw that Jonathan could not contain his laughter. He did his best to cover his amusement at Riverdale's expense by commanding his friend to admire his son. Riverdale relaxed his facial features that had been taut in annoyance, and complimented the Westfields upon being presented with the young viscount.

At that moment, Lady Anne exited the maze looking quite concerned. Elinor asked, "You could not find her Anne?"

"No, I could hear her weeping, but the maze is quite complex and I could never find my way to her. I kept to my left, an old trick my father once taught me in exiting a maze, or else you would be searching for me as well."

Westfield, Riverdale, and Mr. Cowper did not wait to be asked. Jonathan returned Stephen to his mother and then the three of them entered the maze to locate the weeping Miss Morgan. Anne was about to follow when Elinor stopped her. She said, "You have done enough Anne. Rest. They will find her. Edward may have already done so."

She asked, "Lord Felton is here?"

"Yes," replied Elinor. "He arrived shortly after you entered the maze. He went in search of you and Miss Morgan as soon as Bell indicated that you were lost, though I think he was concerned for your welfare more so than Miss Morgan."

Anne blushed as Bell exclaimed, "I thought he was going to bite my head off. You should have seen the look he gave me when I knew not where you were."

"It was unkind of you to leave Miss Morgan behind," chided Anne.

Bell whimpered, "It was not intentional. She kept lagging. Mr. Cowper and I would stop and wait for her and then it seemed she simply disappeared. We retraced our steps to no avail. We thought perhaps, she found her way out and raced to exit the maze to see. We were surprised she had not come out."

Anne smiled, "Do not worry. She will be found." Anne turned as she heard Miss Morgan's praise to Lord

Felton, "How will I ever repay you for finding me, my lord. I feared I would never find my way out. If I live to be a hundred, I do not think I will ever venture into a maze again."

"Nonsense," replied Lord Felton. "You must not fear the labyrinth. Did you know they are designed for contemplative exercise of the mind and body? A meditative walk through a maze can foster peace and tranquility. I shall on another day, escort you myself and show you the path to follow, so that your fear does not overset you."

Miss Morgan fluttered her eyelashes at Lord Felton. Anne found her anger rise as she saw Lord Felton's charm reap the favor of Miss Morgan. She excused herself before he could address her. Edward watched as Lady Anne walked away and then saw Elinor sway her head in disapproval. He wondered, *"What did I do?"*

Elinor rose and asked Mrs. Tate to accompany her to settle Stephen down for a nap. Mrs. Tate respected that Lady Westfield preferred to care for her infant son versus always handing him off to his nanny. The Westfields had brought their whole entourage, but it seemed to Mrs. Tate, their servants were left to their own devices, more so than to caring for the little viscount. Mrs. Tate told Bell that she should retire and freshen up for supper. Her exertion, she chided, had put the blush to her cheeks and tussled her hair. "Heavens!" she whispered, "You have not perspired?"

Bell crimsoned and asked Miss Morgan if she would like to accompany her upstairs. Elinor noticed that the young girl was hesitant to leave Edward's company. She raised an eyebrow to Edward and then said to the girls, "It is best we all retire for the afternoon. I suggest Edward, you wait for the others. You may inform them that Miss Morgan is well and resting in her room." She then herded everyone towards the manor, Miss Morgan acquiescing, knowing better than to disobey a countess.

Later, Edward searched for Anne, but could not find her. He guessed that she must have retired to her room. He wondered where Catherine had wandered, and why she was not taking better care of her companion. He found his uncle in his study and asked, "Do you know where Catherine is, uncle?"

Beaumont replied, "She is on an errand visiting the wife of a tenant whom the dowager called friend in her youthful days."

"She rides alone?" chided Edward.

"No, no," retorted Beaumont. "Mr. Chapman escorts her."

He asked, "Did she take her maid?"

Beaumont frowned, "I did not think to ask? Do not look so disturbed, nephew. It is Alistair. You trust him, do you not?"

He answered, "That is beside the point. His grace, your nephew, would think you negligent in your duties if you allow his daughter to roam free like a country girl. You best check her behavior."

Beaumont barked, "She is your guest, your responsibility. I am too old for this nonsense, Edward. You handle it."

"Very well," replied Edward in a voice delivered to soothe his uncle's frustration. He walked over to close the doors to the study. His actions drew Beaumont's attention. He asked, "What is it, Edward? Is something wrong?"

Edward smiled. "No, uncle. I just wanted a private moment with you. I do not know if you have noticed, but I have grown to admire Lady Anne. I would like to know, how you would feel if I paid my addresses to her?"

Beaumont laughed. "Oh, Edward! Tell me, is it a love match?"

Edward grinned at his uncle's sentimentality. He answered, "I believe so, but I have not confirmed her feelings for me. We have just begun this journey that you so intuitively call love. Tell me uncle, do you like her? Will you approve of her becoming the next Marquessa of Beaumont?"

"I am a sentimental fool Edward," replied Beaumont. "Or else I would have married years ago. If you have been fortunate to find love, then I am all felicitation for you. Lady Anne is of impeccable character and she has proven through her short stay with us, that she has the grace, compassion, intelligence, and fortitude to claim the role of your wife. I like her immensely and have no problem seeing her as mistress of Beaumont."

"I am so glad uncle that you approve," replied Edward. "I would have married her anyway, but it would have grieved me to have caused you injury."

Beaumont professed, "I am proud of you nephew, for knowing your heart and having the strength to follow it."

The festival was a great success. Alistair had organized the tenants to host booths that displayed homemade wares, exhibited local talents, proffered drinks and treats to everyone's delight. Beaumont's staff set up multiple tables and placed a tremendous amount of food on them. The servants manned the tables and replenished every dish as they were consumed. Lemonade and ale flowed heartily. There were pie-eating contests, spinning contests, sheep catching foolery contests, and awards were given out for best pie, best jam, and best woolen textiles. However, the event that drew the largest crowd was the sheep shearing contest.

Everyone gathered in the large barn. Each participant had their designated spot where they would shear. The experienced shearer's worked alone, while the inexperienced apprentices and Edward all engaged a partner to hold their sheep. Edward knew he could not win the contest, but he hoped to finish before one or two of the young lads in the competition. He reminded himself it was all in good fun, but when he spied Lady Anne in the audience he feared of humiliating himself. He had not expected any lady of gentility to watch since all the men were shirtless. He did not see the Tates or Miss Morgan, but was not surprised to see Elinor by Anne's side. Beaumont, Westfield, and the Duke of Hartford were among the crowd. Edward surmised that Riverdale attended to the Tates and Miss Morgan.

Edward smiled as he caught Anne's eyes and saw her smile in return. He wondered if her mirth was directed at him or with him. He was pleased that she did not pale and swoon at the sight of so many men stripped of their shirts. He turned his attention to Mr. Cowper as the moderator called the audience and shearers to attention. Upon the signal, all the shearers would start. The first man to complete the task would win the event. Everyone pretty much knew that Gabriel was the most talented of the group and expected him to win. The contest truly began after Gabriel finished. It mattered not who finished first but who finished last. That poor man would be teased indeterminately. Edward knew if he could only outrace at least one of the apprentices, then he would earn the respect of his tenants and save himself from embarrassment. He hoped that he and Mr. Cowper had worked hard enough the last week to place respectably in the contest.

In anticipation, he found his body tense as he waited to hear the official start. He held his clippers in his hand, watching as the moderator raised a pot over his head to bang it with a ladle. The race was on and Edward watched Mr. Cowper pull down the sheep and place him on his rump. Edward instinctively placed the clippers on the sheep's stomach and began to clip down its belly. He and Lawrence had developed over the week's practice a rhythm to their work. They were each so concentrated on their task that they did not hear the hoots and holler when Gabriel finished first and raised his hands in victory.

Lawrence skillfully changed the position of the sheep while Edward clipped. Then he laid the sheep flat on the ground while Edward took the last of the fleece off the sheep's hindquarters and tail to finish. Lawrence released the sheared sheep and stood to chuckle at Edward whose arms were raised to indicate their completion. It took them a moment to gain their composure and see there was still a flurry of sheep shearing. They both laughed heartily when they realized that most of the young boys were still shearing and they had not embarrassed themselves by finishing last. Edward quickly scanned the crowd to find Anne. Her hands were clasped together against her bosom, her eyes were bright with excitement. He watched as her lips mouthed the words, "Congratulations!" And he felt ridiculously happy.

As lord of the manor, Edward was not able to spend much time with Anne or any of his guests. His popularity from making a good show at fleecing, pulled him from one group of tenants to another. It pleased him to see everyone enjoying the festival. As he made his rounds, he found himself always aware of where Anne stood. He liked that she immersed herself with his tenants and local gentry. He laughed when she tried her hand at spinning and kept apologizing for her lack of skill. He watched her as she hoisted a young girl up to look over the top bar of the corral, so that she could watch the folly of the older children chasing sheep, in hope of catching one. He marveled at her beauty, her inner soul as well as her outer façade. He witnessed her tenderness in dealing with his neighbors and tenants, acknowledging how much she belonged. He prayed that he could secure her as his wife, and hoped she would give him a sign that his suit was welcome.

Anne was enjoying herself. She felt at peace in this country that had so much to offer in its landscape and people. As the day progressed and the festival was wearing to an end, she took in a view to last a lifetime. A cool breeze brushed her cheeks and she unknowingly brought her fingers and rubbed them across her lips. She remembered Lord Felton's kiss and wondered, *"If papa had not died, would I have married and known the passion that I feel with Lord Felton?"* She chided herself for thinking so formally of him in her thoughts. She determined from this day forward, he would always be Edward in her mind.

She did not regret giving in to her emotions. She was only disappointed that Edward, like all the other promising men in her life, wanted only one thing from her. She was surprised how at five and twenty, she still had to keep vigilance over her virtue. She had thought that Edward admired her, or at least valued her friendship. Alas, she was sorry to discover he was interested in only an alliance that was far from respectable. *"What was it he said before he kissed me, I hope to call you more than friend."* She did not know if he was offering her a *carte blanche* where he would agree to anything to acquire her as his mistress or merely wanting to trifle with her. She could not wait to find out for she feared her heart was already engaged and her vulnerable state made her situation dangerous.

She had hopes that his attraction for her could evolve into something more respectable, but watching him charm Miss Morgan reminded her of his notorious reputation for being a rake. Did she not warn Elinor last year when he first attempted to seduce her? How could it have transpired that now he is among those she calls family?

She had to admit that Edward had stellar characteristics and that she liked him well. Who could not when he doted on his family and seemed to care for the downtrodden? Has he not aided the Tates? And who else but Edward would help the man who tried to place a claim against his inheritance. It was not common knowledge, but she had learned about Mr. Cowper's outrageous attempt of usurping Edward's right as heir. She could not imagine anyone else who would have approached the situation with compassion and calmness, but she reminded herself that Edward was a tried and true bachelor and she could not be one of his conquests. She had little but her respectability, and it was the foundation for her livelihood and her connections to the titled. She realized that if she stayed, she placed her future at risk, so she decided she would leave tomorrow with the Tates and Lord Riverdale. She knew she was making the right decision. She needed distance to put her feelings for Edward into perspective.

# Chapter Fourteen

Anne looked at her reflection in the gilt wood mirror above her dressing table. She wore the high-waist light blue crepe dress trimmed in white lace that she had worn to the opera the night she shared the Duke of Hartford's box with Edward. She remembered feeling quite admired under his scrutiny and hoped he would think so again. A single set of pearls graced her neck and ears. Over her long white gloves she wore her mother's bracelet, even though the clasp on the bangle was weak. She rarely wore the jewelry fearing its loss, but Anne wanted to feel close to her family on what she thought would be a momentous evening in testing her will power. She convinced herself she could wear the bracelet, as long as she kept a vigilant watch over it, always checking to ensure that the clasp was indeed secure.

She thought she was ready to make her way to the ballroom, but felt her body tremble. She extended both her arms out in front of her and spread out her fingers.

She could see them shaking. Her stomach was fluttering and her knees were weakening under her nervousness. She knew this would be her last intimate evening with Edward and she was concerned her fragile will was not strong enough to escape his advances. She determined her best plan for safety was to stay within a crowd, so as to eliminate any of Edward's attempts at seduction. She shook, knowing that more than anything, she wanted to feel Edward's arms around her once more. She jumped as she heard a knock on her bedroom door.

"Enter," she commanded. Anne smiled as she saw the Countess of Westfield cross her threshold.

"Oh, Anne!" exclaimed Elinor. "You look simply lovely."

"Thank you, Elinor," replied Anne. "You are always the picture of perfection. You could be in rags and still your beauty would shine through."

"Fustian," laughed Elinor. "I have sent Jonathan ahead. I thought you would like me to accompany you downstairs. I understand the tenants and local gentry have been arriving in droves this past hour. Beaumont and Edward must feel hard-pressed to stand in greeting for so long. Hopefully, we will be the last to enter. I dread standing in wait for others to arrive."

Anne smiled and countered, "You hate being ogled at Elinor. I do not blame you but it is a burden *a diamond of the first water* must own."

Elinor smirked, "You are too ridiculous Anne. You look magnificent yourself and I shall respond in kind later this evening after you have complained about your unsolicited admiration." She then saw the filigree gold bangle encrusted with gemstones on Anne's wrist and remarked, "Oh, your bracelet is remarkable. Is it an heirloom?"

"Yes," answered Anne. "It belonged to my mother. My father, in one of his rare sentimental moments, gave it to me. It was the first gift he gave to my mother. I guess he knew that his profligate lifestyle would force him to sell off all the family jewels and in a moment of weakness he remembered me." She continued soberly, "He was a horrid gambler and a reckless businessman, but I never doubted he loved me."

Elinor looked compassionately at Anne and said, "Who could not?" And then with glee in her voice, she commanded, "Come, I know that Edward anxiously awaits us, as should Jonathan."

Anne felt her body tremble when Edward embraced his hands over hers to welcome her. He noticed her bracelet right away and marveled at its design. He complimented its beauty and then bent close to her to whisper, "Perhaps, like your beloved Cinderella, you will lose your bracelet and then your prince charming will return it to prove his devotion."

Edward's comment discomfited Anne. Before she could assemble a worthwhile witticism, the Duke of Hartford came to escort her onto the dance floor. She had agreed to dance the opening set with him.

Edward looked down the line of gentlemen and smiled as he saw Lord Riverdale partnered with a girl of the local gentry. It seemed he was not the only one dancing, who wished they were partnered with someone else. He guessed that Mr. Cowper had beat Riverdale to the punch by asking Miss Tate for the honor of dancing the opening set. He noticed Anne smiling at the Duke of Hartford. After his conference with his grace where he proclaimed his intention, Edward found himself comfortable seeing them together. What totally surprised him was that his cousin Catherine was partnered with Mr. Chapman, his man of business. He knew Catherine's father, the Duke of Aubry, would not be pleased that his daughter was communing with what he would consider the help. Edward made a mental note to talk with her about her behavior. He knew he would have to seek her out, for he realized as of late, she was becoming noticeably absent.

Thc music began and Edward found himself taking the role of dance instructor, directing his partner Miss Morgan in her steps. The quadrille was a complex country dance and it was clear to Edward that Miss Morgan had little practice in dancing it. He recollected his dance lessons with Lady Anne and Miss Tate. He found himself releasing a chuckle or two at the memory. He was enjoying himself, not so much dancing with Miss Morgan as being reminded of the fun he had during those sessions with Anne.

Anne's body tensed every time she heard Edward laugh. *"The gall of him,"* she thought. *"First, he whispers to me, suggesting he might be my prince charming and then he blatantly flirts with Miss Morgan in my presence."* She knew she should be happy that he just proved he was the rake she knew him to be, but her heart was not logical and she was heartbroken that her feelings for him were not reciprocated. She told herself Edward was not worthy of her affections, that she was blessed with friends who cared about her. She concluded she did not need a man in her life in order to be happy. She smiled at his grace, grateful for his friendship, and made up her mind to ignore Edward and have a good time.

Edward walked briskly toward Lady Anne the moment he released Miss Morgan to the care of Mrs. Tate who somehow became regarded as the chaperone for her and her own daughter Bell. He smiled as he approached her and was dumbfounded by the scowl that graced her face. He dismissed it as none of his doing, made his bow to her and asked, "I hope you will give me the honor of this next dance, my lady?"

Anne quickly rebuffed him, "I fear you are too late, my lord. I am to dance with Lord Westfield."

He frowned and said, "Well then, will you save the following set for me? I have been looking forward to dancing with you all day."

"I am sorry to disappoint you, my lord," retorted Anne. "Perhaps if you had approached me sooner, as you did in Miss Morgan's case, you would not now be disappointed, but I am afraid my dance card is full."

Edward scrutinized Anne's face. He thought her reply was intended as a slight. He was ready to beg her forgiveness for not being more diligent in asking for a dance, when the strings sounded indicating the set was ready to begin. He said, "It seems that Westfield is tardy. Allow me to escort you to him." Before Anne could argue, Edward grabbed her elbow, rather roughly she thought, and led her over to where the Earl and Countess of Westfield stood. Anne was happy they were not dancing and hoped that somehow her deception would not be revealed.

"Westfield," called Edward. "It is unlike you to keep a lady waiting. I believe you have promised this dance to Lady Anne."

Jonathan was about to argue in his defense when his wife spoke up. "I secured the dance on your behalf dear. I expected you would want to dance with our son's godmother and feared, reasonably it seems, that her dance card would fill the moment she made her appearance."

Jonathan looked at his wife whose eyes beseeched him to do her bidding. He smiled and said to Anne, "Forgive me Anne for being so remiss in my duty." He proffered his arm and escorted her unto the dance floor.

As they walked off, Elinor berated Edward and asked him, "What have you done that she abjures you?"

"Is that what she is doing?" asked Edward. "I have done nothing." Then in a hurt voice said, "I thought she might welcome my addresses, but clearly she abhors my advances so I will desist."

Elinor calmed and in an effort to pacify him said, "I do not think she dislikes you. I warned you that her trust towards suitors is fragile. She was not adverse to your kiss in the grove. You must have done something to make her believe your intentions are not honorable. Have you declared yourself, or was your dubious statement of wanting to 'call her more than friend,' her only guide to your intentions?"

Edward's demeanor showed Elinor that he had not declared himself to her before he even responded. He said, "No, I have not paid my addresses, but she must know that I desire her."

Elinor rolled her eyes and replied, "No doubt and for that reason alone she is probably keeping her distance."

Edward's eyes had widened in enlightenment. He asked, "You did not secure the dance for Westfield?"

"No," answered Elinor. "You must fix this, Edward. I will not forgive you if you hurt her."

Edward smiled, his mood improved once he realized that Anne's countenance was a shield she was hiding behind to protect herself. She was not in aversion to him. *"No,"* he thought, *"she would not have kissed me with such passion if she did not care."*

He waited for the dance to end and resolved, *"Yes, I will fix it."*

When Jonathan returned alone, Edward walked off in a huff to search for Anne. Jonathan stifled a chuckle before he found his wife frowning at him. He said, "I thought you wanted to keep Anne from Edward, so I secured Riverdale as her partner for the next dance."

Elinor tried to be angry, but could not when she remembered all the hoops that her husband went through last Season to secure her hand. She mused, "Well, if their love is meant to be, then it will prevail. We are a perfect example of an absurd courtship." They both laughed.

Jonathan continued, "If he is worthy of her love then he will do what he must to secure it. Do not worry. Felton is more than competent in acquiring a wife."

"Yes," sighed Elinor, "but will it be Anne?"

Edward watched from the sidelines as Anne danced with Riverdale, too happily, he thought. He knew her partner's affections to be engaged elsewhere, so their partnering did not disturb him. What bothered him was that Anne thought him dishonorable in his attentions. He recollected his past behavior towards her and saw nothing wrong aside from the kiss he stole from her in the grove. He chided himself for waiting so long to declare himself. He could see how she could misinterpret his actions. What did she say about Miss Morgan? Did she think his behavior improper towards the young girl? Edward grinned. *"Maybe,"* he thought, *"she is jealous."* *"Yes!"* He discerned, *"She is jealous!"* He laughed, unfortunately out loud and found Lady Anne scowling at him.

As soon as the music stopped and before Riverdale could lead Anne off the dance floor, Edward approached them and said, "Riverdale, you have saved me from searching for my partner. Thank you for delivering her safely into my hands."

Riverdale bowed to Anne. He said, "Your servant, my lady," before relinquishing her to Edward and walking off to find Miss Tate. Edward could tell Anne was enraged at his arrogance, but managed, while she chided him, to lead her towards one of the open French doors that allowed the evening's air to cool the dancers. She berated him. "I am sure I told you my dance card was full. I did not want to make a spectacle in front of Riverdale, so I said nothing. However, I cannot dance with you."

"Good," said Edward as he pushed her out onto the terrace. "I do not want to dance either." It was then that Anne realized she was alone with Edward, the one thing she did not want to do.

"Anne," he said as he wrapped his arms around her in an embrace, "You must know how I feel." Edward found he could not resist the lips that were only inches from his own. He tightened his hold, bringing Anne closer before placing his mouth on hers, pressing gently but thoroughly, until she succumbed and kissed him back. He was enraptured and gave into his feelings. His hand moved up her back and found its way into her hair. He heard some pins drop to the ground, as a flock of curls broke free. He broke their kiss to declare his love when he saw her eyes and knew he acted rashly. She pushed herself away from him and ran before he could speak. As she left the terrace, he heard a clink and looked down to see she had dropped her heirloom bracelet. He picked it up, ran his fingers over the gemstones before putting it in his coat pocket.

He did not wish to cause a scandal by running after Anne, so he did not follow her into the ballroom. Instead, he entered the garden and made his way into the manor through another door. By the time he reached the ballroom, he learned from Mrs. Tate that Anne had retired to her room, complaining of a headache. He would have went to her, but found himself being detained, as guest after guest, began to express their gratitude for the spring festival, and to bid their good evenings as they left and took their leave.

Edward rose early. He wanted to take care of his business affairs before his guests broke their fast, so that he could devote the day explaining his erratic behavior to Anne. As he headed towards his uncle's study, he ran into Mrs. Tate who apparently was looking for him. "I extended my gratitude to your uncle last night, my lord, but failed to extend you the same courtesy. I am happy I have found you before we left."

Edward panicked remembering the Tates arrived with Anne in his grace's carriage. He asked, "Do you travel in the Duke of Hartford's carriage?"

"No, no," replied Mrs. Tate. "Lord Riverdale has provided his family's carriage. He is escorting Bell and I to his family's country residence. He is to introduce us to them. I do hope they will approve of my Bell."

He consoled her in saying, "What is there not to like? I have never known Riverdale to bring a lady home to meet his family, so you can be sure his intentions are honorable. Have faith in his affection for your daughter, Mrs. Tate. I am sure he will not fail you."

"You are too kind, my lord," responded Mrs. Tate. "I cannot thank you enough for your benevolence towards me and my daughter. I hope our paths cross again in the near future."

"The pleasure is all mine. Shall I escort you to your carriage?" asked Edward.

"No," she replied. "It is not necessary, but thank you, my lord. I bid you well."

He bowed in acknowledgement and proceeded to his uncle's study. He was surprised to see the door open and his cousin Catherine exit. He was even more surprised to see that she had been alone with Mr. Chapman.

Edward raised his eyebrow in disdain and chided Mr. Chapman. "This will not do, Alistair. What were you thinking having my cousin without chaperone in your company?"

"She entered of her own accord, my lord, and shut the door herself," replied Alistair. "I made her leave immediately."

Edward asked, "What did she want with you?"

"I am sorry, my lord," he answered. "But your cousin has made herself quite distracting these past few days interrupting my work. In a moment of frustration, I called her spoiled, stating that her only purpose in life was in seeking those entertainments that amuse her. She did not respond well," Alistair chuckled, "to my criticism."

"And yet," responded Edward, "she still seeks you out."

He replied, "I think she is bored, my lord, and looking for purpose to prove me wrong. She asked that I assign her a task to show me that she is capable. When I refused, she left abruptly."

"This does not sound like my cousin. She cares not what others think. There is more to this than you are telling me," stated Edward. "I noticed you partnered with her in the quadrille. Exactly, how many dances did she favor you with?"

Alistair stalled in his answer, so Edward said, "Never mind." He walked over to his uncle's desk where Alistair had been reviewing some account books. Alistair quickly relinquished his seat to his employer and waited for his direction. Edward sat down and instructed his man of business to take the seat across from him. Edward placed his elbows on the desk and clasped his hands to rest his chin on them. He leaned forward, steeled his eyes at Alistair and said, "I have not pursued your private business, Alistair, because it is precisely that, private. But you must know that an alliance between a duke's daughter and my employee, even one that is a gentleman is insupportable."

Before Edward could finish, Alistair remarked, "Yes, I know. I made an error in judgment by enjoying Lady Catherine's company. I have tried to rectify it by making myself disagreeable."

"My cousin is too intelligent to fall for such a ruse," remarked Edward. "You have no plans to resolve your issues with your family?"

"No!" hissed Alistair.

"Then," replied Edward, "since I cannot evict my cousin, I shall send you away to take care of some business that I have neglected. You may return, once Catherine has returned home. Does this meet with your satisfaction?"

"Since when do you ask the consent of one of your employees, Felton?" asked Alistair.

He laughed, "That is the first slip you have made since you came to seek me out for a position, Alistair. And to answer your question, I have never commanded my friends, whom you know I consider you one."

Edward spent the next hour reviewing his account ledgers with Alistair before removing himself to the breakfast parlour. He was surprised to see it empty. He surmised that everyone was sleeping in after a late and exerting evening. He ate a sparse meal, his stomach anxious over his impending interview with Anne. He made his way to the library where he uncharacteristically opened one of his uncle's cherished volumes of Wordsworth. He searched for the poem, "Daffodils," and read the prose, reflecting on his tête-à-tête with Anne in the knot garden and felt hopeful once again in his suit for her.

Another hour must have passed before he started to hear the commotion of his guests making their way into the public rooms. He was surprised when Elinor entered waving a piece of paper in her hand. Edward was ready to laugh at her discomfiture until he heard her say, "She is gone, Edward."

"Who?" although he soberly guessed it was Anne.

Elinor answered, "Anne. She writes she did not wish to disturb me. The Tates asked her to accompany them to Riverdale's home. I guess the Tates thought there was strength in numbers. She promises to write when she returns to London. She mentions nothing else, other than to express her gratitude to you and your uncle for your hospitality. She said she left a note for Beaumont and his grace.

"She left nothing for me," confirmed Edward.

Elinor's apology, "I am sorry, Edward," broke his reverie.

He felt challenged rather than defeated, thinking, *"She runs away because she believes my intentions dishonorable. She looked hurt when I kissed her last night, not revolted."* To Elinor, he said, "I need not your sympathy, Elinor, but your good wishes. I am not so easily swayed to give up my pursuit of one I wish to call wife."

Elinor beamed and hugged Edward. She said, "Jolly good for you, Edward. You are the man I always knew you to be. Do you intrude on the Riverdales then?"

Edward laughed, "The heir to a marquis is never an intrusion. I shall simply grace the Earl and Countess of Riverdale with my company."

Before Elinor could apply her own witticism, Catherine burst into the library all a fluster. She was quite angry as she looked at Edward and demanded, "What have you done, Edward? Where did you send him?"

Elinor gave a sympathetic look and without saying a word, left the two cousins to battle out their differences.

Edward in a hauteur tone asked, "My dear cousin, you take me unawares. Whom exactly do you speak of?"

"You know exactly that I am referring to Alistair," replied Catherine. "I want to know where you sent him."

"You forget yourself, Catherine," chided Edward. "It is improper of you to address my man of business on such intimate terms and furthermore, my business affairs or the whereabouts of my staff is none of your concern."

Catherine balked and instead of pursuing a line of questions she knew would not be answered, she left. Edward was about to exit when his uncle entered, himself waving a piece of paper. He announced, "She lives!" Edward resolved that his departure was to be delayed. He commanded his uncle to calm himself and sit down. He then asked, "Who lives?"

Beaumont replied, "As his grace instructed, I immediately sent off a missive to my sister regarding

Alana's family. He was right that the gossip did indeed turn into some local history. Alana's sister lives. She is a baroness and lives not too far from the Duke of Aubry's estate. She will grant us an interview. She is anxious to meet Mr. Cowper. My sister writes she was unaware of his existence or that Alana herself had survived her child's birth. Will we leave immediately, Edward?"

Edward knew his pursuit of Anne would have to wait. He had given his word to help Mr. Cowper find his grandfather and he would not disappoint his uncle by breaking his promise. He was aware how important aiding the boy was to him. It seemed to Edward that since Lawrence's arrival, his uncle had received a new lease on life. His mission to aid Alana's grandson had somehow assuaged any guilt he felt over not being able to protect the woman he loved years ago. Edward knew he would do whatever was necessary to keep his uncle in good spirits. He was happy that Beaumont embraced life again. Then, he realized that with his uncle, Mr. Chapman, Mr. Cowper, and himself departing, there was no one to act as host for his guests. He approached Westfield for direction. Edward's main concern was for Miss Morgan who appeared to have been cast off by his cousin. He wanted to ensure she was not left behind when everyone took his or her leave. Westfield assured him that if necessary, he would safely escort her back to Town himself. Westfield was saved the trouble, for later that day, both a furious Lady Catherine and a complacent Miss Morgan took their leave. The Duke of Hartford planned to return to

Westfield Mansion with Elinor and by the time Edward, his uncle, and Mr. Cowper departed, Beaumont Manor was left with only its staff to occupy it.

Edward and Mr. Cowper rode on horseback while Beaumont was conveyed in his stately coach. Lawrence's equestrian skills were improving daily. Like his mentor, he now preferred to journey by horse rather than by carriage. Beaumont's adversity to travel, slowed his carriage to less than the normal ten miles an hour that a fresh team of horses could cover. The dull ride added two extra days to their trip. The much-used North Road proved tedious, with ruts and potholes jarring the carriage and making horseback riding dangerous. More than one horse was known to go lame stepping into a crevice, so Edward was happy when the Aubry Estate came into view, and he knew they had reached their destination. Finally, they would be able to rest their weary bodies in a familiar setting. He sighed, wondering where Anne was and what she was doing.

# Chapter Fifteen

Edward learned from the butler, that both the Duke and Duchess of Aubry, along with their children, were still residing in Town. He deduced that his cousin Catherine and her cohort Miss Morgan must have decided to make their way back to London, to finish attending the balls and fetes of the Season. Catherine was not one to isolate herself at Aubry, when she could be the center of attention among her numerous beaus.

Edward looked forward to seeing his grandmother, the Dowager Duchess of Aubry, who usually resided in her dowager cottage located a mile away. She had moved there when her eldest son acceded to the title and married. The dowager was quick to relinquish her responsibilities to the new duchess. She announced, "There can only be one mistress of the manor," and helped the new duchess into her role by removing herself to her current home. The cottage was a misnomer, for it was quite an elegant mansion that was fully staffed and could accommodate at least four families. The dowager was famous for hosting her own small soirees and attending one became a bragging right among the *bon ton*. Only a significant few had ever experienced the personal hospitality of the dowager in such an intimate setting.

However, to placate her son, his grace, she removed herself to the "big house," whenever he left to live in Town with his family for the Season. She always sojourned with them during the Christmas holiday. She feared, before long, he would command her to hire a companion. She knew he worried about her being alone as she grew older, but she constantly proved she was more than capable of managing her affairs. She preferred her independence and privacy to that of a dependent. Edward always wondered if she relished her privacy because she had a *bon ami* that no one, especially her son, knew about.

Frenton, the Duke of Aubry's butler, saw to it that they were made comfortable. Both Beaumont and Edward had rooms in the family wing that were reserved and kept prepared for when they visited. Only Mr. Cowper found himself set apart from his mentors, as he was placed in a wing established for guests. He was awestruck of the room's opulence and was hard-pressed to imagine how a family chamber could be more exalted. He assumed that an inferior room would be given to him, being a person of insignificance, a commoner, so he was mesmerized when he entered the enormous suite. The emerald green damask canopy curtains on the tester bed drew his attention first and he immediately relished the idea of sleeping in such comfort and luxury. The beautiful embroidered counterpane matched the split window curtains tied back with silk rope tassels and corresponded with the paintwork of the room. It was a peaceful chamber full of verdant and mahogany color. The multitude of furnishings gleamed from their embedded oils. Lawrence marveled at the intricacy of design in the room, from the plasterwork ceiling representing a scene from Greek mythology to the Axminster medallion carpet below his feet. He began to study one of the many oil landscapes on the wall, when he remembered he was expected to join his lordships in the Sun Room to meet the dowager. Unsure of how to make his way, he pulled the room's bell cord to summon a servant to escort him.

Edward was first to enter the yellow painted stateroom that smelled of lilacs. His grandmother loved the sweet smell of the flower to the chagrin of her daughter-in-law, the reigning duchess, who always came home to an abundance of bouquets displayed throughout her palatial home. Although Edward had more than once seen his aunt's nose crinkle at the potent fragrance, the duchess never outwardly complained. Ever since the dowager relinquished her role gracefully, and continued to treat her benevolently, the duchess was happy to allow the dowager to fill her house with fragrant lilacs while she was away.

Edward had always liked the Sun Room. He liked the way the numerous tall arched windows framed in white let in an abundance of light. It was hard to feel gloomy in a room that breathed warmth. As he entered, he heard his grandmother's voice before he found her arranging one of her lilac bouquets.

She said with a hint of mirth, "Edward, Welcome. It is good to see you. I was hoping that Catherine and Miss Morgan accompanied you as well."

He asked, "Why is that grandmother?"

The dowager grinned as she made her way to one of the sofas and sat down. She patted the seat next to her and Edward made his way over to sit beside her. She said, "I know you are searching for a wife, Edward. Miss Morgan was not offensive to the eyes and she seemed like a biddable girl. I thought you might fancy her."

Edward answered, "So Catherine informed me. She made the announcement in front of my guests with no thought of propriety."

The dowager laughed, and then asked, "Did she cause you much embarrassment, Edward?"

He retorted, "May I ask, when you have ever seen me dally after a girl right out of the school room, and when have I ever favored a biddable girl? I am no green boy, grandmother, only interested in a pretty face!"

"My," replied the dowager. "Are you not out of sorts. Perhaps you should explain what has caused your discomfiture."

Edward wanted nothing more than to unload his troubles upon his most beloved grandmother. She was the one, through all his growing years who offered him support and consideration. Whenever his titled cousins or other children of the aristocracy tried to make him feel inferior, she was always there to console him and strengthen his resolve in knowing that he was equal to those who thought themselves superior. It was she and his father who taught him that character was the measure of an aristocrat, not the title. He thought she reveled more in his inheritance from Beaumont than he did. He knew she thoroughly enjoyed flaunting his new title, at those who once shunned him. As a future marquis he would outrank many families of the peerage, who for years had looked down on him because of his connection with trade.

He was just about to confide in his grandmother when he checked his response, because he saw his uncle and Mr. Cowper, aided by a servant, enter the Sun Room. The dowager rose and greeted her brother affectionately. She then looked to Mr. Cowper and back to her grandson for an introduction.

"Grandmother," began Edward. "Allow me to introduce you to Mr. Cowper who is in our charge. I believe uncle wrote to you regarding our quest in finding his family. Mr. Cowper, I present my grandmother, the Dowager Duchess of Aubry."

Mr. Cowper made his bow. He thanked the dowager most heartily for welcoming him into her home, and soliciting an interview for him with the Baroness Litford.

The small party were happy to lounge and be idle after days of travel. They spent time reading in the library and walking the grounds before dressing for supper. Over their meal, Edward asked Mr. Cowper if he liked to fish. He suggested they could spend an hour at the duke's ornamental lake after their interview with his aunt. Edward assured Lawrence that the lake was fully stocked with fish, offering a very sporting and amusing way to pass the hour.

Lawrence asked, "Do you not think my great aunt will be able to direct me to where my grandfather lives?"

"I do hope so," answered Edward. "But we would need to wait until the next day to seek him out. I do not know if there is much travel involved, but we would not want to come upon him at the supper hour."

"No, of course not," replied Lawrence. "You are right that we must wait. I would like to try fishing. It is funny that I lived near the sea all my life and never tried it. Of course, I never had much of a father's influence. Ironically, my own father died at sea when I was but a child."

Edward asked, "Are you happy staying with us, Mr. Cowper? I know that I have selfishly asked for you to remain for my uncle's sake."

Lawrence was surprised at Lord Felton's questions and said, "First, I wish you would call me Lawrence, my lord. You have made me feel like family, opening your home to me, offering me a job, and providing me with a purpose. I have nothing but admiration for you and your uncle and I must confess that I will regret the day when I must separate from your company."

"When and if that day comes, Lawrence," replied Edward. "It will be because it is what you desire. You have a home and employment at Beaumont Manor for as long as you like."

"Thank you, my lord," replied Lawrence.

Baroness Litford and her two daughters were waiting for Beaumont, Lord Felton, and Mr. Cowper in their informal parlour. They were all surprised to learn that Alana had lived all these years in the seaside resort of Worthing with her daughter and grandson. They were led to believe that Alana had died in childbirth, and the baroness was dealing with much regret and anger. Regret to have missed the time spent knowing her elder sister and anger that her sister had never tried to contact her or their parents. She realized that perhaps Alana had corresponded. Her parents never forgave their eldest and most treasured daughter for eloping with a mere captain in the king's army. Alana was considered the beauty of the family and therefore, its greatest hope for making a superior connection in marriage. Their parents, the Viscount and Viscountess Atwood were high sticklers and looked for Alana to raise their prominence in Society through marriage. They had preferred the suit of

Beaumont, heir apparent to a marquis at the time and highly connected. It was known that the Duke of Aubry was expected to offer for Beaumont's newly *come-out* sister, so the Viscount and Viscountess Atwood were enraged when Alana refused Beaumont's addresses in favor of her beloved captain. It especially angered them, when they commanded her to accept Beaumont's suit and she chose to run away instead. It was assumed that she eloped with her captain. Her parents only mentioned Alana's name once and that was to announce that Alana was with child and was now dead to them.

The baroness, in reflection, realized that she had once seen Alana's husband. Years ago while she still lived in her parents' home, she was upstairs when one of her servants informed her that a military man had forced his way into the house demanding to see the viscount. She hurriedly made her way downstairs fearing for the safety of her father. She expected to see a brawl; instead, she saw a bereaved looking man exiting her home. She asked the hovering footman whom she expected had been eaves-dropping, what the name of the intruder was. He replied, "A Captain Nathaniel Poole, I believe madam."

She remembered seeking out her father, asking him what the man had wanted, and who he was. She recollected that he simply replied, "His business was nothing of significance." And so although she was disturbed, she did not pursue it further. She assumed her father, as usual with his arrogance, had insulted a neighboring family and their son had come to seek satisfaction."

Baroness Litford watched as Beaumont and Lord Felton, with Mr. Cowper behind them, entered her sitting room. She had chosen the smaller parlour, hoping it would make a more intimate setting for their interview. She wanted to make her great nephew, Alana's grandson, comfortable.

Edward knew that Lawrence was anxious, so he took the lead with his uncle, giving Lawrence a chance to collect himself. Lawrence was indeed quite nervous. He was not sure what to expect. Would it be a loving reunion or a cold interview? Was the baroness feeling quite put upon for his trespassing into her life? Lawrence meekly followed Beaumont and Lord Felton into what seemed to be a small sitting room.

Edward made his bow to the baroness and greeted, "I am Edward Brentwood, the Earl of Felton, my lady. Allow me to present my uncle, The Marquis of Beaumont and your sister's grandson, Mr. Lawrence Cowper." Beaumont bowed in greeting, then took a step to the side to give the baroness a view of her nephew. Lawrence stepped forward, bowed and said, "Thank you for seeing me."

The baroness took a few minutes to take in his countenance. She then said, "You must favor your father, Mr. Cowper, for your coloring is not that of an Atwood. Come closer, please." Lawrence hesitantly approached the baroness and looked deeply into her eyes searching for a connection. She responded in kind and then asked, "I dare say, you will think I am impertinent, Mr. Cowper, but will you accommodate me and remove your cravat, open your shirt collar, and allow me to inspect your neck?"

Lawrence laughed, remarking, "My grandmother always said it was a mark of nobility, but I thought I inherited the birthmark from my grandfather." He then removed his cravat and loosened his collar to once again reveal the crescent shaped mark that provided his only authentication to his mother's family.

The baroness noted the birthmark and then asked her daughters to look at it. She said, "You have Alana's laugh, Mr. Cowper. You may not favor her in looks, but I dare say you must have her disposition. She used to laugh all the time, did you know that?"

"Yes, my lady," answered Lawrence. "I remember her laugh well. Many a times, her cheer prevailed when frustration and ire should have been the outcome. She always seemed to find the joy of a situation when no one else could."

Baroness Litford smiled and said, "I am afraid I have been negligent. Allow me to introduce my daughters. May I present Mrs. Sarah Clayton and Mrs. Anne Hodgson. They are your cousins, Mr. Cowper."

Lawrence eyes beamed as he realized he had family.

Edward on the other hand, inwardly sighed at the introduction of the baroness' daughter Anne, who reminded him that his heart was engaged elsewhere.

The baroness continued, "Please sit down gentleman." She then looked to her eldest daughter Sarah, asking her to pour from the Sevres tea set that rested on the mahogany table before her. Looking back upon her guests, she said, "I must admit I was very surprised to learn that my sister Alana was alive all these years, and that her grandson was seeking me."

Mr. Cowper asked, "You did not know she lived?"

"No," she answered. "We all thought she died in childbirth. She had a daughter, your mother then?"

"Yes," replied Lawrence.

The next half hour was spent accommodating her nephew, answering those questions that lay heavy on his mind. She explained what she knew of Alana and why she thought she died in childbirth. When Mr. Cowper asked about Alana's husband, his grandfather, she gave the only name she knew, Nathaniel Poole, who might be the one he sought.

She asked, "What name did Alana use while she lived in Worthing, was it not Poole?"

He answered, "My grandmother went by the name of Morrison. Is it possible that you misunderstood the footman or recollect any other gentleman of her acquaintance at the time with that surname?"

"No, I am sorry, Mr. Cowper," replied the baroness. "I knew of no Morrison. However you must realize I had not yet made my debut, so my society was limited and Alana did not confide in me."

Edward intervened, saying, “Do not look so downcast, Mr. Cowper. This may be the reason my agent could not find a record at Gretna Green, perhaps your grandmother used an alias when she married.”

Lawrence beseeched Edward’s eyes, “Would that have been legal, my lord?”

A hush surrounded the room. The baroness broke the quietness by explaining, “The birthmark you have on your neck, Mr. Cowper, is a most discriminative family trait. It has managed to mark the first born of each generation. My father had it, Alana had it and I dare say your mother had it. My brother, the late viscount, found it most disturbing that he had not inherited the symbol. Over the years, the birthmark authenticated the reigning viscount. Most of them, you see, were first born. ”

Beaumont and Lord Felton raised their eyebrows to one another in acknowledgement. They were aware of the dubious remark the baroness had just made. They knew that the deceased baroness’ brother had been unmarried and therefore left no heir. Viscount Atwood died decades ago in a dueling match, supposedly defending the honor of the one he loved. It seemed his beloved did not mourn him long, for she married shortly after his demise.

The baroness also noted that Mr. Cowper’s birthmark authenticated the reigning viscount. Lord Felton was not one to mince words, so he asked, “Who was your brother’s heir?”

The baroness smiled, set her teacup down. Edward noticed that her daughters moved towards the edge of their seats, straightening their posture in anticipation, he thought, of some breaking news. Edward looked at Beaumont who ascertained the impending announcement as well. Mr. Cowper enwrapped in his own thoughts was unaware of what was about to transpire.

"As I expect you know," explained the baroness. "My brother was not married at the time of his death. His will followed my father's wishes that were clearly outlined in a patent letter. In the event he failed to produce a male heir, his inheritance would pass to the eldest male born of Atwood blood that bore the mark of the Atwood nobility. I bore two daughters, who also bore only daughters. The estate has been in abeyance awaiting its rightful heir."

Edward and Beaumont simultaneously looked at Lawrence who seemed to be oblivious to the news that was being revealed. Mr. Cowper, sadly asked, "Do you think your agents will be able to locate Nathaniel Poole? I find myself torn from wanting him dead, so that my grandmother did not spend her life grieving for him in vain, and wanting him alive, to learn why he left her alone without protection. What kind of man deserts a woman with child?"

The baroness reached over and patted Lawrence's hand. She looked into his pitiful eyes and said, "Do not think the worst, Mr. Cowper. If Nathaniel Poole is your grandfather, I expect like myself, he was told that Alana was dead. The pale face of the man I witnessed that day was tortured with grief. I hope for your sake that he lives and is able to answer your questions."

She then looked at Beaumont and stated, "I will write you a letter of introduction to my family's solicitor. You will need to have him presented at court in order to stake his claim.

Lawrence not understanding the breadth of her comments looked to Lord Felton for clarification. He asked, "What claim?"

Lord Felton answered, "Your grandmother spoke the truth when she said you bore the mark of nobility. She was correct in raising you as a gentleman. She somehow knew your future would bring you back into the fold of her family. You are the rightful heir to your great grandfather's estate and title. I congratulate you on your inheritance, Viscount Atwood."

Lawrence was speechless.

Everyone could see that Mr. Cowper was overwhelmed by the announcement. The baroness suggested that they retire the interview and reconvene for supper. She said, "There are many questions I have regarding my sister and your mother. Plus, I would like you to meet my granddaughters, your other cousins, Mr. Cowper." She continued, "I did not want to besiege you during our first meeting, so they have been waiting patiently to be introduced. If it meets with your approval, perhaps you would sojourn a couple of days with me so that we can all become familiar. I am sure you would like to venture over to Atwood to look at your properties. While the lands are still worked, I fear our ancestral home was left to rack and ruin without a proper steward to oversee its care. It will be nice to see it brought into fashion once again. It has weighed heavily on my mind and my daughters' minds, that none of us had a son to inherit the title. I am happy to know that my father's estate will return to its former glory under your stewardship."

Edward could see that Mr. Cowper was ready to swoon. He decided the best course of action was to remove him as quickly as possible. He said, "Until supper, my lady. I will have Mr. Cowper returned at six o'clock."

"You and your uncle are most welcome, my lord," replied the baroness.

Lord Felton answered, "I will need to make sure that my grandmother herself did not make plans for the evening, but thank you."

Edward helped Lawrence rise from his chair, grabbing his elbow and lifting him to a standing position. The baroness bid him good day as did her daughters. Lawrence simply nodded and allowed Lord Felton to escort him out of the house. The all-knowing butler had Beaumont's carriage and their horses ready, waiting for their departure. Edward tied Lawrence's steed to the back of Beaumont's carriage and carefully assisted both his uncle and Lawrence inside. He then mounted his own bay horse and instructed the coachman to make way. Edward realized at that moment, his duty to Mr. Cowper was just about to begin. It would be weeks before he could forward his own wishes to secure Anne's hand in marriage. He sighed, knowing his lack of pursuit would only prove Anne's worst opinion of him.

It was decided that Beaumont would accompany Mr. Cowper to supper and stay the few days to accommodate Baroness Litford's request. Edward chose to stay with his grandmother whom he had not visited in a while, and to dispatch those letters necessary on behalf of Mr. Cowper. He promised, however, to attend to them both early the next morning, so as to journey and inspect the young lord's estate. Edward smiled, happy that Mr. Cowper would indeed prosper.

Edward's grandmother came upon him just as he finished his correspondence. He intended to dispatch his mail through his own couriers, wanting to ensure their secure and speedy delivery. One letter went to his agents whom he had engaged on Mr. Cowper's behalf. He instructed them to begin a search for a Nathaniel Poole, retired of his king's army, and to investigate a wedding between him and an Alana Atwood, or him and an Alana Morrison. He had told them to broaden their search. Initially, he had supposed Mr. Cowper's grandparents eloped, so the investigation into their marriage focused on Gretna Green. In case the captain had obtained a special license, Edward instructed his men to investigate the London churches and if Mr. Poole's birthplace was known, to search the churches in that county as well.

Another letter went to the Duke of Hartford informing him of Mr. Cowper's identity and fortune. He asked for his grace's help in gaining an audience with the Prince Regent, to validate the young viscount's claim.

Then he wrote a letter to the Atwood family solicitor, informing him that he would be accompanying the Atwood heir to London to settle his affairs. He told him that Baroness Litford provided a letter of introduction.

His last letter went to the Earl and Countess of Westfield, informing them all of what had transpired. At the end of his missive, he asked if Elinor had news of Anne. Edward sealed the last letter and stamped his ring bearing Beaumont's family crest onto the soft wax. His uncle gave him the family heirloom as evidence that he was indeed his heir apparent.

The dowager asked, "Am I interrupting you, Edward?"

"Not at all," he replied. "I have just finished my correspondence. Is there anything I can do for you?"

She answered, "That was to be my question. I know something weighs heavy on your mind, Edward, aside from Mr. Cowper that is, and I wish you to unburden yourself to me. You use to come to me when you were troubled. Let me help you."

"I fear," said Edward, "the follies of love can only be resolved by the parties involved, but I thank you grandmother for your concern."

She asked, "Your heart is engaged then, Edward?"

"Dreadfully so," he answered.

The dowager then asked, "Who is she?"

"Lady Anne is a gentleman's daughter," answered Edward. "However, through no fault of her own, has over the past years, earned her way by providing the service of chaperone for the *bon ton's* debutantes. I never noticed her until Lady Westfield forced her upon my acquaintance. I will admit that I disliked her initially. More than once, I found that her enjoyment was at my expense. She riled me from the beginning, always seeming to get the better of me." Edward laughed. "Jenkins feared I would suffer from a serious malady, if I did not resolve my feelings towards her. I fear he may be right if I am unable to secure her."

The dowager asked, "And why would you not be able to secure her, Edward? Has she another suitor?"

"Not that I am aware. The fault is no one's but my own. I was reckless in not professing myself, allowing my ardor to act without thought. Lady Anne has spent her last years diligent in protecting her virtue against those that behave dishonorably. Unfortunately, I did not make my addresses known, only my feelings for desire were imminent. I fear I scared her away before I could offer for her."

"Oh, Edward," laughed his grandmother. "How delightful that you found a girl with such will power and good sense. I must meet her. You will bring her to Aubry before you wed."

"I do not think it possible after her stay at Beaumont," he said. "She will not trust my intentions. I plan to procure a special license and show her my intentions are honorable. I will marry her that day if she pleases."

"Nonsense," replied the dowager. "You will marry in a manner befitting your title. I shall come to London with you and make sure that all transpires as it should."

Edward laughed. He knew better than to argue with his grandmother and he had to admit that it would be nice to have her meet Anne. It could not hurt to have her in his corner, so he responded, "We leave within the week I hope."

# Chapter Sixteen

Edward was welcomed at the Litford home with much glee. Mr. Cowper, Viscount Atwood, was smiling in anticipation of his arrival. Edward noticed his uncle was in good spirits as well and deduced they enjoyed a pleasant evening. He greeted, "Uncle! Atwood! How are you this morning?"

Edward saw the confused look in Lawrence's face and explained, "Mr. Cowper, you must get used to your new title. Once your claim is validated, you will be Viscount Atwood. The world as you know it will not acknowledge you through your birth name but through your title. You must expect getting used to being called Atwood or my lord."

Lawrence's mouth dropped open. The significance of how his life was about to change suddenly impacted him. He said, "I do not know how to be a lord, my lord."

"You must address me as Felton, Atwood," he replied. "Your grandmother raised you as a gentleman, so you are very accustomed to the propriety of the sphere you are about to engage. As for the management of your estate, Beaumont and I will guide you. Relax, you are not alone."

Lawrence smiled and felt the tension leave his body. "Thank you, my lord, excuse me, Felton, you have been very good to me."

"You are very welcome," replied Edward. "But you must not feel so much gratitude. You have done me a great service in revitalizing my uncle. Until your arrival, I saw my uncle removing himself from Society and I feared he was falling into melancholy. His whole focus was on settling his affairs for when he left this world. You have renewed his spirit, giving him a new goal, that of locating your father, to center his attention. I have seen him invigorated, so you see, it is I who am indebted to you."

Lawrence chuckled. "It is hard to picture Beaumont anything but full of life. He has become incredibly dear to me. I understand why my grandmother set him up as the example for me to follow. I am glad I was arrogant enough to approach him and that I have been good company for him."

Edward smiled at the thought of Lawrence considering himself arrogant. He was far from it. He asked him, "Are you ready to see your inheritance Atwood?"

Lawrence replied, "Indeed, my lord, I mean Felton."

Beaumont's carriage slowed their progress, making their journey a good three hours. Edward thought that on horseback, he was only an hour away from the Aubry Estate. He thought it was funny how Mr. Cowper's inheritance would be so close to his father's ancestral home. Baroness Litford had warned them that her brother's will had left no provision for the maintenance of the Atwood Home, so over the years, the house fell into ruin. At first, she tried to maintain her ancestral home, but her husband, after a decade of not producing a male heir to succeed the title, tired of reaching into their own coffers to care for it. The best she could do was to remove the family heirlooms and items of value that were at risk unguarded in an unoccupied home. The Atwood family solicitor, after taking inventory, allowed the baroness to hold in trust the family jewels, china, silver, paintings, and a few pieces of furniture that she knew her mother treasured. She had the rest of the house covered in white cloth and all the windows boarded. However, as soon as the estate showed signs of abandonment, someone broke through a boarded window and vandalized the property. The thieves, perhaps in trying to pilfer the window curtains, tore the brocade swaths from their rods and damaged the wallpaper in the process. It seemed the furniture was too heavy to remove because none was missing, though a high boy was tumbled down the stairs. The only items the thieves absconded with were a couple of gilt wood mirrors, a porcelain urn and an Aubusson carpet. The theft bereaved the baroness and she felt the violation deeply. She refused to monitor the estate, since without funds there was little she could do to protect it from trespassers. The fear of seeing her ancestral home continually vandalized kept her away.

It was a disappointing site to see. What must have at one time been a rolling verdant lawn that preceded the Atwood Home, was now a parched area overgrown with crabgrass, nettle plants, and dandelions. The yew hedges and willow trees that flanked the house were overgrown and encroaching. The broken statue and bird fountain that graced the center of the drive, reminded Edward of a forgotten sentry who died protecting his post.

The Atwood Home was indeed weather beaten, dilapidated, and boarded up. The baroness had given them a key to open the estate house, but Edward quickly saw that the front door was damaged and hanging awkwardly. He placed his foot on the front panel and gave a stout push. The door swung open immediately and gave them entry. He brushed the cobwebs away from his body as he entered the house. He found, aside from a single beam of light that threaded through a broken slate board that barred the window, the interior was without light or fresh air. The room was heavy and stagnant from years of enclosure. Edward held his hand up to his uncle and Lawrence to halt their entry. He exited quickly and went to unbar two of the windows. He braced his foot against the exterior wall and pulled the slate boards off the nails that secured them against the window casement. He then entered the home again to raise the windowpane to let in the much-needed cool breeze. He saw a rustic candleholder on a nearby console. Surprisingly, he found some tallow candles and a tinderbox on the floor nearby. The candles looked gnawed on. He expected there were vermin in the house. He picked up one of the candles and opened the tinderbox to remove the flint and steel. He gathered a piece of tow, a small scrap of broken flax fibers, into the tinderbox and then scraped the flint down the steel to produce a spark that eventually lit the tow aflame. He quickly lit the candle before the tow extinguished. Edward turned to find his uncle and Lawrence watching him. He entreated them to be chary when making their way in.

The neglected years had done much damage. Water spots stained the walls and ruined the flooring. Wallpaper hung loosely. There was chipped paint, loose balustrades, damaged rugs, cracked windowpanes, tarnished wall sconces, grimy chandeliers, and overall filth. Lawrence was overwhelmed that this horrible place was his new home. Edward saw him tremble and placed his hand on his shoulder. He said, "Do not fear. It can easily be put to rights. I expect the structure is sound. It only needs to be thoroughly cleaned and refurbished. I am sure upon further inspection, we will find a few of the furnishings are salvageable."

Lawrence looked at Lord Felton in disbelief. He could not fathom how he could possibly restore his ancestral home to its past glory, and more importantly, could not comprehend why he would want to try. He queried, "How? Or more importantly Why?"

Edward smiled and said with ease, "The first question I will answer light heartedly and simply say that men and money will put your home to rights. The second question deserves a more profound remark. You fix it because this is your inheritance and your responsibility. The welfare of its occupants, your future family, your servants, and your tenants rest on how well you manage it. You must not fail them."

As they began to exit, they came upon a local tenant. He said, "Who goes there?"

Edward bellowed, "The rightful heir of Atwood. And who are you?"

"I am sorry, milord," replied the tenant. "I am Matthew. I was driving home and saw the carriage in the driveway. Since its abandonment, I cross the property to shorten my trip home. I have often scared away many intruders, mostly young lads who find amusement in breaking into the Atwood Home to prove their bravery. Over time, gossip has turned into folklore and the rundown house is thought to be haunted."

"Well Matthew," replied Edward. "We are indebted for your loyalty. Let me introduce you to the new Viscount Atwood who was in the process of inspecting his property."

Matthew sputtered, "Viscount Atwood?"

Lawrence surprisingly stepped forward and said, "Yes, I am Viscount Atwood. I am pleased to meet you."

Matthew replied, "Not as pleased as I and your other tenants will be, once they learn of you. They, like myself will want to meet with you and share their grievances. We have been left to our own for over a decade and there is much to complain, with respect of course."

Lawrence looked to Edward who answered on his behalf. "Viscount Atwood will be happy to meet his tenants. He will want to inspect his properties. If you would be so kind as to create a list of tenants and a map for us to follow Matthew, we will see to visiting them."

Matthew complied, expressed his happiness that a lord would reign again at Atwood to manage his properties and left. Beaumont asked, "Why did you not bring all the tenants together nephew? It would have saved time. Now, our trip to London will be pushed out another week."

Edward answered, "I feared a crowd would turn into an angry mob. It is better that Atwood allow his tenants to act as host. His visit will serve two purposes. First, he will get to know his tenants and second, he will be able to inspect his land and learn about his tenants' needs. The week will be well used and since we do not know how long we will be in London, it is best that Atwood make a good impression with his tenants while he can. It will only benefit him in the future."

Beaumont had no desire to repeat the tedious and excessively long day drive to the Atwood Home, so he decided to remain at Aubry. Meanwhile, Edward and Lawrence did their duty in making their daily trips to visit Atwood's tenants, inspecting the boy's newly inherited land. Both Edward and Lawrence traveled with more speed crossing the Aubry Estate on horseback versus the winding and rutted roads that snaked around the vast ducal property. While Lawrence was not as proficient a horseman as Edward, they still managed to make the trip within an hour. The rides to and fro each day lightened their spirits and they were happy for the fresh air and exercise.

It surprised Edward that under such neglect of supervision, the tenants' fields were producing high yields of crops. The tenants were generational farmers and he could see that they took pride in managing their piece of land. They discovered their tenants' main complaint was the absence of a landlord to negotiate a price for their crop. Without a nobleman to speak for them, they were left at the mercy of the wholesalers who took advantage of their lack of education. Edward noticed the evidence of neglect with many of the cottages needing repairs. For as long as the estate remained in abeyance, the tenants had no one to bring their complaints, but now that there was a Viscount Atwood, they expected him to do his duty to them. Edward helped the young viscount assure his tenants that he would be an attentive landlord. He also reminded them that the Atwood Home was inhabitable, so it would still be a while before the lord was in residence. Until then, Edward said that the viscount would send a man to see to some of their most important and basic needs. The ones that affected their welfare and livelihood, such as rotted roofs and collapsed irrigation ditches. Atwood's tenants were very agreeable and liked the young, good looking heir who treated them with compassion. They professed they were very happy that the heir had come home.

It took over a month before Edward and Lawrence were able to inform his uncle and grandmother that they would be ready to leave in a couple of days for London. Edward had sent for Alistair. He knew he could leave Atwood's affairs in his hands. Alistair would be tasked to restore the Atwood Home and to complete the list of tasks noted for each tenant. Edward gave Alistair full authority to hire all necessary laborers and staff for the new home. After the summer, when they returned, he expected to hand Atwood the keys to his restored home. When Lawrence asked how he was to pay for all the work, Edward simply replied, "easily."

It was obvious to Edward after inspecting Atwood's properties that Lawrence had deep coffers. He knew the Atwood solicitor, as executor of the estate, collected the tenants' rents. There was no doubt that once Atwood's claim was validated that he would come into a large reserve of money, since it was evident that no funds were ever dispersed for maintenance or improvement. Edward was more than confident that Lawrence could afford the renovations and if not, unknown to Lawrence, Edward was more than capable of covering the costs tenfold.

The day before they were ready to depart, Edward finally received a letter from the Westfields. "Ah!" ascertained Edward as it became clear why a reply from Elinor took so long, "She sent it post."

Elinor wrote of her happiness for Mr. Cowper's good fortune and then cut to the heart of his concerns. She wrote that she had waited to hear from Anne, before writing, because she knew that was his primary interest. It appeared that Anne was enjoying her stay at the Riverdale country home where the whole family was in residence, becoming familiar with their third son's betrothed. Elinor passed on Anne's news that the Earl and Countess of Riverdale were more than gracious to her and that Riverdale's older brother was most attentive. "Damn!" shouted Edward.

He found himself crumpling the missive and stopped himself before any more damage could be done. He straightened, smoothed the parchment out, and began to read it once again. Elinor wrote that both Bell and Riverdale had his parents' blessing. They were to return to Town to read the banns and to finish the Season, hosting a ball to announce their son's engagement to Miss Tate.

Edward thought it was fortuitous that Bell's links to trade were removed after her father died and the business was taken over by a partner. Miss Tate it seems, would not suffer his fate of being ostracized by the "taint" of trade," instead she would simply be accepted into Society as an heiress. Of course, he recollected, that Lady Jersey had sponsored her entrance into Almack's. No one would ever dare to contradict her judgment, regarding who is or is not acceptable in Society. Edward smiled over the Tates' success. He returned his attention to Elinor's letter to read, "Riverdale has begged our attendance at the Ball. I have hesitantly agreed, leaving Stephen to the care of his nannies and his grandmother Amelia. I know I need not worry, but you know how I hate to separate from him. Jonathan assures me we will be no longer than a sev'night from home. I hope to see you in Town, if your business takes you there."

*"Indeed it does,"* thought Edward.

News of the newly found, young, and devilishly handsome Viscount Atwood was already spreading like wildfire through the *ton's* notorious grapevine. Upon their arrival to London, the Prince Regent, as a favor to the Duke of Hartford, granted Lords Beaumont, Felton, and Atwood an audience with him, where he proclaimed Lawrence Cowper, to be the new Viscount Atwood. No sooner was Lawrence recognized by the Crown, did Edward's silver salver begin to fill up with numerous invitations for balls and fetes addressed to Atwood.

The week that followed was a social whirlwind. In addition to taking care of Lawrence's business with his solicitor, Edward found himself ensconced into Society and attending functions that he would rather had declined. As busy as he was though, Edward managed each day to shove one of his calling cards under Anne's door to her closed up apartment. To Edward's chagrin, Anne had not yet returned to London. Each day, he hoped to find her at home. Instead, he found himself shoving another calling card under her door, scribed on the back, "until tomorrow."

Edward's valet, Jenkins, was readying him for the evening's amusements. Edward had done his duty this past week outfitting Lawrence as befitting a gentleman, then introducing and accompanying him into Society. The *marriage mart* mothers were happy to welcome the young man, whom their daughters found nothing to complain about. Lawrence was young, amiable, and ready to please. He was overwhelmed at first, but not adverse to his newfound popularity. Edward watched him keenly, making sure he was not sabotaged into having to offer for a girl, because he forgot the propriety of the moment.

Jenkins had just finished brushing his master's coat when a knock was heard at the door. Edward commanded, "Enter," and was surprised to see his uncle cross the threshold. He asked, "A moment of your time Edward?"

"Of course, uncle. Are you well?" he asked.

"Very much so though I am a bit troubled," replied Beaumont.

Edward dismissed Jenkins, and bid his uncle to sit down. He asked, "What is it that bothers you?"

Beaumont replied, "I am feeling quite guilty that I, though unintentionally, interrupted your pursuit of Lady Anne. Your grandmother informs me that I have encroached on your time to the point that I may have jeopardized your own personal wishes. I do beg your pardon and ask if there is anything that I can do?"

"Nonsense," replied Edward. "Lady Anne was committed to attending the Tates to the Riverdale's country home to meet his parents. I expect her stay, like my own to Aubry, lasted longer than expected. All will be put to rights as soon as she returns to Town."

Beaumont smiled, and stood in enthusiasm, "She has accepted your offer then, nephew?"

"No," replied Edward who saw his uncle's smile diminish. He continued, "But I have every confidence she will. Do not worry, uncle. I will prevail, now tell me what else concerns you?"

Beaumont explained, "I am much concerned that Atwood will fall prey to one of these *marriage mart* mothers that hound us. Lawrence is too green to discern the machinations of debutante mothers. They will do anything to attach their daughter to a titled man of property. He must seem like a puppy to them, eager to please and easy to train. He does not have the wherewithal or Town polish necessary to protect himself."

"I agree," he replied. "What are you suggesting?"

"Well, if it does not complicate your personal wishes, I would like to take Atwood on a *Grand Tour*, the Mediterranean, Greece and the Italian coastline, but that would require you to oversee the completion of Atwood Home, as well as continue to manage my affairs and your own. It is an overwhelming task, but one I know that you are capable. You have been managing my estate for the past year, so really it would only seem that you would be adding Atwood's affairs. What do you think?"

"I think it is a wonderful idea and will benefit you both. I ask only that you wait until I marry. I would like your presence, uncle," replied Edward.

Beaumont queried, "You are confident that Lady Anne will accept?"

"Yes," replied Edward.

# Chapter Seventeen

Anne arrived home and opened her door to a flurry of calling cards, floating about her skirts as she walked into her apartment. A brisk breeze hurled the cards further into her hallway when she reached down to pick them up. She was quite astonished to find that they all belonged to Lord Felton. She gathered up the lot of them and placed them on her silver salver. She then directed the footman, following her into her home, where to place her bags.

The Countess of Riverdale had been quite adamant on having her coachman and footman convey her home safely. The Riverdale town home was a bustle of activity with the servants readying rooms for family members who were due to arrive to attend the Riverdale Ball. An announcement had already been placed in the Gazette and the first banns were to be read this Sunday, at St. James Church, announcing her son's betrothal to Miss Annabelle Tate.

Mrs. Tate had been quite generous to Anne, paying her handsomely for her chaperone services of Bell. She complimented her diligence and stratagem on securing her daughter's place in Society, and could not thank Anne enough for all she did. Mrs. Tate still marveled at the fact that Lady Jersey herself had sponsored Bell's entrance into Almack's. Anne countered Mrs. Tate's compliments, insisting that Bell's character and charm won over the Almack's Patronesses. Nonetheless, Anne accepted her more than generous fee, with sincere appreciation. Mrs. Tate directed Anne to purchase a new evening dress for the Riverdale Ball, stating, "As lovely as you look in your light blue crepe dress, it has been seen one too many times. You must purchase something new!"

Anne spent the next hour sending off a note to her abigail alerting her that she was home and to return to service. Anne gave her leave when she first went to visit Beaumont Manor knowing that the marquis had more than enough servants to attend her. Now that she was home, she was anxious for the company and the help. She did not look forward to unpacking her bags herself. Even more importantly, propriety dictated that she have another woman living with her to corroborate her virtue. Heaven forbid someone should knock on her door and find her alone.

Anne was weary. Being all smiles and attentive to one's hosts and charge was exhausting. She looked forward to retiring early after she had a cup of tea and reviewed her mail. She was lounging on her sofa, sipping her chamomile brew when she remembered the mass of cards that Lord Felton had left for her. He had been on her mind ever since she left Beaumont Manor. She was in constant debate with herself, arguing whether or not her decision to leave was hasty. One moment, she congratulated her forbearance in not allowing his lordship to seduce her. In another instant, she chided herself for being too scared to learn specifically what Lord Felton proposed. Were his intentions honorable or not? She knew she only doubted him because she had opened her heart to him. He was a rake, nothing more, but then she would remember the day she spent with Edward in her apartment showing Bell how to dance. She grinned remembering how he modeled the proper way for a debutante to use her fan. She saw Edward playful and witty. It was at that moment when she knew her heart was engaged and that she had fallen in love.

She looked at the back of each calling card. She saw that each one was inscribed with the same message, "until tomorrow" and dated. She counted eleven in all. She deduced that he did not miss a day since he left the first card. She wondered if he would come tomorrow. She wondered why he came. Anne looked down at her bags, sighed, and realized she would have to carry the bags upstairs and unpack herself. When she placed the callings cards back in the silver salver, she happily spied her abigail coming from the back of the apartment. She guessed she must have entered from the back door, and exclaimed, "Oh, Mary! I am so glad you have come!"

"It is a good thing I came, milady, or else I expect you would have lugged those bags upstairs and unpacked them all by yourself instead of waiting for me," she chided.

Anne replied, "Mary, I have missed you. Tell me all the *on dit*. What gossip have I missed?"

Mary began to ramble, "Did you know that Lord Felton is in Town. He is all the rage, though the other servants tell me that their mistresses have set their caps on him. They say he is the most charming man, knows just how to treat a woman and he cuts a very fine figure in his evening dress. Some of the ladies think he favors them. They say he is out every night amusing himself. What did you think of him when you were at Beaumont Manor, milady?"

Anne's ire began to rise. She realized she should have been assuaged to learn that all her assumptions about him were correct. He was as she thought, a good for nothing rake, but instead of feeling relieved, she felt angry and spewed out a diatribe, "The nerve of him to flirt and who knows what else with other ladies, if indeed they are ladies. Then to call on me during the day! The gall of him! I shall chide him when I see him. No! I shall not see him. He can go to the devil as far as I am concerned. He will not play fast and free with me!"

Mary was dumbfounded, not knowing why her mistress was angry or whom she was angry with, but when Lady Anne gave her a self-satisfying nod, Mary nodded back in loyalty and then helped her weary mistress into her nightclothes and bed.

Like clockwork, Edward raced up the steps to Lady Anne's apartment. He was prepared to shove a calling card out of habit under her door, but to his surprise, after dropping the door knocker, he heard the commotion that indicated the door was about to open. Mary curtsied, greeted, "milord," and waited for direction from the nobleman in front of her. Edward handed his calling card to her, asking when her mistress had returned. Mary replied, "Last night, milord. If you will wait here, I will see if my mistress is receiving callers." It did not take long for Mary to return, flummoxed and stuttering. She said as she returned his calling card, "I...I am so...sorry, milord, but my mistress is not at home."

Edward was too tired of his pursuit of Anne to be angry. He raised his eyebrow at the abigail who defensively took a step back. Edward laughed, saying, "No, I am afraid I am sorry to contradict your mistress' wishes." Edward briskly strode past Anne's servant and made his way to her sitting room, where the abigail had just emerged. Mary followed tentatively, after shutting the front door behind him. Edward burst in to find Lady Anne breaking her fast with a cup of tea and a biscuit. He smiled when he saw her color rise in her cheeks and her eyes widen. She looked to her abigail who said, "I am sorry, milady, but he did not believe me."

"That is all right, Mary," answered Anne. "I should have known his lordship would not yield to the letter of propriety."

Edward chuckled. "I am sorry, my lady, to intrude on your repast, but I have waited long to see you, as evidenced by the numerous calling cards I left for you."

Anne could not help but scowl. She felt her posture stiffen and exclaimed, "I do not know why you would have a need to see me Lord Felton for I am far from desirous in owning your acquaintance. If anything, I would expect your evening pursuits would keep you sleeping away the day."

He was surprised at her churlishness and countered, "I know not what gossip fills your ears, my lady, but my conduct is above reproach. My only purpose in attending any Society is in aiding Viscount Atwood." He continued with a smirk, "Perhaps, since I have been forthcoming, you will apprise me of what transpired between you and Riverdale's brother, the colonel this past month?"

Anne wondered how he knew Riverdale's brother was attentive to her and then she remembered her letter to Elinor. She retorted, "I see Lady Westfield keeps you informed of my affairs."

Edward replied, "Enough of this nonsense. I have come to pay my addresses to you."

Anne responded, "Do not! I am not interested in your games, my lord. I know that you trifle with me and I must ask you to desist and leave."

Shocked at her disbelief in his honorable intentions, Edward began to explain, "But, Anne, you must let me profess my ardor…" Before he could finish, Anne ran out of the room.

His better senses checked his behavior to chase after her. He took his leave, but not before he gave her abigail his calling card again, dated and inscribed with "until tomorrow."

Anne did not want to take the chance at being home should Edward come to call. She decided that today was as good as any other day to shop for her new evening dress for the Riverdale's Ball. She took Mary with her to Bond Street and left Lord Felton disappointed in having to leave yet another calling card.

Edward found his courtship, if paying daily attendance to Anne's abode is courting, nothing more than a battle of wills between himself and her. He realized she expected him to give up to prove his intentions were indeed not honorable. He was determined to prove her wrong. He would spend the rest of the Season, longer if need be, dropping off his calling cards to show her he was very serious. He decided he should place an order to his engravers, to make sure he had enough cards ready and on hand for his use. Nothing would prove more frustrating than for his best-laid plans to go awry, because he lacked a sufficient store of calling cards.

He had just entered his town home when Beaumont. in a very excited manner, informed him that one of his agents was awaiting him with news of

Lawrence's grandfather. "The boy," he exclaimed, "is unnerved with anticipation. Hurry, Edward! They await you in your study."

Edward learned that Captain Nathaniel Poole, retired, lived in the coastal town Southwick, sadly in the same county that Alana had lived her life. The agent informed them that Captain Poole lived with his niece and family. The agent went on to say that as yet they had not found evidence of a wedding between Alana and Captain Poole in either London or Gretna Green, but that they were still looking. As instructed by his lordship, Captain Poole was not contacted. Edward thanked the agent who supplied him with the captain's address before he left.

Lawrence was the first to speak, "Will you go with me, Felton? I fear, I could not approach him alone."

"Of course," replied Edward. "And you uncle, do you wish to accompany us?"

"No, no," replied Beaumont. "I do not think I could handle the sorrow of what might transpire. It is enough that you attend Atwood. I will await you here. Is there anything that I can do for you, while you are gone, nephew?"

He smiled, replying, "As a matter of fact, there is, uncle." Edward explained his strategy of pursuing Lady Anne. Beaumont thought it all nonsense, but being a sentimental fool, he heartily agreed to deliver one of his nephew's calling cards each day that he was away.

Edward did not wish to be gone too long, so he easily convinced Lawrence that they would reach

Southwick faster if they rode cross-country instead of taking his carriage and sticking to the roads. The seaside town was less than fifty miles from London. Leaving early, acquiring fresh mounts along the way, and they could easily make their destination before sunset.

They arrived in Southwick weary after a day in the saddle, but Edward could see, *fagged* or not, Lawrence was as jumpy as a cricket in anticipation of meeting his grandfather. They lodged at the Ships Inn and ate in a private dining room, discussing over their meal how best to introduce themselves to the captain. Edward thought that Captain Poole might not receive the honorable viscount, considering his history with the family. He decided that the best course of action was to present his own calling card and request an audience with the man. Once inside, he would make the introductions that would announce that Lawrence was Alana's grandson and see if the Captain would admit to an acquaintance. It had never even occurred to Lawrence that his grandfather might deny knowing his grandmother. Edward chided his thoughtlessness and then realized it was better the young man be prepared for all eventualities.

Edward had paid the ostler handsomely to watch and care for their horses through the night. He did not wish to learn the next day that their mounts had mysteriously wandered away. They woke early. The inn provided them both with a reasonable meal to break their fast and then to their relief, they found their horses saddled and ready for their use. Since Edward's agent had drawn him a serviceable map, he did not need to secure directions that would feed those local *gossipmongers* curious to know their business. Both of them marveled at the coastal landscape and Lawrence became misty eyed as the salt-water breeze reminded him of Worthing, and his now deceased family. Edward left him to his reflections until they neared the cottage of where Captain Nathaniel Poole resided. It was a quaint two-story Tudor style home that had the markings of a feminine touch. Box planters filled with spring flowers lined the windowsills and wisteria clung to the trellis that arched over the gravel path to the front door.

He knocked heartily and waited for the door to be answered while Lawrence dug deep into his pockets, fidgeting from side to side. A matronly woman opened the door, surprised to see what she knew were men of nobility. Their dress and countenance marked them as aristocrats. The woman curtseyed, asking, "May I help you, milords?"

Edward presented his calling card and asked if Captain Poole would receive him on a matter of the utmost importance. The woman, whom Edward surmised was Poole's niece, knew nothing of propriety, of first seeking her uncle's approval in receiving guests. She simply said, "My uncle is taking his daily constitution in our back yard. He likes to sit out in the sun and watch my grandchildren while they are at play. If you will follow me, I will take you to him."

Edward and Lawrence complied, making their way through the cottage until they exited a door that brought them outside. Sitting on a wooden bench sat the now aged Captain Nathaniel Poole. Like Beaumont, his features reflected those of a man of years, white hair and aged lines. However, Poole's erect posture and jubilant nature from watching his grand nieces and nephews tumble about the lawn, marked a contrast to Beaumont's introspective countenance. Captain Poole bellowed out a laugh each time the children tripped on their own feet and fell into the soft rolling grass. Edward watched him rise as soon as he spied them. He noted by the quickness of his movements that the captain did not live an idle life. He was tall, maintained a strong body, and possessed a bravado that Edward expected had first lured Alana to his side.

"Julie," he asked, "who have we here? I did not know you expected such esteemed company?"

She replied, "They are here to see you, uncle. I will bring some tea." Julie then gathered her grandchildren and brought them inside to give her uncle some privacy with his guests. Edward saw that Captain Poole was at a loss for words, so he began the introductions as he had agreed with Lawrence.

"Captain Poole," he greeted. "I am Edward Brentwood, the Earl of Felton. I act on behalf of my uncle, sir, the Marquis of Beaumont, whose duty I discharge on his behalf. I am honored to present to you,

Alana Morrison's grandson, Lawrence Cowper, Viscount Atwood.

The captain stared at Edward as though he spoke a different language, then comprehension set. He sharply turned his focus to Viscount Atwood. Disbelieving, he asked, "Alana's grandson?"

Lawrence stepped forward, bowed in respect and then asked, "I have come to learn, sir, that you are my grandfather and I would like to know why you deserted my grandmother while she was with child."

Captain Poole took a step backward and found his legs crumble beneath him, as he balanced himself on the bench he had recently sat. He slowly took his seat once again, cradling his head between his hands to collect his composure. He looked up at Lawrence and asked, "Alana lives?"

Both Edward and Lawrence sighed, happy their worst fears were not realized. It seemed Alana had not been abandoned. Julie came upon the scene, hastily set down the tea tray and took a seat next to her uncle. She grabbed one of his hands and found it trembling. She asked him, "What is it, uncle? What news grieves you so?"

Captain Poole answered, "Julie, Alana and my child lives!"

Julie looked back in response, "Your family survived?"

Lawrence quickly intervened, "No, forgive me. My grandmother and mother have both passed. Until my recent inheritance, I was without family. I was searching for a connection when I first set out looking for you, Captain Poole."

"I had a daughter," sighed Nathaniel.

Edward watched as the look of first shock, then joy, finally grief, crossed the Captain's face. Julie stayed by his side as Lawrence explained his life with his grandmother and mother in Worthing. He then asked why his grandmother went by the name of Morrison."

Captain Poole replied, "When I learned Alana was with child, I would not let her accompany me on campaign. She feared her father would find her unprotected and drag her home. She was terrified he would hide her away until she gave birth, and then give the baby away just so that he could annul our marriage. To appease her fears, I allowed her to come up with an alias to live by while I was away." Nathaniel grinned, "Alana had a sense of humor. My father's name was Morris and I am his son. She chose Morrison as her alias."

"You were married," confirmed Lawrence.

"Indeed. I loved Alana and would never dishonor her." He smiled, "my colonel had purchased a special license to use for himself, but upon being refused and hearing my plight, he gave me the special license. He was my best man and witnessed my betrothal to Alana in a small chapel near Aubry. I would not travel with Alana unless we were man and wife."

"But why?" asked Lawrence. "Did I never know you?"

"I left Alana situated in a small apartment in Bath. I was quite pleased that my salary would have allowed me to place her among a Society befitting her station. While on campaign, I, along with others in my company, sustained injuries. The wounded and dead were reported. It was not until I returned to Bath, that I learned my name was negligently reported as deceased, and that my wife had moved out of the apartment where I last saw her. I assumed that her father had found her and dragged her and our baby to Atwood. I went directly to collect them. Instead, I was told that Alana had died in childbirth. I fell into despair. If not for my sister and my beloved niece with whom I now live, I know not what would have become of me."

Edward watched clarity return to Captain Poole's eyes, once he finished his introspection and returned to the present. He looked up at Viscount Atwood and asked, "You are my grandson?"

Lawrence smiled and answered, "Yes. If you will acknowledge me."

Captain Poole, stood up and embraced the young man. They then made their way into his niece's cottage to retire to her common room. Julie went to task to put together a cold collation, while the men exchanged questions and stories. Nathaniel was hungry for information about the wife he lost and the daughter he never knew. Lawrence asked as many questions, yearning to learn about his newfound grandfather. At the end of their meal, Nathaniel was disappointed that his grandson had to return to London the next day. Lawrence informed him that he had some social commitments that he was honor bound to attend, but at the end of the Season, if it met with his grandfather's approval, he would return to visit. His grandfather was sentimentally appreciative of his thoughtfulness.

Before Lawrence mounted his steed, he reached into his saddlebag and took out a medium sized black velveteen pouch. He walked back to the doorstep, where his grandfather and Julie stood prepared to wave them off. Nathaniel watched as Lawrence pulled out from the pouch a gold gilded hinged frame. He opened the frame to show his grandfather the two small miniatures that were housed on each side. Lawrence pointed out the picture of Alana. He said, "She told me that she had this painted while you were away on campaign. She was going to give it to you when you returned. The other picture is my mother, your daughter. Grandmother had it done for me after my father died. You see I was sad that I had lost my memory of what he looked like, and I became afraid that one day I would forget my mother's face." He then gave the frame to his grandfather and said, "I would like you to have this, sir. It is your family, aside from myself." Nathaniel's eyes formed tears as he took the memento and embraced his grandson.

He said, "Thank you, Lawrence. I cannot tell you how dear these miniatures are to me. I will hold them in trust for you."

As Edward and Lawrence trotted away, Edward remarked, “That was very kind of you, Atwood.”

Lawrence replied, “I have a lifetime of memories to reflect on, it was only befitting that he should have something of them.”

# Chapter Eighteen

Beaumont banged the brass doorknocker to Lady Anne's front door. When no one answered, he shoved his nephew's calling card under the door. Anne found she could tell the time by the arrival of one of Lord Felton's calling cards. Each day, at precisely eleven in the morning, Edward would shove a card under her door and her abigail Mary would deliver it to her. Mary knew not to answer the single tattoo, but to wait for the calling card to be shoved over the threshold. It was a daily ritual and one that Anne soon drew solace in, knowing that Edward had not proved himself false as yet.

This time however, after flipping over Edward's calling card, she found herself surprised at the changed inscription. Instead of the consistent note of "until tomorrow," it read, "until when." She wondered if Edward expected her to respond. She placed the card in her pocket contemplating if she should respond. Her fears got the better of her and she reluctantly ignored the query.

The next day, she found herself hovering near the bay window that provided a view of her front steps. She was both excited and nervous over what Edward would do next. She was therefore surprised when she saw Beaumont apply himself to her front door and then bend down to deliver what she expected was Lord Felton's calling card. She waited for Mary to deliver the card. Anne turned the calling card over and found that nothing was written upon it. She went to her desk to inspect yesterday's card with the previous cards she had received and deduced that yesterday's card was not written by Edward.

She became angry, thinking that she had become some piece of folly for Edward's entertainment. Beaumont was part of the ruse. Who next? Who else would place cards at his direction? She decided she would end the game tomorrow and give Edward, Beaumont, or whoever else dared to act in his stead, a good piece of her mind.

The next day, once again positioning herself by the bay window, she watched as Beaumont climbed her front steps. She hurried to open the door and found him bent over in embarrassment. He said, "Oh, my dear, you are home. Good, good." He then went on to say, "You will forgive me and not tell Edward that I forgot what I was supposed to write on the back, will you? It seemed so simple at the time, but I am not quite good at all with this sentimental jumbo, you know."

Anne was dumbstruck at his perplexed state and simply responded, "Indeed, my lord. Perhaps, you could simply inform your nephew to desist and then we will all be quite happy."

Anne thought Beaumont looked very sad when he said, "Oh, dear, I fear I have ruined everything. No, no. You must not judge him by my error." Before she could speak, Beaumont turned around, dropping his head in despair as he walked down the steps of her town home. Anne flabbergasted, thought she could hear him chiding himself as his groomsman helped him into his carriage. She realized she was still gawking as Beaumont's carriage left and quickly closed her mouth.

Later that afternoon as she worked on her correspondence, she heard Mary open the front door. She was waiting for her to come and announce her visitors when instead she saw a regal elderly lady enter her parlour with the Marquis of Beaumont following. Mary was nowhere to be seen. Lady Anne surmised that the Dowager Duchess of Aubry, sister to Beaumont himself, had graced her home with her presence.

As Anne rose to greet her guests, she said, "It is unlike my abigail to neglect her duties and fail to announce you."

The dowager grinned, liking the girl's audacity, and replied, "I sent your girl to bring us some tea. I am Edward's grandmother. I thought it high time we met."

Though Anne did not like the imperial attitude of the dowager, she knew better than to argue with her. She decided with undo patience to sit through the impending tête-à-tête with as much sanguine as possible. She directed her guests to sit around a small console where Mary would set the tea service. Mary brought the much-needed refreshment and hurriedly left the room closing the doors behind her. Anne raised an eyebrow, looked at the dowager and asked, "Perhaps, you would like to pour?"

The dowager laughed, saying, "Don't be churlish, my girl. I am not here to offend you, only to set to rights whatever my brother may have jeopardized, while acting in my grandson's stead."

Anne queried, "I know not what you mean, my lady?"

She answered, "Fustian. For whatever reason, you do not trust Edward's addresses. I am here to tell you his feelings for you are honest and worthy of reciprocation."

"An honest man, my lady, does not play games. And certainly," glaring at Beaumont, "does not recruit others to enjoy in the game," replied Anne.

The dowager turned her head to reprimand her brother with a steely look. Then she explained to Lady Anne, "My brother meant well. Edward was called away on business, yet still, he cared to entrust his uncle to continue in his pursuit. He did not want you to believe he wavered in his devotion to you. You should be complimented by his attention, instead of annoyed by it."

"Lord Felton, I fear has misled you," answered Anne. "He is interested in me as a conquest, not a love match. Perhaps you should hold an audience with him when he returns. I am sure he can assure you that his heart is not engaged."

"You are wrong," replied the dowager. "I am very well aware that my grandson's heart is engaged. What of your heart Lady Anne? What does it hold for Edward?"

Anne blushed and bowed her head. She found she could not speak.

The dowager said, "You are a fool not to trust your heart. I will leave Edward to pursue his own interests, for he can do it better than I, but I can stand witness that he indeed knows his heart. He trusts it enough to offer for you. It is a shame that you cannot trust your own heart."

Anne finally found her voice and said, "It is difficult to believe in a rake, my lady. I have been desired before and have learned that such feelings are not honorable ones. To trust that Edward's passion for me to be of a lasting and genuine nature, would require him to reveal his addresses in a public forum, not hidden on a darkened terrace or a secluded garden. I thank you for your visit, but I do not believe that Edward loves me."

"I will trespass on you no more, Lady Anne," responded the dowager. "But, I leave you to contemplate that you will never find love, if you do not open your heart."

Edward returned home to find his uncle and grandmother in his parlour. They were in a very solemn mood, quite opposite to Lawrence's cheery disposition and garrulous chatter, who took no notice to the state of Lord Felton's family. Edward allowed Lawrence his moment, recalling his reunion with his grandfather and then upon his leave, Edward initiated an interview with his elders.

He asked, "What has happened that causes you to fret even when Atwood shares his good news?"

Beaumont's grim face looked to his sister. She announced, "I am sorry, Edward, but my brother has fumbled in your pursuit of Anne. I tried to put the whole situation to rights, but may have made matters worse."

Edward, who had been standing, went over to a chair opposite his grandmother, sat down and queried, "Tell me all."

His grandmother went on to describe how Beaumont forgot what to write on the back of the cards, how Anne had caught him in the act of delivering the card and chided his participation in Edward's folly. She then explained how she tried to assure Anne that Edward's intentions were honorable. His grandmother finally concluded, "I am sorry, Edward, but I do not think her heart is engaged. She said nothing less than a very public declaration would convince her that you were serious. I believe she only wishes to humiliate you in front of the *ton*."

Edward bellowed a laugh as he watched his grandmother dab the corner of her eye with her laced handkerchief. "This is no laughing matter, Edward," she reprimanded.

"Indeed not," responded Edward. "But if I must make a fool of myself to win her hand, then a fool I am."

"But, Edward," exclaimed the dowager. "What if she refuses you?"

"Then," answered Edward, "I will pick her up and carry her off like any man that knows better of his lady's love than she."

"You would not," she chided, "Why, it would be scandalous."

Edward smiled and retorted, "No more than a refusal to my proposal. Cheer up grandmother, I am about to make the Riverdale's Ball the success of the Season."

Oddly enough, Edward was far from nervous as he entered his own carriage for the Riverdale Ball. He wanted to be prepared in the event he had to resort to carrying Anne away. His uncle and grandmother, on the other hand, were completely racked with nerves. Had he been in their carriage, he would have been privy to all their concerns, regarding how his actions might place him at the fringes of Society yet again.

Edward patted his pocket and smiled. He recollected the list he had compiled over a month ago when he attempted a calculated approach to locating a wife. He had forgotten all about it, only discovering the piece of paper last night while he was reviewing some personal correspondence. He smiled at the providence of falling in love with a woman who met both his logical and emotional needs. Anne was witty, beautiful, passionate, and so much more. How he hoped he prevailed in winning her affections.

He spied Lady Anne the moment he entered the ballroom. He noted she had purchased a new gown. She was enchanting in a high-waist emerald green crepe dress that glittered from all the glass beads and silver embroidery that trimmed the low cut square bodice and flounced hemline. Her long emerald green gloves were an extension of her puffy crepe sleeves, and Edward saw how gracefully her skirt moved when she walked. Her tendril curls bounced in rhythm.

Edward had intentionally arrived late, hoping to time his entrance with one of the favorite waltzes that were so in rage. He heard the strings sound and watched as the Duke of Hartford collected Lady Anne to dance. Edward was glad that he was about to intrude on one who would understand and not add to the scene he was about to create. He prepared himself: all or nothing, he thought. He found his grandmother and uncle on the sidelines watching. He noticed how they held their posture regally and saw that they both delivered their most supportive smiles and nods.

Anne curtsied to the Duke of Hartford who came to claim his dance. She had saved the first waltz for him and was finally beginning to feel some peace. Ever since the day of the dowager's visit, she realized that whatever had transpired between her and Edward had finally come to an end. Her solace came from knowing the decision was completely out of her hands. She knew her demand for a public display of affection from Edward would end any attempts he had at seduction. After a good cry, she resigned herself to what was her destiny, spinsterhood. She found contentment in knowing she was a respectable lady of good birth, earning her own living and able to call more than one person a friend. She could easily live her life satisfied.

His grace had just joined his hand to hers and placed his other hand on her back when she saw Lord Felton on the perimeter of the ballroom. *"He is back,"* she said to herself. Perhaps it was because he was no longer a threat to her that she saw him as the handsome and desirable man she knew him to be. He looked exquisite in his black and white formal dress. She noticed he stood akimbo and smiled as he caught her eyes taking in his countenance. Anne trembled in response and then missed her step. His grace held her firm until she regained her balance. He then asked, "Are you all right, my lady?"

"Yes, yes," she replied. "I am just clumsy I fear. I am so sorry. I did not step on you, did I?"

"No, not at all," replied his grace.

Anne was happy to see Edward was gone when she returned her view to where he had stood. When his grace abruptly stopped, Anne returned her gaze to him, only to find, he had released his hold of her and was delivering her into Edward's hands.

She scolded him, "This is not your dance, my lord!"

"From this day forward, Anne," he replied. "All dances are mine."

Anne stared at his grinning face, and exclaimed. "I do not believe I have given you liberty to address me so intimately, my lord, nor do I care for your duplicitous comments." She began to turn and leave when she felt his hand on her wrist.

He brought her close to him and said, "I will do your bidding Anne to secure your hand, but beware, we will wed either by your wishes or mine."

The swirling couples that flanked them became aware that some scene was unfolding within the center of the dance floor. Slowly, one by one, the couples began to stop and form an audience around Edward and Anne. Anne remarked softly, fearing scandal, "Do release me, my lord, you are creating a scene."

Edward bent down on one knee while still holding on to Anne for fear she would bolt. Anne recollected her comments to the Dowager Duchess of Aubry and realized what was about to transpire. Her heart fluttered and nerves made her body tremble. Edward smiled as he loosened his grip on her. He said quite loudly, so the crowd could hear his prose:

Nothing in the world is single;
All things by a law divine
In one spirit meet and mingle,
Why not I with thine?

"Shelley," she realized. A jumble of emotions went through her body. First was her discomfiture of the unfolding scene she was ensconced in, and second was the excitement in knowing that Edward indeed loved her.

Edward saw the fear in Anne's eyes and released his hold. He wondered if his intuition had failed him, and that her heart was truly not engaged. He reflected that perhaps his own feelings for her had blinded him. His anger began to rise at his stupidity. He rose and said, "I am sorry, Anne. My love for you blinds me. It never occurred to me that you may not return my feelings. You need not fear for your reputation. Only I will suffer for tonight's folly. Do not accept me if your heart is not engaged, for I will settle for nothing less than a love match."

He reached into his pocket and clasped Anne's heirloom bracelet, that once belonged to her mother, on her wrist. She noticed he had the clasp repaired, the bracelet polished and the gemstones secured. A number of diamonds were added to enhance its magnificence. He drew her gloved hand to his lips and kissed it. He said, "I love you, Anne. Will you do me the honor of becoming my wife?"

Anne looked into Edward's eyes and could not fail to see the gallant man before her. He was indeed her prince charming and she smiled at the similarity between Edward's proposal and Rossini's opera. He understood her well, declaring himself in a way that realized her fairy tale dreams. An exclamation distracted her and she noticed the music had stopped. The room was silent, except for Edward's proposal floating about her. She spied in the crowd that surrounded them, ladies with widened eyes and gaping mouths, and males with smirking grins. She looked back at Edward who whispered, "only agree to a love match."

Anne smiled, trusting in her heart and in his. She replied, "Yes, I will marry you." The crowd burst out in applause. The Countess of Westfield who had been holding her breath was the first to approach her. She said, "Oh, Anne. Do tell me it is a love match that you have made?"

Edward raised his eyebrow at Anne. Feeling her tension leave her body, Anne laughed and joy filled her. She replied, "A love match, indeed!"

# Acknowledgements

Thank you Alicia Floyd, my amazing editor, for your astute corrections and insightful advice.

Thank you Christina Brusaca, my wonderful technical designer, for formatting the book and photographing the cover layout.

Thank you Debby Ring, my good friend, for sharing your expertise and answering all my equine queries.

My family has always noted my enthusiasm for Jane Austen novels and the Regency period, but it was my youngest son Jonathan who suggested I write my first story and encouraged me to put my pen to paper. Once I started writing, both my sons, Lawrence III and Jonathan, leant me their ears. I want to thank them and all my readers for sharing their opinions and encouraging me. I would not have thought to publish without the encouragement of my family and friends, so thank you all for your love and support.

A special note of appreciation to my husband Larry and my parents, Mama Dee and Papa Ern, for all that you have done for me.

# About the Author

Teresa Sweeney is a wife and mother of four adult children. She loves to read, write, and a myriad of other things where she can use her creativity and imagination. She takes great pleasure penning historical romance novels that focus on the charm, wit, and banter of courtship. Visit her website www.teresa-sweeney.com for the latest information on her novels.

www.ingramcontent.com/pod-product-compliance
Lightning Source LLC
Chambersburg PA
CBHW030518310726
48979CB00010B/1714/J
*9781940319001*